Described as 'short and spiky', Phyllis Foundis was raised in a tower in the 70s. Her early loyalties were split between C.S. Lewis and Michael Jackson. And by the time she'd mastered the moonwalk, she'd spent her parents' life savings on books.

In a career as varied as the places she's travelled to – America, Canada, Europe and Japan – Phyllis has been an advertising copywriter, written a Seinfeld episode, interviewed Sam Neill and had herself – with manuscript – delivered in a box to a London publisher. She's also sky-dived, walked on hot coals and ballooned over the English countryside in search of the Cernes Giant. She married her own giant – Kym – on a Greek Island in the Summer of 2001.

Phyllis' passions are roasted red peppers, Sydney and cashmere.

# the virgin club©

a novel by phyllis foundis

StarScribe

*in association with*
BookSurge UK Limited

www.the-virgin-club.com

ISBN 1-904672-01-9

phyllis@the-virgin-club.com
www.the-virgin-club.com

LEGAL NOTICES



Typeset in Caslon 11/13pt by StarScribe Productions, London.

First Published in Great Britian 2003 by BookSurge UK Limited.

## acknowledgements

All writers need a support system like the one I've been blessed with. Kym Borrett (my beloved, preemptive gold digger); through my light and shade moments, good and blah days – you've been there. I love you. I thank my incredible parents Barbara and Dino Foundis who love me in spite of my shattering all the Good Greek Girl rules! Huge love and thanks also to the following creative giants; Sam Bauers, Susan Chernin, Madonna Ciccione, Lachlan Colquhoun, Menna Elfyn, Freedom Publishing, Jennifer Gayapersad, D.A. Green, Miri Jassy, Lisa Pember, Ty Newydd, Roz Reynolds, Alessandra Wollaston. And finally, to Betty and Sally – we're all 'guest speakers' now.

NB: And to anyone I know who thinks they recognise him/herself between these pages – er, you're wrong.

For my AJ,
world's greatest virgin buster.

# 1

# Daddy's little girl

I was born yesterday.

A heavier-than-average baby at nine pounds something with a messy crop of soot-black hair, squinty eyes and dimples in all the right places.

I was born to be a Good Greek Girl. To tread the path. Never upset the norm, or defend individuality. Never question, why. Somewhere in my baby album, there's a tiny picture of me taken a few days after I landed on the world. Dad cradles me. Proud. Expectant. He has a shaving cut covered by a little white piece of paper just above his chin. Mum stands beside him. Wide smile. Beehive high. Skirt grazing the tops of her perfect knees.

I was the keeper of their dreams.

Dad took charge of my photo album; all pink with vanilla-scented pages. He collected my first words like stamps. Mama. Baba. Cat. Honey. Girl. And when I had my first haircut, Dad stood by with a small plastic bag ready to collect the curls that fell from my head. He turned to the first page and stuck my ringlets beside a grinning, bow-legged stork. Years later this lock would come unstuck only to be replaced by a strand of permed hair.

I would always be little. Intact and frozen in time – like that shiny lock of hair trapped under a film of yellowing sticky tape. Never allowed to grow. Never let her go. The little girl with the big brown eyes. Always adore her, always protect her. Keep her, closed. There she is eating ice cream from Daddy's spoon. There she is chasing boys with her plastic gun.

There, there little one. There, there.

Mum bundled me up in my bassinet so Dad could take me for long drives in his taxi. Just him and me, a sleeping city and endless road.

As he drove, Dad hummed *Santa Lucia*; a rich melody I could never get enough of. Many years later, he would take me back to those long drives and hushed Italian lullabies ...

'You used to hum like this ... Hmm. Hmm.' he laughed softly. 'You were such a smart, baby. Very, very smart.'

'How did you know I liked the song?'

'I knew,' Dad smiled, 'I just knew.'

☆☆☆

It's a crowded, smoky, Greek nightclub. Our table is littered with the remnants of a huge meal. Souvlaki sticks snapped in two sit high on our plates, prawn tails rim my mother's dish, oyster shells lie empty on my father's plate. I poke at the dry chips left on mine.

'Eat them.' my mother says.

'Eat them to be a strong little girl.' Dad strokes my fringe.

I make a face.

The manager comes to sit with us. He pinches my chin with thick fingers, dry like an old clothespeg.

'*So* beautiful … how old is she, five, six?'

'Seven.' I snap.

'Oh and very clever too,' he smiles at my parents. His teeth are the colour of cheese.

'You should see her bellydance.' Mum beams.

'She'll have to do a floor show for us!' he coughs and lights another cigarette, 'huh baby?'

I shake my head and look at my shoes, willing them to turn to ruby and whisk me home. Dad puts his arm around me.

'Come on, everyone wants to see you.'

I shake my head again, faster this time so my hair bobbles click against each other.

'Leave her. You know how stubborn she is.' Mum frowns and looks away.

I tug at her sleeve. She ignores me and the manager pushes a wet, boozy kiss into my cheek.

'Come on darlin'. Show us what a great little bellydancer you are.'

I feel his saliva slowly drying on my cheek. If I sit very still, like an insect playing dead, if I don't flinch, or even gag as his spit slides down my skin, my predator might lose interest.

'Well, if she doesn't want to … ' the manager winks at my parents and walks off.

I poke my tongue out and drag the palm of my hand

over his kiss. Mum glares at me. I turn my attention to the singer. She has gold lips, a green sequinned dress, and frizzy hair that spills all the way down her bare back.

The manager is back at our table again. He whispers something in my father's ear. Dad seems worried and keeps looking at my mother who shrugs her shoulders. The singer gets tangled up in her microphone cord. I'm fascinated.

'What are we going to do now?'

My mother's voice pulls at me. I look at her. She's biting her lip. Dad's wiping his brow.

'Your Dad hasn't got enough money for the bill sweetheart,' the manager says.

I shouldn't have had those chips. I didn't even eat them all! I stuff the leftover fries into my mouth. Mum slaps my hand. 'Yucky! They're cold.'

'M-ma,' I stumble.

'They want your father to wash the dishes,' my mother says.

Wash the dishes? Poor Daddy. This is the worst thing in the world. No. We can't let it happen. There has to be another way.

'But there is another way … ' Mum says slowly, smoothing my hair.

The singer's still tangled up but she's singing the chorus anyway.

'… if you dance … if you bellydance, they won't make your father wash the dishes.'

I purse my lips. The singer has crouched down mid-verse to loosen the cord around her stilettos.

'Let him wash the dishes Mama.'

'Let your father wash the dishes?' Mum's eyes widen. 'Imagine his embarrassment!'

The singer untangles herself.

'Just dance like you do for me at home … '

… when she puts the music on and I tuck the corners of my nightie into my panties and writhe and shimmy to the beat and move my hips around. Side to side. Backward, forward. I seduce. I curl my body like a snake. She clicks her tongue, 'Aaahhh, you little tart!' And I make love to air. She hugs me, kissing me hard on the forehead …

'Say yes like a good little girl.' my mother says.

The music has stopped. People are murmuring at their tables. Glasses clink.

'Do it for Daddy.' my father says.

The manager sucks another drop of nicotine from his cigarette. Mum pulls me close and smooths my hair again. She adjusts the bow on my dress. Dad folds his arms.

My heart tumbles about in my ribcage. But I have to do this. For our dinner. For Dad. The singer comes to sit at our table. I get a close up of her sequins – some are falling off. The band begins to play and the music floats over to me. The percussion tugs at my dress, egging me on. I feel sick. But I take a breath when the manager announces,

'And now I'm proud to introduce a very special little dancer,'

My world blurs. I can't see the people watching me. I can't even hear the music. But I'm standing on that shiny parquet floor and I'm dancing for my Dad. All my best moves. I can hear applause, whistles, but I keep moving, jiggling gently on the spot, more and more … the meal was probably expensive, all those chips … keep swaying … I see Mum clapping in time. She's whistling through her fingers now. Dad's just smiling. And I'm still dancing, but my arms are getting sore, held above my head, splayed little fingers drawing circles in the air. A flashbulb explodes.

Another moment is wedged in time. The little girl dances, happy that Daddy won't have to wash a single dish.

☆☆☆

I didn't sleep with a teddy bear. Or a dolly with woollen blonde hair and a sewn-on smile. A flat and floppy pillow shared my dreams every night. Pillow was tougher than the troll who lived behind my curtains. Better looking than my pop star pin-ups. Truer than my university pals. My unlikely lover on those hot summer nights when all I wanted was something cool between my legs. I'd drift off in his 'arms', gazing at the glow-in-the-dark stars stuck to the ceiling. My parents' conversation providing the perfect soundtrack from the bedroom next door.

I lived with them right through to my mid-twenties; cocooned in a world of curfews.

In the mornings I'd be woken by the sound of my mother chatting on the phone; rapid-fire gossip with various Aunts and the Greek hairdresser who called daily to hear what her stars had in store from the pages of my mother's Greek newspaper. Mum would read out the horoscope and pepper the paper's predictions with her own opinions.

I waited until she said goodbye before calling out.

'Mama!'

'Are you awake my Nariman?'

Nariman, the daughter of a long forgotten Egyptian King, and my mother's nickname for her lazy princess.

'Yes Ma. I'm awake.'

She pushed my door open. It made a 'shoosh' sound as it rubbed against the dark floral carpet.

'Good morning, all morning.'

Mum bustled about my bedroom, opening windows and pulling dusty curtains aside.

'How can you sleep with no air?'

'I like it.' I said and buried myself deeper under the covers.

Sometimes on these mornings, Mum sat on my bed and let me stare up into her face … eyes the colour of espresso, high cheeks plump and pink, brows dark like olives and tweezed to perfection.

Mum put her head on my chest and I breathed in the rose scent that lingered on her nightie. I kissed her, wrapped my arms around her. She nibbled at my neck, gripped a fleshy part and wouldn't let go. Her bite was strong and I laughed, tugging at her hair, sticky in parts from too much hairspray.

She sat up and pinched my breasts.

'Still you wear that old thing? I don't believe it fits you anymore.' Mum pulled at a sleeve on my faded pink T-shirt.

'It's a good nightie … keeps me cool.'

'This is not a nightie, it's a baby's thing. Come, get up.

You want hot chocolate?'

If I couldn't sleep, if I felt faint or queasy, or for no reason at all, a hot chocolate was the cure-all. Still is.

There's some jittery 8mm film of us stashed somewhere …

Mum's just woken up. She smiles at me through her messy fringe and laughs as I try and climb into the arms she still has wrapped around a pillow. I am determined to wrench her arms free … to hug me. The camera goes in for a shaky close-up of her sleepy grin. She lets go of the pillow and I bury my head in her flannelette nightdress, gently suckling on my bottle of hot chocolate. Her large breasts cushion me. I seem to be falling asleep and the teat from my bottle slips out of my mouth just as the camera runs out of …

'I want coffee, Mama.'

'Coffee's for old women. I will boil the milk.'

The door shooshed as she left.

I peeled off my t-shirt. It had a picture of a tiny girl and her kitten on it. She had big eyes, brown pigtails and a pink mini dress. Beside her, in black block letters, were the words,

*Daddy's Little Girl.*

I wore that shirt for as long as I could. But, as the years melted away, my T-shirt grew dull; its pinkness squeezed out from one machine cycle too many. The little girl's smile had cracked in the fabric. Her clothes had faded too.

But I clung to her.

My name is Agni.

Agni is Greek for pure.

Mum took one look at me when I was born and decided I was the purest little thing she'd ever seen. Clean and sweet and perfect.

Agni – the Good Greek Girl.

The one you work with. Play with. The pretty girl you met at a party once. Your sister. Best friend. Confidante. Your Good Greek Girl. Daddy's little girl.

# 2

# the virgin's apartment

I used to wear my fringe so long it tickled the tops of my eyelids. It was thick and heavy like the curtain in front of a movie screen. And I spent hours flattening its bounce with straightening irons, twisting it into little plaits for a part-time frizz and slicking glitter gel through it when disco reigned.

Other girls loved their Barbies, I loved my fringe. But with the onset of puberty and the demise of the Bay City Rollers, warped logic took my hairstyle hostage. Suddenly, my luscious fringe became more than just a source of trichological pride.

Somewhere between emerging nipples and the fall of a tartan-clad boyband, I decided my fringe would hide my neon; that lurid sign that flashed on my forehead,

*Good greek virgin girl. Do not approach unless ready for commitment.*

My neon glowed brightest on first dates. And blinked fearlessly through the rain. Sometimes even strangers noticed it.

On the first day of my first office job, I was passing a

construction site on my lunch break. Cement trucks rumbled back and forth. Jackhammers jacked. Diggers wrenched bulks of earth from the ground. Utility belts swung from the waists of workmen. Short, tall, hairy, firm and floppy men. Men with cigarettes dangling from their mouths. Men with tattoos of snakes and breasts. The air was choked with tar and testosterone.

I swooned.

A flash of suntanned flesh caught my eye first, then a well-developed bicep. Tight bums shrinkwrapped in workshorts filled my vision too. The sun beat down as I stared and my summer dress clung to me like a needy child. Then I saw him, straddling wood, flicking a hammer up and down like a toothpick. I watched as he grabbed a gulp of water. Drops stuck to his stubble and I swallowed when he swallowed, tasted my lips as he did his.

He looked over. He smiled. He stood up and began walking towards me. Muscles burst through dark blue cotton. Closer and closer. He grinned again and mouthed the words, *nice dress*.

My neon zapped to life.

I dropped my gaze and walked faster. Careful what you wish for. Careful what you wish for! I slammed a hand to my forehead and from the corner of my eye I saw him trip and fall over a bunch of cables. I didn't stop. But the sound of '*Fuck!*' collared me. I spun around.

He was on his back moaning. Sparks were flying.

God, how I wanted to push up my dress, jump that fence and run to him. I'd hold his head in my lap and soothe him like the time when, as a teenager, I cradled the bleeding hand of a carpet layer in our bathroom.

'You're squeezing too tight,' he winced, his blood dripping onto Mum's fluffy pink bathmat.

'Sorry!' I released my trembling grip and more blood oozed from the gash in his finger.

I had watched him all morning from behind my magazine; down on all fours in my bedroom banging loud floral carpet into place with his knee. I wasn't allowed to distract him.

'Sharp tools,' my mother said.

I rested the magazine on my chest. 'Have you been laying carpet long?'

'Long enough.' He turned to look at me, his sweaty, olive skin glistened in the light. 'You in highschool, uni?'

'Last year of highschool. I should be studying but,'

'... but who likes studying right?'

'Right.'

'Yeah, I finished highschool couple years ago.' He stood up and stretched.

'Can I get you a drink?'

'No thanks. Gotta keep moving, busy day today.'

'Okay.' I returned to my magazine, for a second. And then I was back studying the perfect curvature of his spine as he stretched.

Maybe I stared too hard, gave him the evil eye or something, because he lost his balance, fell backwards onto a carpet knife and sliced his finger. The blood gushed instantly spraying my cream-coloured wall. His olive skin washed out to white.

'Mama!' I cried.

Next thing I know I'm in the bathroom holding his

bloody hand in a white towel. I didn't know where his trembling hands ended and mine began.

'Does it hurt?' I whispered. A warm sensation rose up between my legs. I squeezed my thighs together.

'Yeah, tighter … wrap the towel around tighter.' He moved closer and the metallic smell of his blood filled me.

'I don't want to hurt you again.'

'You won't.'

My mother rushed in. 'Where the hell your father put the bandages?'

I shrugged. Mum saw the white towel, now drenched red, and frowned.

'Why are you using the *white* one?' she hissed in Greek and handed me a striped kitchen towel.

'What did she say?'

'She, uh, wants to know if you'll need stitches.'

'Not sure … what do you think?' He peeled the towel away from his wound. More blood trickled down his wrist and onto my jeans.

'Shit, sorry.'

My mother made a loud *tut-tut* noise and quickly dabbed at the stain on my jeans.

'Mum it's only blood,' I laughed nervously and pushed her away.

'I told you not to bother him didn't I?' she muttered in Greek.

'What's she saying?'

'She has a great stain remover.' I smiled and relaxed my grip on his hands.

My mother spat more Greek, 'don't get his blood on you again!' and rushed out.

'Where's she going?'

'To find you a bandage … let's run your hand under some water.'

Warm water fell on his hand and he flinched. I nudged the door shut with my foot, put my arm around his shoulders and …

'Why did you close the door?'

Mother burst in holding a pair of her beige pantyhose. I sprang back.

The carpet layer grinned. 'She really *is* going to dress the cut isn't she?'

Mum pulled his hand from mine and wrapped it in another towel before securing the makeshift bandage with her pantyhose.

'There!' she said, 'you be alright. Go see the doctor … and you,' she motioned towards the door, 'go clean your bedroom.'

'You okay?' I asked, reaching out to touch his pantyhose.

My mother nudged me away. 'Don't be stupid, he is alright,' and then she added, in Greek, 'go clean the blood before it dries on your bedroom wall!'

'What did she say?'

'She hopes you'll come back again when your cut heals,' I replied and dashed out.

☆☆☆

When Madonna first burst onto the pop scene in a flurry of crucifixes and overgrown eyebrows, she became one of virginhood's greatest neons. Here was a woman shamelessly hurling the notion of 'touched for the very first time' onto dancefloors around the globe.

I prayed she would be a one-hit wonder.

Virginity wasn't meant to be sung about on a gondola with a lion roaming hungrily in the background. Virginity was meant to be hidden, not applauded. This wasn't Ancient Greece where the Parthenon was built in tribute to the virgin Goddess Athena. And this wasn't the Ancient Middle East either where sacred books were bound in the skin stripped from a virgin's inner thighs. No. This was the modern world where the only Greek virgin worth celebrating was thick, green and dressed salads.

My parents shone a very flattering light on virginity. It was sex that was a no-no; a forbidden 'flesh-press' sanctified only by marriage. When love scenes appeared on TV, Dad shouted, 'Yucky!' loud enough for his eight year old daughter to hear. I heard it then. I hear it now. And sometimes I still watch love scenes through slightly parted fingers.

As a little girl, the most terrifying thing on television was Rod Stewart's video, *Tonight's the Night*. It epitomised all that sex was to me. Mysterious, scary and smeared in Vaseline. How could the girl be so calm at the mercy of Rod in his satin shirt?

Rod gazed into the camera, red wine in the foreground, roaring fire in the background.

'*Nobody's gonna stop us now*,' he threatened.

Then he lead the girl by the hand up those white stairs. You never saw her face. The camera panned down from her long brown hair to her white sandals. What was going to happen once they reached the top? What was she letting herself in for? She climbed the stairs in a trance. A virgin to the sacrifice. No argument. No questioning. Will it hurt? Will you take that ridiculous satin shirt off? Nothing. She just followed.

But it was different with Prince. In *Under the Cherry Moon*, a virgin lay in a candlelit cave. There were no stairs to climb or satin shirts to negotiate. She clutched his hands and he dug deep inside, moving over her like a gentle wave.

Playground gossip picked up where rock stars left off. Someone said you did it – whatever 'it' was – with your clothes on. And I revealed this pearl at a family gathering. All the cousins were there. The fashionable, flare-trousered goddesses who huddled in a bedroom to gossip and practise 'boy moves' on big white pillows jammed between their legs.

I peeked around the bedroom door. My beloved Pillow came flying out at me.

'No baby pillows allowed!' one cousin yelled and the door was shut in my face.

But I didn't budge. I stayed behind that door straining for a tidbit that would earn me kudos in the playground. I pushed a corner of Pillow into my mouth and sucked as a cousin revealed her latest fashion tip; for ultimate sex kitten effect, she wore her crocheted bikini top with the crocheted holes positioned just over her nipples.

I sucked a little more until my eyelids fluttered and closed.

'*That's* not right. You are *such* a baby! This is how you do it,'

My eyes flew open.

'Course I won't be wearing any clothes … '

I sprang out of my foetal position and fell backwards onto the door – it creaked open.

'Agni you little sneak – get out of here!'

'People have sex with their clothes on,' I said. 'Don't fib! People have sex with their clothes on. I know all about it.' I said.

The girls glared at me for a moment before opening fire with their pillows.

'You don't know what sex is!' one cousin roared as a pillow hit me in the face.

'Yeah, her parents probably won't tell her about it until she's twenty!' another cousin shrieked, her pillow narrowly missing a vase of flowers on the landing.

I ducked, holding Pillow out as my shield. Then I scrambled to my feet and lunged at them. Tears scorched my eyes. I yelled. I kicked. I was crying so hard I couldn't see their stupid, beautiful, angry faces. Before I knew it I was back downstairs with the adults. No one would talk to me. And when the flare-trousered few emerged, I tried to redeem myself.

I tugged on a cousin's flares.

'You know, you're right,' I raised my hands, pretending they were naked bodies, 'yeah, you're right. If they had clothes on, they'd be far away from each other like this, but if they don't have any clothes on … '

I clapped my hands together and looked up at her but she had turned away.

☆☆☆

In the 'heyday' of my early-twenties virginity, I worked in an advertising agency populated with screamingly confident sexualities. Lolly was counting the days since her last 'fuck'. She was on day 26 and on full alert for her droughtbreaker.

One day she skipped into the office yelping something about the rain tumbling down. Everyone gathered around her, except me. I stood at the water cooler sipping lukewarm water from a paper cup, a familiar rhyme on my lips.

*Down came the rain and washed poor Incy out.*

'Well?' A woman with a head full of red curls bounced up and down.

'Do we alert the press?' said the guy from accounts.

Lolly motioned for everyone to move in close. Then she cleared her throat, pushed her hair off her shoulders and began,

'Well, he was *gorgeous*,'

'Yeah?' The redhead grinned.

'And tall,'

'Hm … ' The MD's secretary swooned for effect.

'And he bought me dinner at an exclusive restaurant,'

'Flashy bastard.' The guy from accounts folded his arms.

'And we went back to his place for plunger coffee.'

'Come to *mama*.' The redhead began to bounce again.

'And then we *tore* each other's clothes off,'

'Come on spit it out, I put my calls on divert for this.' said the receptionist.

And then Lolly of the broken drought burst out laughing.

'I already did!'

'Did what?'

'Spit it out!'

'Bullshit.' The MD's secretary pushed her.

'He got his money's worth then.' The guy from accounts nudged her in the ribs and walked off.

'You sucked his dick?' The receptionist rolled her eyes and returned to her desk.

'That's it?' The redhead stopped bouncing.

*Out came the sun and dried out all the rain.*

Lolly beamed. 'Drought's over!' she said and threw her hands in the air.

'Yeah, you did it,' The redhead gave Lolly a small pat on the back, 'er, well done.' she said and walked away.

Lolly turned to me but the loading instructions on the water cooler had suddenly caught my eye.

☆☆☆

Dog-eared and soaked in Fanta. That sums up my first encounter with a penis.

I had just come out of History class to find a friend standing with a group of very excited girls. They were watching the resident tough girl, fishing something out of a garbage bin.

'What's she doing?' I whispered.

'Rescuing our education.' she replied and craned her neck for a better view.

'What?'

'Some senior girl brought her sister's Playgirl magazine to school ... she almost got caught with it, so she dumped it in the bin. The tough girl's getting it back for us.'

'Why?'

'Why? For our own good that's *why*. Come on.'

I dragged my feet and joined a bigger bunch of girls standing by the bin.

'What's the best thing to come out of a cock?' one girl giggled.

'Wrinkles!'

Tough Girl looked up from the bin.

'Will you kids shut up? I'm trying to fucking concentrate!'

The group fell silent. I inched behind a nearby tree. You didn't mess with Tough Girl. She could crumple you with a look, devour you with a hissed 'fuck off'. She was short and built like a stack of bricks and she was always covered in bruises.

'This is a place of learning,' Tough Girl finally announced in a voice that would have looked more at home in a suit and flat leather pumps. 'And we are here to learn.'

She shook the pages of the magazine and showered the asphalt with drops of Fanta.

'Ladies I present to you – the *penis*.'

Tough Girl flipped open the magazine and there it was; a soft, thick sausage-like creature nestled between a pair of shaved thighs. I didn't want to look. I didn't want to look away either. My stomach flipped over. And Tough Girl kept turning the pages for her hysterical, breathless audience.

'Look at the veins in that one, it's like my Dad's street map!'

Centrefolds were yanked out and studied. Naked men with blinding white teeth and plastic tans grinned at me. There were dicks in every size, shape, colour and mood swing. Some had longer fleshier tips you could tie knots in. Others had clean, bald tops shaped like the mushrooms that grew in my Grandmother's garden.

My stomach turned again. There must have been a mistake. Surely we weren't expected to have sex with a fungus. I turned to walk away. There was nothing more to see here.

'Hey you, catch!'

I turned around in time to see the magazine tumbling towards me in slow motion. I reached out to cushion its fall but pulled away at the last minute. Laughter erupted among the girls.

'It won't bite.' Tough Girl yelled. 'You are *such* a virgin!'

'I just don't … want Fanta on my fingers.'

A teacher's voice tore across the schoolyard. 'What are you girls doing out of class?'

'We're having an anatomy lesson Miss,' Tough Girl called out, quickly stuffing the magazine into her bag.

'Get to class now!'

'Yes Miss!' the girls chorused and I followed them to the next period. Media Studies.

☆☆☆

Dad ferried me to and from everywhere; school, university, work. We drove thousands of miles together and there was always time for a wisecrack, a lecture. Always time to read each other's horoscope.

'Do I have lucky stars today Agni?'

*Change is beginning to make its presence felt in your world. Don't fight it. Don't be alarmed by it either. Saturn, the great planet of change, can work in your favour – if you only let nature run its course ...*

'All bullshit.' Dad swung around a corner. 'you always were my lucky star ... from the day you were born.'

He also ferried me to and from my childhood. Then one day, as a newly annointed twenty-something, I interrupted the nostalgia.

'What if I have sex before marriage?'

'What?' my father swerved to avoid a dog, 'good girls don't talk like that.'

That was rich coming from Dad; the man who had lived the heady life of a single nightclub muso through his thirties. The man who turned lots of 'good girls' bad when they succumbed to his goofy sex god charms – slicked-back dark hair, Roy Orbison glasses, gap-toothed grin. He enjoyed strings of one-night stands with leggy dancers called Ursula and Lola. But every night, as he played hypnotic Latin American tunes on his piano accordion, he'd peer out into the audience at the latest round of 'good girls' – the demure young ladies with the well-spun hairdos and pastel micro-minis. They were the band's pickings for the night and when I was old enough to understand, my father justified his conquests with a flick of his bushy eyebrows and the words,

'I was a hot young man Agni. That's what we did.'

Then, decades after sharing a school playground, my mother walked back into Dad's life. She was Liz Taylor in miniature. He was hooked. And the Lolas and Ursulas were history.

A lifetime away from loosened beehives and showgirl romps, my father diluted his past for my benefit. Between traffic lights, he'd sneak in a bit of,

'I know you're not a little girl anymore,'

'Dad, stay in the lane!'

Then, when the lights turned green,

'Agni, you're a woman now I understand, just be careful, you know … AIDS,'

It was more than I got from my mother though who insisted she was sick of sex.

She looked up at me from her potato peels.

'Once he spills inside you, it's over. He's had his release. And then you have to clean up his dirtiness. That's sex dear Agni.'

And I was expected to say, 'Yuck, really?' So I did.

'That's sex. If you like it, do it. I don't care. He'll have his fill. Sex will steal your purity. The man will go to someone new. But marriage is different. It's respected.'

'Come on Mum, you must like sex, you love Dad right?'

'It's not everything,' she said, turning down the heat on the stove.

'Yeah, but you love Dad. Don't you enjoy sex, being close to him?'

'Oh, for heaven's sake. Why are you asking this? You have nothing to do?'

'I am a *virgin*.' I hissed. '*Tell* me!'

'You are a *flower!*' she snapped, 'and don't you forget that.'

'I just want to know.'

'Nothing to know. You will have sex, don't worry. Don't get itchy. It will come and pass and you will get sick of it.'

'What else Mum? Talk to me.'

'Not about stupid things. Do you want chips or mashed potatoes?'

'It's not stupid.'

'Tell me what you want Agni!'

'I want you to tell me about sex.'

'Christ! What do you want me to tell you? Yes, I love your father, he's my husband isn't he? But sometimes, in bed, I can't be bothered. You get sick of sex after a while, now, do you want chips or mashed potatoes?'

'Mashed potatoes.' I pouted just as frustration sneaked up on me.

'I bet you love it.' I said. 'Yeah, you love sex Ma. You're just pretending to be the Virgin Mary so I won't screw the next man I meet 'cause Mum says it's the best thing ever!'

Mum looked at me. She sighed and pulled the glasses off her sweaty face.

'I'm going to make chips.'

☆☆☆

My mother was sick of it. My work colleagues couldn't get enough of it. And there I was, the virgin in the middle. Who could I reveal myself to?

On Fridays our office lunched at the local Thai restaurant. I nibbled on sweet and sour pork. They swallowed bottles of wine and bowls of laksa.

'Truth or dare?' someone asked me as the dishes were cleared away.

'Dare,' I replied.

The office hearthrob, Roman, plucked a red chilli from his bowl.

'Eat this,' he smiled, 'or tell the truth.'

The truth? I took the chilli. I stared at the dripping, fermented mess it had become. It didn't even look like a real chilli anymore. But I swallowed it, whole and fast, so my tastebuds wouldn't catch on. And then I got a small round of applause.

'That's some secret you got.' Roman winked.

A few months shy of my 25th birthday, I started planning my getaway. A sabbatical in Greece. The promised land. The permissive land. On the Islands I would unfurl …

I slipped my bikini top off and lay on Santorini's black volcanic sand. And the old fisherman said *tut-tut* as he hauled in his slippery catch. I wore midriff-baring tops with torn denim shorts. My mother said only nightclub dancers dressed like that. I nibbled ear lobes and tasted sweaty lips. Smashed my body up against hard English boys. Breathed in mouths drenched in alcohol. Kissed on deserted beaches at dawn. And wandered drunk through sleeping villages where my date and I groped each other until a light was flicked on above our heads and an angry voice cried out in the night.

I waded through the crowd in my favourite nightclub; it was always smoky and packed with the stench of cheap perfume. I climbed up on a bar, negotiated the pools of spilt bacardi and cola and moved as if I were dancing in front of my mirror at home. Sweat stuck to my body like the t-shirt that clung to the Adonis setting spirits on fire behind the bar.

I slipped one heel off and touched the nape of his neck with my toe. He grinned up at me wiping away puddles of cola at my feet.

The following day I met up with a group of girls from my hotel. We stripped down and spread out on rocks jutting out from the base of the cliffs. I closed my eyes and let the sun's fingers stroke colour into my skin.

'It will take the sting away.' the Adonis said smothering my sunburnt breasts with the homemade Greek yoghurt he'd collected from his mother's fridge.

'You begin all your first dates like this?' I said and gasped as the yoghurt skimmed my goosebumps.

'Don't worry,' he smiled. 'I'll lick it off.'

I looked down at myself. My nipples looked like little maraschino cherries.

'Delicious.' he whispered and devoured me like an expensive dessert.

They called him DJ Yanni. He had hands like a drag queen's. Soft and manicured. Big. And every night I went to the club to watch him spin his records. I loved the way his fingers skimmed over vinyl coaxing a mish mash of melodies into one with the flick of a wrist.

One night as he drove me home, I marvelled at how easily he changed gears and crossed himself when we passed a church.

'I bet,' I began slowly, 'I bet you can't make me come while you drive.'

'Sounds like an easy bet,' he laughed.

A few minutes later, his hand wedged between my thighs, we passed another church and he pulled his fingers away to cross himself. I couldn't believe it.

'Er, ah, ah, I … ' I began to say, between urgent breaths.

But before I could ask my DJ to show reverence with his other hand, he'd already crossed himself, changed gears and made me lose the bet.

☆☆☆

My last night in Greece was spent in Athens, in a double bed, alone. My uncle snored in the next bedroom. The music from the bar downstairs thumped up through the floor. Lyrics soaked in innuendo ripped through the room and high-pitched giggles floated over my bed.

There's a whole city out there full of penises, I thought. Yes. Of course. Yes! A whole city. How could I have missed it. Oh the possibilities.

But what could I do? Ask a few passersby to draw straws for my virtue?

# 3

# late night porn and parmesan

A conversation with Sex.

The Virgin trembled.

'So you must be, Sex.'

'Yes I am,' Sex said.

'Pretty humble for such a famous thing.'

'Humble, famous, obscure, nothing, everything – anything you want.' Sex said.

'Anything.'

'Yes. People like to paint me different colours to suit their own perceptions of what I ought to be ... mysterious, dirty, fun, evil, exciting,' Sex said.

'Yeah, yeah, I get you.'

'You do? But I thought you were a virgin.' Sex said.

'No, I mean, yes, yes I am a virgin.'

'Right,' Sex said.

'You think that's right. You think it's OK to be a virgin?'

'OK, terrible, funny, awful, fantastic.' Sex said.

'Which one?'

'All of them. None of them.' Sex said.

'You're not making any sense.'

'I don't have to. People can accept me. Or not.' Sex said.

'How can people accept something they know nothing about?'

'What's to know? I feel good. Or not.' Sex said.

☆☆☆

When people spoke of first time sex it was always in terms of fruit and flora; to be deflowered, to lose your cherry. Devirginisation was my term. It erred a little on the industrial side, but I preferred it.

I arrived home from Greece determined to let everyone believe I was well and truly devirginised. Magdalene came to visit soon after and she was the one to convince.

Mag was my only Greek friend. But that's where our similarities ended. While my mother bought me linen for my 'marital bed', Magdalene's took her and her boyfriend mattress shopping. I aspired to be Mag. And over the years she acted like some bizarre ATM of sexual experience for me. Everytime I needed to know about something I was too Greek or too good to experience myself, all I had to do was ask her. A newly minted lawyer, Magdalene collected lovers as religiously as she did stilettos. When she went to Greece, she came back with twelve pairs of shoes and sexy stories. My suitcases were so stuffed with fantasies, I had little room for shoes.

I looked at Magdalene sitting cross-legged and confident in our living room; cropped dark hair, floor-skimming, tight skirt. Magdalene oozed woman in her wool blend couture.

'I want to know *everything* about your Greek island adventures!' She clapped her hands like an excited child.

I mumbled something about sunbathing nude on Santorini.

'I hope you used sunscreen,'

'Not always.' I said.

'You know, Greek yoghurt is meant to soothe sunburn.'

'Fancy that.'

Magdalene laughed. 'I know, bizarre.'

She reached into a glossy bag and pulled out a tissue-wrapped thing. It was a negligee. A belated birthday present.

'Happy 25th!' she said and hugged me.

I turned her gift over in my hands. Did I like it, did I really like it? Well I had to didn't I? Every girl gushes over lingerie, it's the hormonally balanced thing to do. But that mock chiffon never did it for me. I preferred my powder blue undies with the puffy lion that squeaked when he was pushed.

☆☆☆

Back at work, tales of debauched weekends raced each other around the office.

'I got totally bladdered and took him home … '

' … fucked if I remember what happened next … '

' … she showed me her split … '

' … so I said yes … '

' … just this once, I told him … '

' … and I said, I just want to see it … '

' ... ten shots of tequila ... '

' ... watch your fucking language I said, there's cunt about.'

' ... eleven pints of lager ... '

' ... and it was pavement pizza for everyone.'

I closed my eyes and whispered *gamoto* – Greek for 'fuck it'. No one noticed in the office, but at a family lunch it was the hottest topic of conversation.

'What did you say Agni?' My uncle cornered me at the barbeque where sausages and souvlakia spat.

'I said, when is that meat going to be ready gamoto!' I replied.

He collapsed with laughter. 'Hey ... hey everyone, come and listen to our little Agni,'

I left him laughing, clutching tongs to his belly, and walked into the kitchen where aunts and female cousins bustled about mixing, seasoning, washing up and stirring.

Standing in a corner chatting on his mobile phone was my older cousin Alexander – or the 'Greek Hulk in designer jeans' as he liked to be called. Alexander bought hair gel by the kilo and mobile phone cases to match his shoes. He also chose his clothes based on their 'bulge potential'. T-shirts had to be tight. Trousers the same. He wasn't above illusory bulges either.

'You want to wear thick socks in this heat?'

'*Yes* Mum ... do I have to wash them myself?'

'Give them to me, you'll ruin them.'

Younger male cousins hung around him like ravenous blow flies at an Aussie barbie.

'Elle stood *next* to you at the bar?'

'Far out! What's she like?'

'Like every other supermodel who comes on to me.'

I stared at him as he chatted into his phone. A pair of sunglasses gleamed in his rock-hard cow-lick. He was, quite simply, Alexander the Great Greek Son.

He walked over, phone clamped to his ear.

'Hi gorgeous … great tan,' he said and grabbed my waist.

'Gamoto!' I shoved him. 'Keep your paws off.'

'Oooooh … didn't we pick up the culture! *Huh? Talking to my cousin … yeah, she's cute – for a cousin, heh, heh … just back from Greece …* ' Alexander poured me a glass of wine, ' *… we're meeting the girls at 5 … yeah cool, later.*'

He snapped his phone shut and handed me the wine.

'You look different Cuz.' he said.

'Good different or bad different?'

'Good, great, yeah great.'

'Thanks. You too.'

'I try.' he smiled.

'Sleep with any supermodels lately?'

'Now that would be telling.' he grinned sucking on his mobile's antenna.

Alex's mother looked up from the sink. 'Meet any good boys in Greece?' she said.

'Not one gamoto.' I replied and sipped my wine.

'Did you say what I *think* you said?' she giggled behind her marigold gloves.

'She's a big girl mum.' my Cousin said and answered his mobile, '*talk to me.*'

'I know that! Get off the damn mobile.' she sighed and handed me a silver platter. 'Take this to your uncle love.'

'Do you see this beautiful girl?' my father said handing

me a souvlaki.

'What girl? She's an old woman.' my uncle grabbed the platter from my hands and slapped it against my bottom. 'How old are you?'

'Too old to be smacked gamoto!' I slapped him back and he roared with laughter.

'Bet that's not what you told the Greek boys,' Alexander plucked the souvlaki out of my hand and took another call, '*yo.*'

'Wouldn't *you* like to know!' I lunged at him but he had already run off.

'*I'd* like to know,' my father grinned and pinched my cheek.

'Hey, what's this pinching, is she a baby?' My uncle handed me another souvlaki.

'Well, you know.' Dad blushed. 'Agni is still my little … ' His voice trailed off.

'We need another platter here!' my uncle shouted.

My Aunt rushed out with two plates.

'Just in time Wife … you can stick around for my joke too,'

'God, not that filthy priest joke again.'

'Sh, my niece will appreciate this one … so there's this priest with one eye,'

☆☆☆

'Telefono!' Mum's voice burst into my room startling me as I drew a line of kohl onto my eyelid. Poo. Queen of the Nile to Groucho Marx in one slip.

'Telefono!'

'Okay, okay. Hello?' I said dabbing a wet fingertip to my eyelid.

'Hi it's me.'

'Oh, hi Magdalene, how are you going?'

'*I'm* fine. How about you? You dropped off the face of the planet!'

'Who me? Nah, hey, uh, how did that rape trial go?'

'Fine, fine, now *where* have you been *Girly?*'

'Well I, work's been just nuts … was he found guilty?'

'Jury's still out. Okay so I'm the crappy friend, I should've called.'

'Still out? You're kidding me! You said it was a cut and dried case,'

'I know, I know, listen we haven't talked for weeks,'

I looked in the mirror. The kohl had smudged. My eyelid was red.

'I haven't had a spare second; barbeques, birthdays,'

'Yeah, yeah, but now the parents aren't around, tell me about the Islands. How were they … *really?*'

'Huh? Hang on, my mother's calling,'

I cupped my hand over the receiver and stared at my red eye. I must have stared at it for five minutes. In the distance I heard a tiny voice.

'Hello? Hello?'

Could I conjure up some breathtaking bullshit?

'Is anybody *there?* Hello!'

'Sorry about that – so yeah, when are you back in court?'

'Agni are we going to catch up *properly or what? How were the Islands?*

'Wha-? Well, God, they're still the same, lots of white-washed houses, lager louts, great tzatziki. Nothing's changed.'

'Nothing?'

'Nothing.'

'Nothing's changed? Or *nothing's* changed?'

Silence.

'Hello?'

I fiddled with the hem of my jeans.

'I'm still a virgin ... no big deal.'

Insides out. Game over. Suddenly I felt more exposed than I ever did when I pretended to be cocky, worldly, devirginised Agni. I looked in the mirror. Both eyes were reddening now and kohl had nothing to do with it.

☆☆☆

He nudged the silk robe off her shoulders and stroked baby oil into her breasts.

'Do you know what you do to me?' he breathed.

'Why don't you tell me.' she said and pushed her thigh between his legs.

*Are you tired of limp hair? Do your bad hair days last for months? Put the air back in your hair and get back the hair you deserve ...*

I pressed 'mute' and wandered into the kitchen for a hunk of parmesan cheese. Hunk in hand, I clicked off the kitchen light and flopped back onto the couch. I pressed 'mute'.

*... there are hundreds of guys and girls waiting for your call now! So pick up the phone and join the party. It's easy, it's fun and you could meet your dream match!*

'I like where you've put your thigh,' he said running his mouth over her breasts.

She groaned. I gnawed on my parmesan. He pulled on her nipples with his front teeth. She threw her head back in a cloud of blonde curls. She moaned. I shuffled a few cushions around.

'You like that?' he pushed her hands down to his crotch and pressed her lips to his ear. 'Tell me how you want it,' he hissed.

'From behind,' she breathed.

' … like the sound of that.' he said.

I chewed furiously on my parmesan.

He threw her over his shoulder like a rag doll and carried her to the bedroom. Candlelight danced on the walls. He lay her down on a big, brass bed. She turned over and touched herself.

Something insistent started up between my legs.

'Turn the music up,' she whispered.

He reached across her body and hit 'up' on the remote control. The hair on his chest tickled her nipples. She smiled and grabbed hold of his head.

'I've changed my mind,' she said and pushed him down between her legs.

'It's a woman's prerogative.' He smiled and lowered his head.

*Finally! A kitchen knife that stays sharp without sharpening! With the new …*

I swallowed my cheese, pressed 'off' and went and stood outside my parents' room. Chorus snoring. I walked into my bedroom, flicked on the light and began to rummage around in the wardrobe. Pushing my way through a mound of baby clothes, abandoned dolls and old high school files, I pulled out a small stack of books wrapped in thick plastic. One title read, *Naturally Original. A guide to the female body.* It was a personal development book from highschool and on the front was a picture of a girl sniffing a lily. I stopped breathing for a second. The snores were still coming loud and clear. Good. I flicked the book open and thumbed through the musty pages. And there it was.

A fading, black and white diagram of a vagina. Fig:12 on page 15, Chapter 5.

I bookmarked the page with a finger and carried it to the bathroom. Locking the door, I sat cross-legged on the fluffy pink bathmat and opened the book.

*... our summary of the female reproductive organs begins at the vulva.*

My mother kept a scattering of make-up on a thin glass shelf above the sink. A red lipstick and two eye pencils in 'cocoa' and 'midnight' fought for space with a shiny Chanel compact – my mother's pride and joy. She gave it a spit polish every morning after she used it before placing it gently onto a square of black faux velvet. I reached up and grabbed the compact. And then, like a move in a bizarre game of Twister, I squatted, holding Mum's Chanel compact between my legs.

*The biological symbol for the female is derived from the hand mirror of Venus – Roman goddess of love and fertility. And our summary of the female reproductive organs begins at the vulva. Unlike the male, a female's sexual organs are almost entirely hidden. The vulva is an effective cover for the narrow tunnel known as the vagina. This is a muscular sheath that acts as both a receptacle for the penis during copulation and a birth canal for the foetus.*

I strained to see my 'sheath'. But all I could see was darkness and the occasional flashes of pink. Mum's foggy compact, my Twister squat and the surrounding pink fluffiness of the mat wasn't exactly conducive to an internal examination. One look at that mat and all I could think of was Mum beating the dust out of it every week.

*Two pairs of fatty, fleshy skin flaps surround the entrance to the vagina and the urinary opening: the labia majora and the labia minora located under the labia majora. The clitoris, situated toward the front of the vulva, is a small structure shaped like a cylinder, not dissimilar to the male penis. It is very sensitive and contains tissue capable of becoming erect when sexually aroused.*

A male penis? I felt like I'd just been introduced to a new friend. I touched its dry little head and a small electrical sensation rippled through me. I pulled away and deepened my squat.

*The fine membrane of tissue protecting the vaginal opening can stretch to accommodate the girth of a penis during first time sexual intercourse. This tissue is called the hymen. See Fig: 12.*

Girth? Stretch? I squinted at the diagram. The criss-cross of lines pointing to faded bits of genitalia alarmed me. So that line ran to … what? Bullshit. None of what I saw in the mirror matched Fig:12. This had to be some kind of sick hoax. I focused back on my reflection, and then, just as the mirror was fogging up again, I saw it.

In amongst the fleshy, flappy pinkness, was a tiny, tiny opening. Tunnels didn't get any narrower. It looked so tight. I steadied my breath and placed a trembling finger above it. Maybe I could poke just a little harder. Maybe I could relieve all my anxieties here, now with one, gentle – push.

The doorknob rattled violently.

'Are you alright?'

# 4

# no hymen, no cry

He arrived. Topless. Torso glistening in the heat. Hard muscles, skin like dark, bitter chocolate. Alluring, fattening all at the same time. I smiled hello from my park bench like I'd just seen an old high school friend and not a seething mass of testosterone I couldn't wait to devour.

'Hey,' he said, sitting down beside me.

His head, almost bald, shone in the sunlight. I imagined my fingers running and skipping across his stubble. Sandpaper.

'You made it,' I said pretending to be more interested in my tuna sandwich.

'Starving,' he replied and tore into my bread with his mouth.

Lips jammed up against my fingers. Teeth scraped against my skin.

'You know I, er gotta get back to work er, soon,' I faltered, pointing to the mayonnaise sliding down his chin.

He smiled, oblivious, and stuck his chin out for me to get it. Colour surged into my cheeks. I inched closer and with a shaky finger, wiped the runaway sauce off. I fumbled around for a tissue until I gave up and licked the cream away before he could see. But he saw and he nodded, motioning to my sandwich for more. I ripped off a corner with crust and began feeding him. He opened wide, eyes fixed on me, and chewed every mouthful slowly. Jaw muscles flexed in his chocolate cheek. And he savoured every morsel as if he hadn't eaten in days. I pushed the last square of sandwich into his mouth. He clamped his lips down over my fingers startling me.

'Full.' he said and lay down on my lap.

Birds fluttered from tree to blossom. A little old lady poked at a bush with her walking stick. An office worker rustled a broadsheet. I closed my eyes and turned my face to the sun savouring the heat that tore through my jeans.

That night we tiptoed down dark alleys searching for doorways to kiss in. Corners to touch on. He pressed his fleshy, brown lips against mine but I didn't taste his tongue immediately. He toyed with my mouth, sucked gently on my lips; deliciously adult kisses that were light years away from the imagined pecks of a tight-lipped sweet sixteen year old.

Sweet sixteen, never been kissed. Definitely a birthday I wanted to forget.

My parents had organised a party for me. They hired a hall at the local club – a DJ was thrown in as part of the deal and Dad booked a live Greek band; he'd play accordion, his brother would bang on the drums and a family friend, famed for his million dollar Lotto win, would pluck the bass guitar. For dinner we'd feast on filo puffs crammed with fetta cheese and spinach, cold cuts and roast pork courtesy of our local Greek butcher, Theo (and I'd 'get' Thanassi his gorgeous 18 year old son 'thrown in as part of the deal'.)

Truth is, cold cut deal or not, Thanassi wasn't mine to 'get'. I just wished he was. Thanassi was the highlight of the grocery route I took with Mum every Saturday. He had curly brown hair that fell in his eyes (he constantly 'lost' his hair net) and a mouth full of steel and elastic bands that somehow added to his magnetism. Girls would file into the shop to giggle and ogle at him over the rows of pork sausages his father made him stuff.

'Tell your girlfriends they buy or they get out.' his father steamed in Greek.

Occasionally, Thanassi caught my gaze, but I'd blush and quickly avert my eyes to his father's chopping block; worn in the middle where scores of knives had sliced and cleavers had chopped, stained at the edges where bits of pink fat clung and blood had congealed neatly in the grooves.

'Mince my meat now so I can see.' Mum warned his father who winked and said,

'Always, dear woman, always!'

'Why Ma?' I asked.

'They put off-cuts in the packaged mince, that's why.'

As usual, Magdalene had set an annoyingly early, if not exotic, precedent for the 'first kiss'. At age thirteen, she'd fidgeted with a boy in the storeroom of a shoe boutique under last season's silver platforms. In the face of such glamour, how could I admit my lust for the heir apparent to a mincing machine?

On the night of the party my butterflies were in full

flight. And when I thought about my plans for the evening, they batted their wings so fast I felt like throwing up. I was determined to kiss Thanassi at my party – before or after the roast pork was sliced up, it didn't matter. So long as I went home far from 'sweet', I'd be happy.

'You look anaemic.' My mother pinched my cheek, 'what's wrong with you?'

'Nothing.'

'Put some more blusher on.'

'No.'

'Yes.'

I got dressed in a cloud of pink dust.

My dress was a knee-length, strapless polyester number in watermelon. The bodice was padded and sprinkled with iridescent sequins and the skirt ballooned at my hips; the height of 80s fashion.

The hall was still empty when we arrived. Empty except for the pink helium balloons and the balding DJ setting up his flashing lights.

'They look like traffic lights.' I said as a couple of overhead fluorescents reflected in his scalp.

'They *are* traffic lights.' the DJ said without looking up.

'Oh, um, well, I'm Agni, the birthday girl … um, have you got lots of cool music?'

'Do you know the chicken dance?'

I felt a tap on my shoulder and turned to see Magdalene resplendent in slut chic. Her hair had been teased until it blurred at the tips. Her eyes swam in a sea of blue kohl. And she wore a skirt that hindered circulation teamed with shoulder pads that swallowed her neck. I wanted to chew my sequins in envy.

Magdalene followed me to the door and took the gifts as people filed in.

'Agni, what a sweet dress!'

'Don't you look sweet,'

'Happy birthday Sweetie.'

All the girls wore pointy, shiny kitten heels and the guys looked like members of Duran Duran with their high hair and white shirts.

Alexander walked in and shoved his sleeves up nervously. Years away from being the Greek Hulk, Alex was just a bony boy in oversized shirts. He loved to roll his sleeves up as far as they would go to give the illusion of biceps (he spent the whole night at my sixteenth birthday party dancing with elbows bent to keep his 'biceps' pumped).

'Happy B Cuz. Cute dress,' Alexander pecked my cheek. 'Magdalene, you look *hot.*'

'Put your tongue back in.' Magdalene looked past him. 'Shit, is that *Thanassi?*'

'How do you know Thanassi?' I peered through the crowd.

Thanassi was coming towards us, sandwiched between two guys in shiny grey suits and a chubby girl with a Cyndi Lauper haircut.

'He sold shoes one Summer,' Magdalene pretended to shiver. '*What* a Summer.'

I felt like someone had punched my butterflies out.

'You said that shoe guy was a lot older than you.' I hissed.

'Three years is older.'

'He stuffs sausages.' Alexander said.

'Who's the scrag with him?' Magdalene frowned.

'Scrag?'

'Yeah, scrag. Tart. Poutana. Slut,'

'I get it.'

Thanassi walked up and kissed me on the cheek.

'Happy Birthday Agni,' he said and I plunged headlong into his aftershave.

'Th-thanks,'

'These are my cousins, Taki, Tony and Loula.'

Taki and Tony nodded and Loula forced her lips into a tight little smile.

'Hi, thanks for coming.' I reached over and touched Thanassi's shoulder,

'I love your shirt.'

'*I* picked it for him.' Loula said loudly and adjusted his cuff.

'She picks all my clothes.' Thanassi grinned.

'How bizarre,' Magdalene said. Loula bristled.

'Don't I know you?' Thanassi narrowed his eyes at my friend.

'Yeah silly, I was hoping … ' Magdalene began.

'Are we sitting near the dancefloor?' Loula interrupted, pulling Thanassi back.

'Yeah, on my table. The one with the balloons.' I said.

'Cool thanks.' Thanassi said and brushed my breast with his forearm as he walked away. 'Sweet dress too,' he called over his shoulder.

'Thanks, I'll … '

'What a *scrag*.' Magdalene huffed.

'Will you stop using that word.'

'Did you see how that slut was acting, and she's his

*cousin.'*

'Incest is best.' Alexander grinned.

'Maybe she's just protective. No harm in that, hey Alex?' I hugged his waist.

'Back off Cuz. Time for the single to mingle.' He pushed his sleeves up and wandered off.

'Agni *there* you are!' A large, sweaty woman pushed through the crowd. 'Do you remember my son Sotiri?' She pulled a stooped guy with a severe buzz cut from behind her back.

Magdalene made a wretching sound and looked away. I nudged her.

'I remember, hi Sotiri thanks for coming.'

'No problem.' he said and shook his mother's arm away, 'I'm having a great time.'

'You just got here.' Magdalene said.

'I know, but the atmosphere is incredible you know?'

'Glad you like it.' I said.

'And you look really beautiful.' Sotiri smiled and his mother fussed with his hair. 'Ma!'

'Don't you think he's grown Agni? Remember when you two used to squeeze his father's back pimples together? God rest his soul.'

Magdalene's mouth dropped open. Sotiri blushed and handed me a blue envelope,

'This is for you.'

'Thank you.' I said and opened the card. Sotiri had copied the signature I'd put on my birthday invitations in his card to me.

'Yeah sweet.' Magdalene linked her arm with mine. 'We'll see you later.'

'What are you doing?' I said as we walked away. 'I was talking to him.'

'You squeezed his father's pimples?'

'What? I got 10 cents a zit.'

'Spare me.' Magdalene cringed and pulled me onto the dancefloor where Thanassi was spinning Loula around and around.

'Let's show that scrag what I'm made of.' Magdalene hissed as she propped up the flagging tease in her fringe.

I tried to do the same but my hair had no tease to begin with. So I got into a self-important groove instead, eyes glued to Thanassi. Suddenly, I felt a pull on one of my saddlebags.

It was Sotiri.

'I wondered whether you might like to dance with me?' he asked.

Magdalene rolled her eyes and moved to another part of the floor.

'Pardon?' I could barely hear him.

'I was wondering whether you'd be interested in sharing this dance with me.'

'What?'

The beat was loud.

'Dance?'

'Sure.'

Loula shrieked with laughter and I turned to see her being tangoed across the floor.

Sotiri smiled, 'she's having fun.'

I nodded and another 80s classic blasted through the speakers. Sotiri slapped my shoulder excitedly and began to bop up and down as if he were on a Stairmaster. I took a few steps back in horror. Sotiri was in the 'zone'. Dancin' up, dancin' down those stairs.

I looked through the traffic lights for a better view of Thanassi. He had abandoned Loula and was almost dancing on his own, eyes closed, moving in time with the beat. The guy was an orgasm in motion. This was my chance. I felt another slap on my shoulder. Sotiri moved closer.

'What's your opinion on the state of modern pop?' His breath was a mix of mint and boiled egg.

'What?'

'Modern pop? What do you think about it?'

I shook my head. 'Too loud!'

I looked back at the spot where Thanassi was but he'd gone. I craned my neck over a couple of people. Nothing. I couldn't see him. I panicked. Had he sneaked away early? I motioned to Sotiri that I'd be back and ran off to the bar where Alexander was talking to a waitress. As I rushed up I caught the tail end of,

'How old do you *want* me to be?'

I pinched him. 'Have you seen Thanassi?'

'Ow! What's eating you?'

'Do you know where Thanassi is?'

'You mean sausage boy?'

'Have you *seen* him?' I shoved him again and the waitress walked away.

'Relax! I think he and some mates went to Bunny's.'

'The disco upstairs?'

'No, Bugs' hangout. Yes the disco upstairs.'

'Thanks.' I turned to leave. Alex grabbed my arm.

'You can't go up there Missy. Over 18 only.'

'So what, I can fake it.'

'They'll want to *see* ID.'

I pulled my arm away. 'Let go.'

I ran out of my party and jumped onto the next lift bound for Bunny's. One, two, three floors later and I stood staring at my lovely butcher boy as he laughed with a bouncer. Thanassi wandered over when he saw me.

'Hey Sweet Sixteen, having a good time?' He put his arm around my shoulders.

Adrenaline sneaked up on me. 'Yeah, you?'

'It's cool. I'm meeting some friends inside, but I'll be back down soon.'

'Oh. Well, can I come in with you?'

Thanassi looked at the bouncer, 'what do you say mate? Do the birthday girl a favour?'

'How old are you Sweetie?'

'I, um, I'm,'

'She's sixteen man. Come on, what do you reckon?'

'Dunno, rules are rules,'

My heart rushed up to my throat.

'I'll only be a minute … please?' I pressed my palms together.

The bouncer smiled and turned to his friend,

'Hey Rog, check this chick out,'

Rog, a guy with a ring through his nostril, turned around.

'Isn't it passed your bedtime Honey?'

I stood up a little taller. 'I'd like to come in for a look.'

'Well,' Rog rubbed his chin and smiled at Thanassi, 'seein' as though you asked so nicely.' He began to unclip the velvet rope just as my father came out of the lift.

'Agni love, time to cut the cake!'

I didn't move.

'Daddy's here.' Rog laughed and unclipped the rope for Thanassi who disappeared into the smoky den with a wink and a wave. I tried to follow him but Dad had grabbed hold of my hand.

'Come on Darling, everyone's waiting for you.'

'Bye, bye Sweet Sixteen.' Rog waved at me, grinning.

I smiled weakly and followed my father into the lift.

'How did they know you're sixteen?' Dad asked.

'Good guess.' I said.

Back on the parquetry floor my cake had been rolled out. It was a tower of choux a la crème with sixteen candles flickering at its base. I wanted a heart-shaped marzipan confection but Mum insisted shoux would be more impressive.

Standing behind my tower, I smiled as everyone sang me happy birthday from their seats. The right side of the room had started before the left and by the time they caught up with each other, the DJ had slapped on Kool & the Gang's *Celebrate*. With the first chorus, Mum rushed up to help me separate the choux balls and Dad took control of the band who had started playing along to Kool. Sadly, the tinny drums could never hope to match the record's jaunty soul.

Next up on the pop chopping block was Neil Sedaka's *Happy Birthday Sweet 16*. The drummer cottoned onto the sugary riff first and followed the track with stomach-churning gusto while Daddy abandoned his accordion in favour of whipping me and my make-believe curves around the dancefloor.

'*Tonight's the night I've awaited for. Because you're not a baby anymore.*'

Everyone clapped and cheered and Dad puffed up. In his skinny grey leather tie and grey shoes, he waltzed me about the floor like a blow-up doll. I looked up and saw Thanassi coming in. He gave me a thumbs up and took a seat next to Magdalene who immediately increased the tease in her fringe. I gritted my teeth between twirls. One more chorus, I thought. One more bloody, sugar-coated chorus.

'*You've turned into the prettiest girl I've ever seen. Happy birthday Sweet 16.*'

I stared into my father's shoulder and pretended to be fine when the entire hall broke into spontaneous la-la-la's along with with Mr Sedaka. I'm dreaming, I thought. Just hallucinating. I'll close my eyes and when I open them I'll be breathing in Thanassi instead of my father's moth-balled shirt. But then, without warning, Dad dipped me and I responded with about as much aplomb as a twig in a storm.

'Happy birthday my darling.' Dad hugged me hard and the guests applauded.

'Thanks Daddy.' I squeezed him back and skidded off across the floor to my table.

'Don't hunch!' Dad called after me.

Back at the table Thanassi was whispering in Magdalene's ear. I went over and draped my arms over their shoulders.

'How's it going guys?'

'Your Dad's quite a dancer,' Thanassi said.

'I know.' I said.

'Get that DJ to put something slow on,' Magdalene said, her gaze fixed on Thanassi.

'He should put a slow track on now.' I replied and pinched her shoulder.

'Ouch!' she said.

'What's wrong?' I glared at her. 'Thanassi wanna dance with the birthday girl?' I ruffled his hair and got gel under my fingernails.

'Yeah, cool.' he nodded just as Loula returned to the table, 'Hey Louls.'

'You're in my seat love.' She looked at Magdalene who pretended not to hear.

'You deaf?' Loula repeated, nudging her.

'Mag, Loula was sitting there.' I said.

'Whose side are you on?'

'No one's. Just move.' I replied.

'Sit in my seat Loula, I don't mind.' Magdalene waved to a chair opposite.

The early strains of A-ha's *Take on Me* filled the hall.

'Guys this is the *best* song,' I said. 'Let's go.'

Thanassi stood up and stretched. I smiled and held out my hand. Loula fixed me with a cold stare. Thanassi took one look at the thunder on his cousin's face and rolled his eyes.

'Come on *Louls*.' he said and lead her away leaving me with my hand still outstretched.

'I'm telling you she's a *scrag*,' Magdalene fumed.

'What are *you* so pissed off about? It's *my* birthday.'

'Oh. My. *God*. You *like* Thanassi don't you?'

'I might.'

'Why didn't you say something?'

'Like you'd care.'

'That hurts.'

'You're obsessed.'

'Who, with that *pussy?*' Magdalene made a face.

'No with you!'

Sotiri appeared at the table. 'Beautiful ladies!'

'Piss off Sotiri.' Magdalene spat and walked off.

'What's wrong with her?'

'Don't know.' I collapsed into a chair.

'No Birthday Girl you have to dance, come with me.'

Sotiri grabbed my arm and notched it up to 12 on his Stairmaster as we hit the floor. I looked over at Thanassi. He was doing a Tourette's impersonation of Simon Le Bon and still looking irresistable. Sotiri grabbed my fingers and twirled me around awkwardly. A-ha moaned.

*'Oh it's better to be safe than sorry.'*

I spotted Magdalene in the corner aiming dagger looks at Loula who caught her glare and gave her the finger.

'Sotiri can we have a break?' I shouted.

His eyes widened. 'Yes! Yes when can we make a date?'

'What? No, break, *break*. Can we stop for a bit?'

'A k-kiss?'

A-ha hit a high note and Magdalene lunged for Loula. I went to move and tripped falling into Sotiri's arms who wasted no time in poking his tongue through my lips. I pushed him back.

'What the *hell* are you doing?'

'You said kiss,' his face dropped, 'didn't you?'

I shook my head and ran to Thanassi who had dropped

to his knees just as Loula went crashing to the floor, Magdalene on top of her.

I pulled at Magdalene's shoulder pads. 'What's wrong with you?'

'That bitch started it!' Magdalene shrieked taking a swipe at Loula's face.

'Fuck off!' she cried pulling herself up to Thanassi's chest.

'You're friend's a psycho,' he said stroking Loula's hair.

My mother rushed into the fray. 'What's going on?'

'I tripped.' Magdalene scrambled to her feet and flicked her fringe.

I shot Mag an angry look. 'Everything's okay Mum.'

My mother narrowed her eyes at Magdalene and took her by the arm. 'Let's go to the Ladies.'

Thanassi walked over. 'We're going Agni.' he said while Loula hovered in the background like a wounded bird.

'Oh,' I said. 'Sorry about … '

He shrugged his shoulders. 'Loula's no angel either.' He leant over and kissed my cheek.

'Hey we're watching the birthday video at my house next week if you wanna come.'

'I'll let you know.' he said and then he was gone leaving me standing alone with egg-breath on my face.

Nearly a decade later, I found myself missing the innocence of sweet sixteen. Almost.

A would-be lover dropped to his knees and pulled my thighs towards him,

'I wanna go down on you.' he whispered.

I fell to my knees too and pulled his beautiful, black

face close.

'Not here.' I said, my cheeks blushed so bright, they glowed in the dark.

'My place then.'

'No.'

'Then where?' He buried kisses in my neck. I reached up and touched his marks.

'Let's … kiss … here.'

He stood up and left me on my knees.

☆☆☆

Another working week had been and gone.

Magdalene rushed around flinging wispy negligees into an overnight bag. I lay spreadeagled on her bed imagining the tales her mattress springs could tell.

'So are you going to sleep with this guy?'

Magdalene looked up from her underwear drawer, red-faced. 'If I told you we were sleeping in two beds 20 feet apart would that make me a good girl?'

I poked my tongue out. 'So when's the penis du jour picking you up anyway?'

'In two hours and I haven't even chosen my shoes!' she ran to her walk-in and snatched up a snakeskin heel. 'You think animal print is overkill for a farmhouse?'

'Possibly.' I replied and picked up a book on her bedside table. It had a deep red velvet cover with faded gold lettering on the spine.

*The Kama Sutra.* I gasped and hugged it. 'Oh my God, when did you buy this?

'I didn't. It's my mother's.'

'She *gave* it to you?'

'No I took it.' she said yanking two pairs of shoes out from behind a wall of glossy boxes. 'Caramel mules or my strappy copper heels?'

I hugged the book tighter to my chest. The velvet itched my skin. 'Is this a special edition?'

'Or maybe bare feet,' Magdalene whispered, admiring her foot in the mirror.

'Mag?'

'What?' she snapped.

'Is this a special edition?'

'God I don't know, who cares?'

'Are you mad? This, this is *the* book on sex!' I spluttered.

Magdalene shrugged. 'So?'

'So why does it have pride of place on your bedside table?'

'Matches the duvet.' She slipped on her caramel mules and went for a walk around her bedroom waving to imaginary friends. 'I'd forgotten how good nubuck feels.'

'Well,' I said, 'I'm going to open it.'

'Knock yourself out,' came the tired reply.

I turned to the first page and slender, brown bodies leapt out. Skewiff fingers, toes, beautiful men and women wearing detailed, blank expressions, writhed and blended into one another.

'These people are contortionists,' I said and flipped to another page where more mocha-coloured lovers bent over backwards to greet me. Magdalene looked over my shoulder.

'Learning anything?'

'Back off,' I snapped the tome shut. 'At least I don't use books as décor.'

'Call me practical.'

'Or vacuous.'

'Come on help me choose.'

'Okay, you're vacuous.'

'Oh for fuck's sake which shoes?!'

Magdalene flung herself on the bed, pushed a thumb in her mouth and sucked quickly.

'I think the copper strappy heels.' she pouted.

☆☆☆

It was Friday afternoon. The boardroom overflowed with drink and laughter and I was late. I pushed the double doors open. A high pitched giggle pinched me.

'Shut up you silly bitch!' someone said.

I tiptoed in and took my place in the corner by the mini-bar.

'Hey love, what can I get you?' The guy from accounts swayed from side to side.

'Just a sparkling water thanks.' I smiled.

'One sparkling water on the house!' he shouted and lunged towards me with a smeared tumbler. The bubbles popped over the side of the glass and splashed down my front.

'Whoopsy!' he hiccuped. 'Hey where are the fucking napkins? Hey! Wait here,' he said and stumbled off.

I looked around, dabbing at my shirt. Cigarette smoke had settled like a grey blanket over the room and someone was skipping through the tracks of an Oasis CD.

'What track's fucking Supernova?'

'It's Champagne Supernova.'

'Put Britney on!'

'She's a virgin,'

'And Madonna's the fucking tooth fairy.'

A secretary with a skinny black ponytail tittered. And snatches of conversation whipped around me. I strained to listen in but it was like fiddling with the knobs on a radio with bad reception.

A blonde with a chin stud spread her palms out.

'I used to work in a supermarket and I swear I could *smell* a woman who came to the check out wearing a sanitary pad … '

I moved along the side of the wall to where an art director in leather jeans was holding court. She was surrounded by a bunch of women with shiny mouths.

'So I get into the cab right … and I'm feeling sick as a dog and the driver, he, he starts taking corners like we're racing in the Grand fucking Prix!'

She clutched her head and shook it dramatically.

'I said stop! Stop you bloody maniac … I wanna get out! But he doesn't hear me does he and by now my stomach feels like a fucking washing machine on *spin cycle.*'

Roman grinned and swallowed some wine. He looked over and winked. I waved.

'Listen, *listen*,' the blonde flailed her arms. 'I yelled stop you wanker, stop! And then he zooms round a corner, I take one look at the window and puke my guts out,'

She slammed her green bottle down on the table. 'But the fucking window was *closed!*'

Her audience burst into spontaneous applause. The guy from accounts tapped me heavily on the shoulder.

'Here you go love!' He pushed a soaked napkin into the wet patch on my front.

'I er, I can do that.' I said and pulled at the napkin, it tore in my hands.

'Aw, now see what you've done. And you've gotta look your best for your birth-' he belched.

'What?'

The creative director stuck two fingers in his mouth and a whistle screamed through the din.

'Listen up, someone's notched up another year on the planet … Agni, where is she?'

I blushed hot red and I felt a hand push my arm up into the air.

'There she is! Raise your glasses … happy birthday to you, happy birthday to you,'

'*And maybe … you're gonna be the one that saves me,*' Gallagher wailed over my birthday song.

A few people cheered and the guy from accounts stuck a wet kiss on my cheek.

'Happy birthday!' he shouted and staggered away.

Roman came over and handed me a birthday card.

'From all of us. Happy birthday Hon.' he said and kissed my hand. 'You look surprised.'

'I am. Everyone forgot last year,' I smiled and opened the card. The messages tumbled out with a handful of star-shaped confetti.

*Happy birthday schnookums.*

*Remember those new wrinkles only disappear when you stimulate them!*

*Sweet 25 and still a Virgo.*

'Cute. Thanks.' I said and closed the card quickly, crushing the stars.

The spongy bass of a Bob Marley classic filled the room.

'Oh yeah, cool tune.' Roman took another sip of wine.

'Yeah it's nice.' I smiled.

'Nothin' like reggae Agni.' he slipped his arm around my waist, encouraging me to move with the beat. I stiffened.

'Hey turn it up!' Roman shouted over my head, 'we wanna sway *mun*,' he twisted his fingers into the creases of my skirt. 'Just relax.'

I looked up into his face. A baby face. Slightly shiny and cherubic. Like Elvis when he loved tender. I found my reggae legs and began to rock unsteadily.

'Like this?' I said, sticking a clammy palm into the small of his back.

'You got it.' Roman tightened his hold and Jamaica came to me.

Sand squeaked between my toes. A tropical breeze ruffled my fringe. I rocked from side to side. Hypnotised.

'*No hymen no cry,*' I sang and salt air stung me.

His grip loosened. 'What?'

'*No hymen no cry,*' I continued looking up through the palms.

'*What* are you singing?' he laughed, pulling his arm away.

A screech of gulls came overhead.

'You can't be serious!' Roman laughed louder and collapsed in a chair. 'Fuck you're a *scream*.'

Quicksand squeaked between my toes. I scraped my fringe straight.

'Hey Agni, wanna have a drink tonight?'

I shook my head.

Roman raised his glass to me. 'You sure? We could talk about … hymens.' he exploded again.

I reached for my bag. 'I, er, I've got a family dinner.'

'Right.' Roman smirked behind his glass.

'She doesn't drink remember?'

A woman sat cross-legged on the boardroom table peering at me through her cigarette smoke. Her eyes were ringed like a raccoon's. She took a deep drag and blew a wonky circle in my direction.

'You don't smoke either do you?' she sneered.

'No.'

'You don't drink, you don't smoke. You don't – *poke.*'

She laughed, squeezing her raccoon rings together. And Roman walked off singing a new set of Marley lyrics.

On my way home that afternoon, I passed a guy selling t-shirts on the pavement. Each one was emblazoned with the promise,

*Sex Instructor – First Lesson Free.*

I tried to imagine a Sex Instructor's classroom. Would it be blonde wood and wrought iron? Or shag pile and animal print?

'The best things in life are free, love.' a thick cockney accent snarled in my ear.

'Wha-?' I looked up.

A man with a gold tooth grinned at me. 'The *best* things in life are free!' he said pointing to the row of t-shirts.

'No capiche senor,' I muttered and scurried away.

I used to think Bob Marley was giving me good advice. I also used to think no hymen would make me all woman. Stuffed full of anxieties, I was convinced sex would cure my ills. But frankly, I didn't need sex any more than I needed a head full of dreadlocks. What I craved was a meeting with other twenty-something virgins.

But what clubs could I join? What self-help books could I buy? I couldn't stand before a bunch of fellow 'flowers' and confess all, not even anonymously. Although sex instructors touted their skills on cotton, I could hardly expect every mid-twenty virgin to advertise.

Desperate to belong to something, someone, I turned down the neon on my forehead and tried to blend in with the rest of the fucking planet.

# 5

# rose-coloured world

Mum came home from bingo with a huge grin on her face and a brown box under her arm.

In a sea of scratchy mohair and blue rinse, my mother had triumphed with a Full House to bring home the much coveted Judder Elite,

*'The latest in multi-pronged, penetrating percussion massage technology.'*

'We don't need it Ma.'

'Do you know how many women wanted to win this?'

The bingo crowd was buzzing when Mum took her seat by the stage that morning.

'The massager is on the Full House table!' a woman with drawn-on eyebrows cackled.

'Oh?' My mother feigned indifference and pulled out her chubbiest red texta.

'Yes and my daughter has one. She says not even her husband gives massages like it!'

'Here comes Bingo Barbara.' a portly woman in yellow polyester called out, 'hello Barbara!'

An attractive brunette in her fifties smiled warmly and settled into a seat on the stage.

'Hello everybody,' she waved, a hefty charm bracelet clunked against the microphone.

'Ooh, she waved at *me!*' an elderly lady struggled to her feet. 'Hello Barbara!'

'Who wants to win that *wonderful* Judder Elite?' Bingo Barbara purred and the hall filled with cheers and wolf whistles.

'Well there can only be one winner. Good luck!' Barbara slipped on her gold-rimmed specs.

And then it was eyes down.

A swift fifteen minutes later, with a call of *Two Fat Ladies*, my mother was on her way to a one-on-one with Bingo Barbara and *Judder Elite* glory.

I pulled the beige plastic appliance out of its box. It looked like a big misshapen bagel.

'We don't need it Ma.'

'Do you know how much this costs?'

'We don't need it.'

'You're fifteen, what do you know about tired muscles?' Mum snatched the massager away and placed it tenderly beside a photo of me with Santa.

I could say the devil made me do it. Or just plain old curiousity. All I know is that I stumbled on paradise that night after my parents went to bed. As the clock struck eleven and another infomercial chattered away on TV, I got better acquainted with *The Judder Elite* – and its promised 3,000 pulses per minute.

The shudder startled me at first when I placed the multi-pronged head on my body. I looked over my shoulder at the blur of plastic massaging me. Quite a sensation. Surreal even. For what human hands could massage so fast, so deeply? I let it judder a few seconds more, before moving it down and over my chest, close to the heart that vibrated against its bony cage. I hummed quietly. Hmmmmm. Like a nervous singer desperate to reach those baritone knots. Lower and lower my beige bagel went until eventually, without thinking, I'd parted my legs. Settling just below my pubic bone, *The Judder Elite* quivered – and waited.

Then a soft, tiny pulse started up inside me, deep in dark curls, sliding up my thighs, climbing higher and higher, penetrating bone and melting muscle, past kidneys and heart, legs now like jelly and, and, and,

Bingo.

☆☆☆

Magdalene rushed up, hair flying in all directions, briefcase beating against her thigh as she walked.

'Okay Girly I have 30 minutes before a meeting. What was so urgent?' She looked behind me and clenched her teeth. 'Why are we standing outside a sex shop?'

'I want to get a vibrator.'

'In broad daylight?'

'Yeah so what?'

'So what?' Magdalene shouted and then turned around to see who'd heard. She lowered her voice. 'So *what?* Agni this *reeks* of trailer trash.'

'Oh relax. It's a perfectly normal, natural thing to do.'

'No, *no*. Your finger is the normal, natural thing to do, *not* … '

A man in an expensive suit walked by, Magdalene smiled nervously and dropped her voice to a whisper again, '*not* a small *appliance*.'

'Anyway, I've already been in and,'

'Well, what do you need me for?'

'I chickened out, okay? There I said it.' I sighed, 'Mag, they're *noisy*.'

'That's right, they're noisy as well as tacky and they don't come with silencers.'

'I panicked. I saw all these, these huge rubber … '

'Stop, stop,' Magdalene pushed her palm in my face. 'I haven't had lunch yet.'

'*What* is your problem?'

'Look do you want a silent sex toy?'

'I suppose so … '

Magdalene grabbed my hand. 'Use this. I've gotta go Girly. Good luck.'

☆☆☆

I was desperate for another job. The allure of my old ad agency had worn off. Actually, I'd just grown tired of being the office virgin. I wanted to start over. I needed to be in an environment where nobody knew me, where at least I could pretend to be wiser than I really was.

Mum couldn't understand. 'Tease them back.' she said.

'I don't want to tease them back. I want to leave.'

'You want to run away.'

'Yeah, so what?'

'Stand up for yourself. Be proud you're a virgin! They should be so lucky to have a sister, or a girlfriend or a daughter like you.'

'Mum, it's time to leave.'

'Better the devil you know.' she frowned. 'If you must leave your job, do it for the better.'

'I am.'

'Are you?'

'Yes!'

'Ah, that hard head … look at me, I had a chance to be the biggest dancer in Egypt, but I said no.'

'Your father said no for you Ma.'

'And he was right. What business did a young girl have getting dressed up in women's clothes, dancing in the smoke for drunk men every night.

'You said the club was nice.'

'Don't change the subject Agni – we're talking about you.'

'You should've run away to dance.'

'And where would I be now?'

'Who knows?'

'That's right. Who knows? Stay where you are. Wait.'

'You said speed has grace in it.'

'And whoever rushes, trips.'

☆☆☆

I was up early, showered and dressed before Mum had time to make me a hot chocolate. I pulled on my new 'pubic skimmers' – tight, ink-blue denims that settled just below my bellybutton.

Mum appeared at my door and screwed her nose up at my 'skimmers'.

'Only nightclub dancers dress like that.'

'Mum.'

'Naked bellybuttons put men on fire.'

'Ma.'

'Well, you have decent shirt. You found it washed and ready my Nariman!'

'Yes Mama – thank you.' I blew her a kiss.

She disappeared into her bedroom and came back with a comb.

'Your hair's flat Agni. Tease it, like this,' she poked the comb into the crown of my hair and all of a sudden I was eight years old again, getting ready for my first Halloween at school …

Mummy pinned a pair of black velvet cat ears to my hairband. Then she covered my lips in frosty pink, drew kohl whiskers on my cheeks and picked the lint off my leotard. I stood on the tips of my black ballet slippers and stuffed Mum's stockings into my panties. I miaowed out loud. I spat and hissed. Mum looked on, proud. *You're my beautiful black cat.* I purred and licked her cheek. She pinched my velvet ear. I curled little hands around my face. Smile. Purr. Pose. Snap. Feline fatale. Mummy told me how wonderful I looked and how much prettier I was than the other girls who shimmered in their sugar plum fairy costumes and teased the boys who came as superheroes, pirates, cowboys and ghosts. Mummy said if the boy I liked chose another girl it was because she was 'loose'. As it happened, my 'crush', the small superman in the red cellophane cape, was more interested in a sugar plum tart.

'You won't look like a tart.' Mum insisted on teasing my hair high. 'I'm only making it fuller.'

I pulled the comb away. 'I'm going to be late for work!'

'Do what you like!' She grabbed the comb and left.

I dragged my fingers through the teased clump and untangled.

☆☆☆

I walked into my new office to find a beanpole in ripped jeans and red lipstick standing on a desk shouting, 'Fuck you!' into her phone. A white t-shirt hung taut over her small, hard-boiled breasts. Her bony fists tore holes in the air. Jab. Jab. All arms. All legs. A living Giacometti sculpture with limbs like long, sawn-off twigs. Her pedestal, her desk.

This was my new art director; the woman I would spend eight hours of my working day with. We were supposed to be a creative team. She'd do the pictures. I'd write the words. We'd exchange ideas, come up with concepts for ad campaigns, we'd brainstorm, go to meetings together. And, if the chemistry was right, we might share a couple of in-jokes, maybe even do a little light-hearted bitching about the suits. It could be fun. Or an absolute bloody nightmare. I stole another look at the fury on her face as she shouted abuse down the phone and decided our pairing could easily turn into the latter.

Please God, I didn't want my mother to be right.

My art director yelled one almighty 'Fuck off!' to her caller and leapt off the desk. She shook her thin mane of mousey hair and I heard her hiss, 'breathe.' before striding towards me, a shaky arm outstretched.

'You must be my new copywriter.'

I swallowed hard and shook her hand. 'Yeah, hi. I'm Agni.'

'Cool name. I'm Allegra.' she smiled and launched breathlessly into the tale of her drunken weekend, speeding sex drive and the moment she propositioned her best male friend.

'Let's fuck,' she'd said. 'But it was like fucking my brother … horrible. That was him on the phone. Says he loves me, the sad fuck.'

We worked well together.

When Allegra talked about her sex-drenched weekends, or 'fuck-ees', I smiled, wide-eyed in feigned admiration. On and on she rambled about this hangover, that lover, this hang-up, that fuck-up. I kept smiling, writing. Wrote headline, brochure, headline and tried to keep my blurbs brief. Her splashy, technicolour layouts had to have 'lots of white fucking space!

Meanwhile, any common ground shook underfoot as she blurted things without thinking; talking fast, fast, fast happy to let her words trip up.

Allegra's free spirit pissed me off. And yet, slowly I found myself warming to her. The more time I spent with this strange creature in torn denim, the more I craved to live in her 'white fucking space'. This unnerved me most of all. This and Allegra's nonchalance towards popular opinion. The girls in accounts whispered viciously about her bad breath, crooked teeth, spent virtue. The computer operator boys sneered whenever they saw her staring at girly pin-ups. But Allegra was unaffected. She loved herself.

She walked around the office in long, confident strides, expletives trailing behind her like kittens clinging to a ball of yarn. She didn't 'fucking care' what the world thought of her.

☆☆☆

I arrived at Magdalene's fancy dress party with a head full of fantasies. Would tonight bless me with a lovely boy? Would a chance flirtation by the canapes turn into something a little deeper than the mini quiches?

Maybe. Maybe not. Didn't matter. I was ready for anything.

My wig was cropped, blonde and tousled. Jeans were baggy with a fashionably frayed hem. Shirt had a bold nautical flavour, navy horizontal stripes.

I rang the doorbell and patted the single perfect mole I'd drawn just above my lip.

Yes. I was ready. Ready to be …

'Huckleberry Finn?' Magdalene looked me up and down.

'What?'

'Why one freckle?'

I touched my face in horror. 'You think I'm … '

'Where'd you get the 'little boy' jeans?'

'I'm Madonna for God's sake!'

'In what lifetime?' she laughed.

'From the Papa Don't Preach video.' I rushed to the

hallway mirror, 'can't you tell?'

Magdalene squinted at me. 'No.'

'I'm going home.' I turned to leave.

'Come on don't freak out,' Magdalene straightened my wig. 'You look good,'

'You think?'

'Yeah, in that 'ol' man river' kinda way.'

'That's it.' I shook her arm away.

'Agni just come *inside*.'

She patted my back and her sleeve jangled. I looked down to see a large silver handcuff hanging from her wrist.

'Who are you supposed to be anyway?'

Magdalene produced a small leather whip from her cleavage and smiled.

'A dominatrix,' she cracked her whip dramatically, 'in Gaultier.'

'Subtle.'

'Couldn't you tell?'

'No.'

'See? Now we're even.'

I set up camp by the canapes, happy to gobble down more than my fair share of diminutive slivers of salmon and brie. Happy to avoid small talk too. Between bites I stared at a man in a duck suit doing a slow twist with a mermaid. The duck had slipped his webbed feet between the parting in her sequinned tail and they seemed to be moving as one. Envy itched me under my androgynous wig.

A Red Indian with flabby pecs walked up.

'Catch the salmon today Huckleberry?'

I pretended not to hear and stuffed a wad of cheese in my mouth. Red laughed and stroked my ear with the tip of his plait. I gave him a dirty look.

'You've got split-ends.'

He grinned. 'Wanna closer look?'

'I've got a boyfriend.'

'So do I, we can party *together*.' He moved in closer, 'what's your name?' he whispered.

I pushed him back and motioned to my red lips. 'Look!' I hissed.

'I know, Huck in drag, I love it,'

Madonna's *Erotic* filled the room and the mermaid returned to her rock with the duck. I grabbed the Indian's plait and yanked hard.

'I'm *Madonna*.'

'Even better.' he smiled, misty-eyed. 'My man and I are *huge* fans. I'll go find him.'

I looked around for Magdalene and spotted her by the stereo, whip cocked, laughing with a vampire as he tried to decapitate prawns with his plastic fangs. They looked over at me and the bloodsucker raised a prawn in my direction. I shot Magdalene an angry look and she came strutting over.

'Why aren't you mingling?' she said, cracking her whip close to my ear.

'I'm guarding the salmon.' I said through clenched teeth.

'Not good.'

'No, it's delicious. Want some?'

'There's *real* talent here Girly.'

'Like the Red Indian?'

'He's a queen.'

'I know that and he just came on to me!'

'Well, it's not my fault your tits are swimming in stripes'.

'Thank you for noticing.'

'Anyway, someone wants to meet you.'

'Really.'

'He's the most eligible penis here my dear.'

'Really.'

'Penthouse apartment,' she continued, 'huge salary,'

'And is this penis Greek?'

'No, I'm telling you the guy's perfect.'

'So why don't you have him?'

'Lips are too thin.'

'You're kidding me.'

'I'm particular.'

'You're nuts.'

Magdalene rolled her eyes. 'Do you want to meet him or not?'

'What is he?'

'Jewish.'

'Mum won't be pleased.'

'Will she be screwing him?'

'Nice.'

'Well?'

'The Jews crucified Christ.'

'And?'

'And I'll be making out with the race who crucified Christ.'

'Making out? What are we on *Happy Days*?'

'You know what I mean.'

'Whatever … are you interested, yes or no?'

'I'll reconsider the Red Indian.'

Magdalene pushed her whip into a thin silver belt on her hips and shouted, 'Ryder!'

In a flutter of batwings, the Count was by my side. Suddenly the music seemed louder.

*'Give it up and do as I say, give it up and let me have my way, I'll give you love, I'll hit you like a truck, I'll give you love I'll teach you how to … '*

'Huck,' Ryder bowed low, his satin cape swished over my frayed jeans.

Something odd tingled inside and I smiled at him. 'I'm not … hi I'm Agni.'

'Very nice to meet you Agni.' he said taking my hand and turning it over gently, placing a small kiss on my wrist. 'You make a very sexy Huckleberry.'

That tingle came again and I took a closer look at my Count. Beneath his thickly drawn eyebrows, lurked a nice face; clear blue eyes, flawless skin. His hair was a thick shock of dark red. Magdalene nudged me with her handcuff.

'Enjoy mingling.' she said and left.

'There she is darling, look, Madonna!' The Indian minced through the crowd followed by the man in the duck suit.

Ryder turned to me, 'You're Madonna?' he asked, puzzled.

'No.' I replied, blushing. 'You were right the first time.'

☆☆☆

'Like fire and a match,' Mother muttered and sprayed a dark golden perfume on her neck. 'What time is he coming?'

'In about half an hour.' I lay on my stomach and fingered the splash of jewellery she'd laid out on her bedspread. I handed her a delicate platinum chain with a single pearl drop.

'Wear this one.'

Mum shook her head. 'I told your father to stay home.' she said and plunged her hand into a little pile of gold chains. She pulled out a gold rope chain with a large crucifix pendant.

'Why?' I sat up.

'It doesn't go with what I'm wearing.'

'No, why's Dad staying home?'

'Because fire and a match shouldn't be left alone.' Mum said and poured her gold and silver back into a velvet box.

'What?'

'I told your father to stay home. You never know what can happen.' She flung open the wardrobe and yanked out a beige raincoat.

'What's going to happen?' I jumped to my feet. 'Ryder's my *friend*. We'll talk, watch TV, we'll, we'll make some popcorn, *nothing's* going to happen.'

'Really? He's an angel?' Mum narrowed her eyes. 'You don't know your worth.' she said and pushed past me.

I followed her into the living room. 'What's that got to do with anything?'

'Talk some sense into your daughter.' Mum said and pulled on her coat.

'What's wrong now?' Dad sighed from behind a wall of

newspaper.

'She wants to turn your house into a brothel.'

'We're going to have popcorn!' I said.

My father stood up. 'Who is this guy anyway?'

'You met him when you picked me up from Mag's party.'

'The guy with the thin lips.'

'What?'

'And big teeth.'

'He was a vampire Daddy, they were false.'

'You want to leave your daughter alone with a vampire? Very nice.'

'Mum he's not ... '

'You didn't tell me you met him.' my mother glared at my father.

'Do I have to tell you everything?'

'You keeping other secrets?'

'Secrets? Woman you're ... '

'Hey! Hey!' I shouted.

'I'm not going anywhere.' my mother snapped.

'See what you've done now?' Dad threw his hands in the air.

'Please Mum, he's a nice guy, and, and we're only friends.' I said.

'They're only friends.' Dad repeated.

'Fire and a match *cannot* be left alone.' my mother spat and began to rearrange the crocheted cushions on the sofa.

Each one was handmade by my grandmother, Yiayia. Some looked like giant sunflowers with their lime green 'petals' and orange centres. Others reminded me of multi-coloured spiderwebs. Yiayia would buy her wool on sale at

Woolworth's and then go on a crocheting rampage well into the night.

'I'm doing this for you,' she'd say and show me her red fingers. 'for your *prika!*'

For my dowry. By the time I was twenty I had enough crocheted cushions, bedspreads and doilies to last me well into the afterlife.

Mum pushed a fist into a spiderweb and shook it before nestling it between a sunflower and another web. She looked at my father.

'Are you staying or will I?'

Dad rolled his eyes, sat down and disappeared behind his paper. 'I'll stay.' he said

When Mum left I joined my father at the kitchen table.

'Dad don't you think Mum's being ridiculous?'

My father put his paper down and kissed me on the cheek. 'she just worries.'

The doorbell rang. I didn't move. It rang again. Dad looked at me.

'Tell him I've gone out.' I said and went to my bedroom.

I buried my head in Pillow and as I breathed in his limp cotton body, I heard the door open, a muffled exchange and then the door close again. The television was clicked on. No point in taking it out on Dad, I thought. So I wandered out to the living room. My boyfriend was sitting on the sofa clicking through the channels. He stood up when he saw me.

'I was going to come and wake you.' Ryder said pulling me into his arms.

'Wake me?'

'Your Dad said you were having an afternoon nap.'

'A nap?'

'Were you dreaming of me?' He laughed and pushed his nose into my neck. 'Mm. You smell gorgeous.'

A distracting warmth drifted up through my thighs. 'Wh-where's my father?'

'Hm?' Ryder's lips began to wander down my neck and into my cleavage. 'Gone.'

'What?' I pulled away. 'My father left?'

'Yeah, he said something about a grease and oil change. What's up Babe?'

'Huh?' my heart somersaulted. 'Nothing, nothing, I, er … want some popcorn?'

Before he could answer, I vanished into the kitchen and lit a gas hob. Its little blue tongues danced about, happy to see me.

Ryder's arms circled my waist. I jumped.

'Little uptight today?' he said. 'Anything I can do?' he pressed himself against me.

I reached up and ran my fingers over his lips.

'Salty or sweet?' I said.

'What?'

'Do you like your popcorn salty or sweet?'

He snapped at my fingers with his teeth. 'Salt…' Ryder began.

I pushed myself up against his chest and he fell backwards onto the fridge. Instantly, he tightened the grip around my waist, moved his hands up my thighs and clawed at my woollen jumper. I pulled him closer, traced his face, his neck and lips with my tongue. Then we moved, kissing, groping, feeling our way into the living room. A snag in the rug tripped us and we fell onto the lounge – my dowry cushioned our fall. TV commercials blared. He pulled me down on top of him, fingertips sprinted across my cleavage, touching, tugging, snatching at my clothes, his hair, jeans, belts and buttons, gloss slipped off, mascara streaked, cushions scattered and a Disney classic returned to the screen. Delirious soundtracks danced in my head and between my legs he rubbed and pinched as the afternoon darkened and tongues, teeth, hands battled more buttons and Dad's keys jangled in the lock …

I leapt to my feet and as the door swung open I switched on the living room light.

'Oh you're home Dad,' I said and looked over at Ryder who had jammed a spiderweb in his crotch.

'It's pouring outside.' my father said and went into the kitchen. 'Why's the hob lit?'

'Yeah uh I was about to make some popcorn. Want some Daddy?'

☆☆☆

Weeks after my first day at the new agency, Allegra started receiving flowers. Blood red roses one day, anemones the next. The girls in accounts tittered and squealed each time an impressive new bouquet arrived at reception. But when she strode up to collect her latest blooms, they'd look away pretending not to be impressed.

'Fucking stunning, don't you think, girls?'

And they'd force a smile through clamped, Chanel-slicked lips.

'Agni! Aren't these fucking *gorgeous?*' She marched into our office and plonked the flowers on her desk.

'Wow. You are *so* lucky.' I said fingering a fleshy petal in the bouquet.

'Luck's got nothin' to fucking do with it.'

'Then it must be love … right?'

'Fuck love, it's lust.' she knocked back some cola. 'and I'm *lovin'* it!'

She plunged her face deep into a pink cluster of roses and a couple tumbled off their stems in shock.

'You want one?'

'No, they're yours.'

'Just put a fucking rose on top of your mac – it'll cheer you up.'

'Cheer me up?'

'Yeah! Look at me grinning like a silly bitch all day!' Allegra plucked a rose out of its green tissue paper and lay it gently on my monitor.

'There! Now smile, Grrl.'

Another thing I grew wary of. She could read my moods. I'd walked into the office that day with a smile on my face and tears in my throat. I'd had another fight with Mum the night before. I was late coming home after another night of striking my match and lighting his fire.

'Ryder's cooking me dinner tonight.' I told Magdalene.

'Good luck Girly.' she said and took a quick sip of her soy-latte. 'Gotta go. Deposition in an hour.'

'Don't go to his apartment.' my mother said and shook the front page of her Greek tabloid at me. 'twenty five girls this pensioner raped in Greece – the monster!'

'Be careful Darling.' Daddy said. 'and come home after the restaurant okay?'

I walked into Ryder's apartment and the smell of sizzling steak rushed out to greet me.

'God Agni … you look good enough to eat.' he said drawing me into his arms.

'Thanks, I think. Candles look *amazing*.' Dozens of little tea lights winked at me.

'Glad you like them, I burnt myself twice lighting the suckers.' Ryder said and disappeared into the kitchen.

'I uh, I always wanted to see what these apartments looked like inside … '

I dropped my bag and walked around touching the furnishings lightly. 'The building looks incredible from the road – I look out for it everytime Dad – everytime I drive by. How many rooms are there?'

Ryder poked his head out from the kitchen. 'Two – the spare's filled with junk though … now Missy, well done, rare, medium rare?'

'Oh, well done thank you.'

'Well done it is. Feel free to look around. I gotta keep my eye on these steaks.'

'Okay.'

I moved around the living room. Charcoal line drawings hung on the walls. Mauve suede cushions nestled in the corners of a black leather lounge. A splash of red shag pile covered blonde wood. In another nook a silver stereo with two little Bose speakers whispered Annie Lennox. I ran my fingers over the TV widescreen.

My mother's face leapt out.

'Monster rapist!' she cried and disappeared back into the dust.

'*How many times do I have to tell you … to keep your big mouth shut?*' Annie sang.

I wandered down a hallway and into the bathroom. Fresh pine smell. White tiles. Navy blue towels. A bottle green bathrobe hung off a hook on the wall. Two bottles of French aftershave and a balm with a label reading Arctic Ice sat on a glass shelf. A silver shaving mirror with a long, knobbly neck poked out at me. Its face was cocked to the side. Hello! I picked up the aftershave and sniffed. Fermented vanilla.

I left the bathroom and followed the hallway down to another room lit partially by streetlight. Bingo. The bedroom. King sized bed. Calico curtains. The outline of an exercise bike in the corner. I peered into the dusky light and just as my eyes adjusted to the gloom, I saw him.

He hovered above the bed.

Eyes large, bulging out from his skull. Grey skin pulled tight over thick, mottled veins. The virgin spread out in white before him. Her face ashen. His fingers, twisted bone. He sneers at me. Gnarled fingernails that shred innocent flesh, they beckon me. I can hear her heart race. Feel her blood ice up. A string of horrors unreels in my mind. He has twenty-five maidens stocked up, locked up in the spare room. Just junk. They wait. Paralysed by angst. Trapped. Starving. Naked and shivering. Yet, the room is heated, warming their flesh for him. Their mouths are bandaged. Eyes too. They cannot see. They cannot scream. And when it is dark and the moon hangs like a slice of tarnished silver in the sky, he takes her. Tearing into her. Over and over. Pressing his bony limbs against her. His rotting nails claw away at her innocence. She drips onto his putrefying flesh and he swallows her. It is done. She is lifeless. He has sucked her purity dry. Soon he will be ready to feed again.

Electricity suddenly lit up the vampire's glare. I screamed.

'I see you've met Nosferatu.' Ryder was standing behind me, breathing down my neck.

I turned to face him. 'Feel my heart!' I said and then a shrill buzz sounded.

'Shit!' he cried. 'the potatoes.' And ran out.

I put my hand to my chest. My heart was leaping about and my panties were moist. I stole another glimpse of Nosferatu; it was a giant copy of the original film poster framed in chrome. He looked wrinkled, dry and washed out by halogen. He'd been caught feeding and now his face was lined in shock. A pair of shrivelled grey lips barely concealed his sorry row of sparse, misshapen teeth. Pupils the size of pin-pricks dotted the glare of his white eyes. He looked desperate. Hungry.

I turned away from him and sat on the edge of my boyfriend's bed. It was soft and the baby blue duvet made a comforting crackling sound as I gathered it up around me. I breathed it in. Man smell. Over in the corner by the bike, a pile of Sunday papers were stacked as high as the pedals. The mirror on the wall had a postcard from Barbados stuck to it. A gleaming golf club was propped up against the wall. And on the floor, near the calico curtains, was a man's g-string. I poked at it with the toe of my boot.

Its cotton folds seemed glued together.

I reached over and grabbed the golf club. I pushed the club under the g-string and picked it up. The 'string slid down the shaft and touched my hand. I flinched but quickly took a sniff.

'You hungry?' Ryder's voice came from the kitchen.

The club fell out of my hands and his g-string flopped to the floor. I turned around and he was at the doorway eyeing his discarded underwear.

'Yeah, yeah, I've got to do a load of washing,' he said with a sheepish grin.

'I don't know which is worse,' I said correcting my posture. 'your taste in underwear or standards of hygiene.'

He stood still for a minute or so just staring at me.

'Oh come on,' I stood up. 'I was only kidding,'

Ryder walked over and pushed his lips through my fringe. 'Wanna skip dinner?'

'*And it feels just like I'm walking on broken glass . . .* ' Annie sang.

'I think it's time we changed that CD.' I said and sprinted out.

Ryder lit a thick black candle on the dining table.

'Red wine?'

I looked at the red liquid in the bottle.

'Got any white?'

'White with steak? A sacrilege!' he smiled.

'I'm a rebel like that.' I said.

'Your wish, my command.' He bowed low.

An hour later we were sitting on his leather lounge sipping home made cappuccinos. I fished some froth off the top with my finger and dabbed it on his nose.

'You shouldn't have done that Missy.' Ryder said in a mocking tone.

'And I'll do it again if you keep calling me Missy.'

'But you *are* a Miss to me.' He stroked my hair.

'I'm warning you.'

'What are you going to do … *Missy?*' He moved closer.

I snatched up another fingerful of froth and smeared it all over his cheek.

'Well my dear Agni,' Ryder took the cappuccino from my hands and placed it on the table. 'you have left me,' he grabbed my arms and pinned me to the leather, 'with no other alternative!'

I laughed and kicked as he lay down on top of me and pressed his face against my neck.

'Stop it! I'm ticklish!' I cried trying to bite him.

'You are *so* sexy.' Ryder whispered in my ear. And then he began to tug gently at my neck with his teeth. I stopped fighting. A lovely sensation pulsed under my skin. He moved his lips to my mouth and dove in with his tongue. I let him and tentatively allowed my tongue to touch his too. A white heat throbbed inside me and I ached for relief. I hugged him tighter, making him push down harder onto me. Ryder put his hand between my thighs and squeezed into the heat that rose there. I moaned.

'Let me,' he whispered with an urgency I pitied. 'Please let me.' he repeated as he carried me into the bedroom.

I lay down on the baby blue duvet and spread my legs. Ryder took his shirt off and climbed on top of me crushing my senses with vanilla. I unbuttoned my shirt and he helped me peel it away. My bra was next. He played with the lace for a second or two, then that too joined his g-string under the calico curtains. Now we were topless in each other's arms. His skin hot to the touch. I hugged him.

'You're lovely,' I said and nestled my head in his shoulder.

We lay there for a few minutes listening to each other breathe. But he couldn't be still. Soon he was up again and on top of me pumping – pumping like we were having sex. He moved his body up, down, his crotch came crashing down onto mine over and over. Nosferatu winked his approval.

'Will you let me,' Ryder said again and this time his hand reached down to my fly.

I stared up at the ceiling, my pubic bone had begun to ache. He pulled my zip lower.

'No.' I said and sat up before he could unzip me.

'What's wrong?' Ryder looked dazed.

'I just don't want to.'

'Not tonight … or ever?' He moved to touch me. I pulled back.

'Ever.'

'What?'

'Well, not until I'm,' I pulled on my bra and fumbled so long with the strap, I gave up and left it undone under my shirt.

'I understand,' he whispered. 'You want to wait until marriage.' He touched my shoulder, 'I like that in a girl.'

'Well I don't.' I said rushing out to the living room. He followed me.

'I've gotta go.' I picked up my bag. 'Thanks for dinner.'

He kissed me behind the ear and squeezed my arm. 'I'll call you.' he said.

'What's going to happen with you?'

My mother's voice was even and low. She was sitting alone in the living room with one weak lamplight on.

'What do you mean?' I said and flicked on the lights. She made a face.

'You're out every night with someone we don't know. He's doing God knows what to you … using you like he's used all his other girlfriends.'

'He's *not* using me.'

'He's not using you? Do you think he *likes* you?'

'Why shouldn't he like me?'

'Look at you! You think I'm blind? You think because I don't understand English, I don't know what's going on? I'm the bigger whore here. I know more than you think. Where's your lipstick?'

'We had dinner. I must have eaten it off.'

'You ate it? Or did he?'

I bit my lip and the barrage continued.

'You don't know nothing about life. This is a man, not a child you tease. He wants a woman, someone who will satisfy him,' she moved closer. 'Are you going to satisfy him? Are you? Are *you* going to be … '

And then she spat the words in my face – *that woman.*

'You live here, you our responsibility, not his, not a man who is using you. Hear me?'

'What if I want to use *him?*'

'Get the hell out of my eyes,' she hissed.

Alone in my bedroom I sobbed. Sloppy tears drenched

the pillow slip Mum had ironed for me that day.

☆☆☆

Days grew into weeks and more flowers kept arriving. Every chrysanthemum, sunflower and yellow-lipped lily was relished by my over-flattered art director. And by the time our office looked like a florist, Greek Easter had come around. It's the time of year when Greeks abstain from dairy, red meat and sex until Christ is resurrected on Easter Saturday morning – or night if you're a Doubting Thomas.

My mother goes by the first, official resurrection which happened at ten a.m – this was believed to be the real time Jesus rose from the dead. But Thomas wouldn't believe until he pressed his fingers into Christ's wounds. And now millions of Orthodox Christians around the world wait until midnight on Saturday before they can tuck into a flesh-laden feast.

Greek Easter always inspires a renaissance of the proud, God-fearing Greek in me. I am proud of my fasting, my ancient religion and the customs that connect me to the Greek psyche – twisted though it can be at times. I've sat for hours inhaling the cooking smells that fill my parents' house in the lead up to Easter Sunday. Sweet and sour scents flood me. Vanilla, port, sticky sugar syrup, the fatty fragrance of clarified butter. My mother bakes hundreds of biscuits drenched in port. And when it's time to polish the dyed boiled eggs, we stand, side by side, in her kitchen. A bowl of eggs in red, blue and yellow sits on the bench top. Mum dabs a few drops of olive oil into a paper towel and hands it to me. Then we polish the dull reds, blues and yellows to life. Here, I am Greeker than Greek. Loyal to my role as Good Greek Daughter.

The day before Good Friday, Allegra gave me three birds of paradise to take home to my mother. I thanked her without thinking, with a hug.

'You're welcome, Grrl.' she said.

Easter Sunday came around and I helped Mum wrap the birds of paradise to take to lunch. My aunt had prepared a huge traditional spread. The whole family had gathered to celebrate and everything was perfect. The nibbles sat motionless in their dishes stabbed together by toothpicks. Cousins, uncles and aunts swapped Easter wishes – Christ is risen, true is our Lord.

Alexander sauntered over to me in a new t-shirt splashed with a familiar message.

'Christ is risen Cuz.' he said planting a kiss soaked in aftershave on my cheek.

'True is our Lord.' I replied. 'Can you turn down the volume on that shirt?'

'You like it?' he grinned.

'I've seen it before.'

'Where?'

'On a pavement. It's not a designer shirt – you alright with that?'

'Ha, ha. Where's yours smart arse?'

'I don't need to advertise.'

'Yeah well, I know what you're thinking.'

'Really?'

'You're thinking I should charge right? A Greek Hulk like me,' He flexed a bicep.

'Aren't the best things in life free?'

'You're a funny chick.'

'Alexander take that stupid shirt off – have some respect.' my aunt shouted from the kitchen.

Alexander winked at me and went out to the garden where the long-awaited flesh-fare sizzled on a spit.

'The lamb will be ready in half an hour!' my uncle yelled, spit-side.

Skewered by a single gleaming rod, the lamb was clamped into place with giant bull-clips. The motor whirred softly. A balding family friend moved in for a closer look.

'That bloody thing's doing all the work for you!' he laughed.

Every Greek man has spit-envy – particularly at Easter. Some spits are manual and fuelled only by elbow grease and ouzo. While others boast shiny electric motors and multiple speed settings. These are cherished, expensive toys and my uncle owned the 'Rolls Royce'. It was a 5-speed, stainless steel Hellenic wet dream complete with a tefal-coated 'fat-catcher' at the bottom. Legend has it he cancelled a family holiday to Greece to afford it.

My uncle puffed up, smiled and took a long gulp of his beer. Then he clicked another button and increased the speed slightly. He nudged the family friend who knocked back a shot of ouzo and stared at the fat that fell onto its slippery tefal bed.

'Lamb looks good.' I said.

Crushed garlic and oregano crackled in the grooves of its scored pink skin. The garden was filled with a rich and tangy aroma. And I inhaled happily, already imagining the taste of smoked meat on my tongue. My uncle reached over and lovingly basted the flesh with extra virgin olive oil, lemon juice and herbs. This lamb would do him proud, I thought. There was nothing like a successfully 'spat' Easter lamb to reaffirm a Greek man's worth.

He grinned again and wiped the 5-speed console with the back of his hand.

'He was up at five this morning polishing that thing with car wax!' my aunt laughed appearing suddenly at my side.

'Haven't you got a salad to make?' he scowled at her.

'Isn't it time you came inside?' she gave him a dirty look.

'I'm busy!' he said, guzzling more beer.

'Yeah, real busy.' the family friend sneered.

'It's *time*!' she raised her voice and disappeared into the house.

'Wha … ' He looked up pissed off but then something registered on his face and he ran after her, baster and beer in hand.

Next minute we were all standing in the living room toasting my cousin Despina's engagement. Years ago, she was an active member of the 'white pillow fellowship'. Now she was going to wear her mother's wedding dress and pretend she'd only had a pillow shoved between her legs.

Despina emerged from behind her chubby podiatrist fiance with red cheeks and a shiny diamond. She poked her new jewel into the crowd of well-wishers. Oooh. The women fawned. Aaah. The men approved.

'We wish them years of joy … and lots of children!' my

Uncle bellowed and then he pushed their faces together.

The happy couple kissed. A few of the younger cousins wolf whistled and little girls hid in their mothers' skirts.

'It'll be your turn next.' I said pointing to Alexander.

'No chance.' he smirked and snapped open his mobile, '*you got me.*'

'No it's *your* turn next, he has too many girlfriends to think about marriage!' My Uncle slapped Alexander on the back sending his phone hurtling into the plush carpet. It landed near my feet.

'Dad!' he shouted and stumbled forward to try and catch it.

'Your phone's too bloody small son!' my Uncle said and escaped to the garden.

I picked up the phone and put it to my ear.

*'Secret Service Ladies confirming your booking sir. Hello? Hello?'*

Alexander lunged towards me. I clicked the mobile shut and handed his phone back.

'It still works.' I said.

I moved to congratulate Despina and her podiatrist and felt a tug on my dress. I looked down to see a small cousin staring up at me. Her eyes were like chocolate buttons.

'Hello beautiful,' I crouched down to face her.

'Will you play with me?' she said and grabbed hold of my arm.

'Looks like you need a rest.' I smiled lifting the sweaty curls from her eyes.

'Please, please, *please?*' she pulled on my arm.

So I followed her outside and chased her around the

garden until my stilettoes abused me.

'Take your high heels off silly.' The little girl laughed and rushed into my belly.

I grabbed her and lifted her into the air. 'What did you call me young lady!' I said spinning her around.

'Silly!' she teased. 'Silly!'

I spun her around some more before we both collapsed on the grass out of breath.

'Now will you take your shoes off?' she said laughing and grabbing at my heels.

'No you cheeky thing,' I said and scrambled to my feet. 'Let's go look at the lamb.'

She screwed her nose up. 'Yucky!' the little girl cried and ran off.

Back at the five-star spit the lamb had turned into a golden, crispy-on-the-outside, moist-and-tender-on-the-inside unmitigated success. The balding family friend was still leering at the 'fat-catcher'. His glass of ouzo was bigger and fuller and he was swaying 'in time' to the roaring motor which had been kicked up a notch or three.

'Does it have to be that loud?' I shouted.

My Uncle smiled and pointed to the bald guy, 'He wants to know why you're still single!'

The family friend plunged two fingers into the lamb's right flank and tore off a piece of fat. He shoved it into his mouth and curled a hairy arm around my shoulders.

'Tell me,' he slurred, filling my face with garlic and grease.

'Well,' I began, wriggling in his grip. 'I'm very busy.'

'You need to find yourself a good doctor like your cousin.' my Uncle interrupted.

‘He’s a podiatrist,’ I said.

‘Same thing,’ he chirped.

‘Why don’t you have a … boyfriend, gorgeous girl like you … ’ The family friend pulled me closer and a shiny streak of fat dripped from his bottom lip onto my blouse.

‘Who needs a boyfriend?’ I said and freed myself from his arms.

My uncle laughed and adjusted his speeds again. ‘Are you a lesbian?’

‘Darling,’ my aunt rushed up. ‘Have you seen Despina’s engagement ring?’

I started to walk away with her when an almighty bang ripped through the garden. We turned to see my uncle’s beloved spit puking putrid-smelling black smoke all over the lamb.

‘What have you done?’ my aunt shrieked.

‘I don’t know, I don’t know!’ he cried, sweat pouring from his scalp as he tried to free the lamb from its clamps.

The balding family friend drained his glass and hiccuped,

‘’Bout time he did some work.’

☆☆☆

Despina’s hens night was billed as the event of the year – second only to her wedding of course. It was held in an Italian restaurant on Gay & Lesbian Mardi Gras night. We were ‘treated’ to cold wood-fired pizza and wilted rocket salad, frozen tiramisu and a male stripper with an infected nipple piercing. It was destined to be a delightfully forgettable evening until someone suggested we catch a cab to King's Cross – Sydney's red light district.

The tiramisu stuck in my throat. Suddenly I was 18 again and riding along in a mini-bus heaving with drunken cousins wearing shoulder pads and fluorescent lycra, singing along to *Material Girl.* This was the hens night I wanted to forget – and not just because of our fashion choices. (I wore a white lace ensemble. My mother had curled my hair into a bun.)

As the mini-bus crawled down the congested main drag of the Cross, I wished for an accident, an earthquake, the Second Coming. Anything would have been better than walking the streets of this place. I was convinced the pavement would split open and swallow me – lace, bun and all. But what could I say? No. Please. Not King's Cross, the pavement will eat me.

We climbed out of the van, and spilled out onto the street.

' … *and I am a Material Girl!*' the Bride shouted and she spun around and around holding her pink veil high above her head. She crashed into me.

'Watch where I'm going!' she giggled and the others linked arms with her and began to march down the street. Dozens of patent heels became one.

'Everybody sing! *You know that we are living, in a material world,*'

I reached up to feel my hairbun. It was now a flat mess at the nape of my neck. I tried scrunching it into shape with my hands but gave up to follow the makeshift madonnas. They walked fast – and not always in a straight line – but their pace was a relief particularly when we passed a woman with mascara tears sitting on a crate murmuring,

'Spare tyre, spare tyre.'

All around us neon lights hollered. *Fresh Pussy 24 Hours. Lusty Ladies – Try Before You Buy. Ex-Marine Strippers.* But up ahead, the sign outside the Sex Toy Superstore was deafening. *Buy One Get One Free!* it promised and a couple of cousins ran inside. A few minutes later they emerged with a handful of penis pens swinging on red plastic cords.

'Hang 'em round your neck.' they said and everyone started grabbing at them.

'Hey, hey one at a time!'

'Can I have an uncircumcised one?' the Matron of Honour shouted.

'I don't do pink dick – got any in black?' another girl cried.

'Here,' the Chief Bridesmaid pushed a penis into my hands, 'have a cock!'

I looked at my new writing implement. It had a pretty smile and two puffy brown eyebrows. He reminded me of Barbie's boyfriend, Ken.

'*Some boys kiss me, some boys hug me,*' Bridesmaid Two sang swinging her pen around like a feather boa.

'*I think they're ok-ay-ay,*' another cousin replied and pulled the pen out of her mouth. The happy penis grin was smothered in frosted beige lipstick.

'*If they don't give me proper credit,*' Bridesmaid Four sang into her penis.

'*I just walk away-ay,*' I laughed and wrapped the cord around my handbag strap.

'Where's mine!' The Bride pushed past me in a huff.

'We saved the best pen till last.' the Chief Bridesmaid replied winking at the cousin with the fattest shoulder pads. 'Wanna do the honours?'

'Close your eyes!' Shoulder Pads said and placed a jumbo-sized penis pen in the Bride's hand. 'Enjoy sweetheart!'

The Bride opened her eyes and squealed. 'It's a *monster!*'

'Press the button behind its balls.'

'What? Where?'

'The balls, there's a little button behind the fucking balls, press it!'

The Bride flicked the button and the penis head lit up and started to wobble.

'It's vibrating!' she yelled. 'I love it!' She jumped up and down.

All the girls gathered for a closer look.

'I want one of those too!'

'Thought you didn't do pink dick.'

'Depends how big it is.' the girl said touching the quivering plastic knob. 'Wee!'

The Bride snatched her pen away. 'Mine!'

Just then a man in a dark suit and purple tie glided into the group.

'I've got an extra present for the Bride.' he said in a low voice.

'And you are?'

'Proprietor of a fine establishment.'

'What sort of establishment?'

He pointed to a hot red sign flashing *99 Spread Legs.* 'You're just in time for the next live show.'

'And what's my present?' The Bride batted her

eyelashes.

'Half price tickets for all you beautiful ladies.' he said. 'right up those stairs.'

'I'm in!' The Bride tied a knot in her veil and stuck her pen in it.

The suit lead them up the stairs as they waved their pens above their heads singing,

*'A material, a material, a material world!'*

Shoulder Pads was last in line, she turned to look at me. 'Come on – the show's starting.'

'No, uh, you go on ahead … I'll wait here.'

She gritted her teeth. 'Oh for *fuck's* sake.' she said.

I bit on a hangnail.

'What's happening down there?' the Chief Bridesmaid shouted down the stairs.

'Missy here doesn't want to see the show.'

I looked away. At this point, the hooker selling herself as a spare tyre was the better woman.

'Just leave her behind … ' Chief called back.

'I promised her mother I'd look after her didn't I!' she replied and turned to me, 'now what's the *bloody problem?*'

'It's not my thing that's all,' I tugged on a bobby pin in my bun. 'You go, I'll be fine.'

'Not your *thing?*'

I shook my head.

She shut her eyes and rubbed the bridge of her nose. Her blue eyeshadow was thick and creased. Her orange lipstick had started to feather.

'Have you ever seen a show like this?'

'No.'

She opened her eyes and glared at me. 'Then how do

you know it's not *your thing?*'

I stared at my feet. The pavement broke into a sly grin.

'I just do.' I said without raising my head. 'I think I'll go home.'

Chief yelled. 'Come on, just leave her, the show's starting!'

Shoulder Pads gave me one last dirty look and then spat, 'Suit yourself,' before turning on her snakeskin heels and clattering up the stairs. Halfway up she turned around,

'If you go home, leave a note with the bouncer.'

'But … but I don't have a pen,' I called out.

'Use your penis!' she shouted over her shoulder and then she was gone.

I wanted to scream, come back, the sidewalk will eat me. But I didn't. I just stood there, frozen. Alone with neon, drug pickled prostitutes and my Ken penis pen. I pulled out a writing pad and began to doodle but halfway through a rose petal, my penis ran out of ink.

Back at the Italian restaurant, I swallowed my tiramisu quickly.

'Forget the Cross.' I said. 'We're not 18 anymore.'

'Hey guys it's Mardi Gras tonight.'

'Yeah. The clubs'll be pumping.'

'Cool, let's go. Just no live sex shows. I promised hubby.' Despina spooned a dollop of tiramisu into her mouth and motioned to a waiter for the bill.

Oxford Street was a glittering sea of sequinned G-stringed bottoms, PVC and tassled nipples. We waded through and managed to get into a club filled with more bottoms and breasts. Everything felt electric. The crowd was so high. I settled back into a velour booth to watch. The conversation zipped around me, look at him, look at her, look at him with him, him with it, her with her … they're kissing … oh wait for it, here come the tongues! Oooooh! One cousin wished she wasn't so squeamish when it came to lesbians, but she couldn't help it, she said, it just looked so unnatural.

There was a woman in our neighbourhood Mum and I often saw on our grocery travels. She was a little on the butch side. Short hair, thick build, in her thirties, Greek and single. An anomaly. Rumour had it she was a lesbian. Whenever we saw her my mother would nudge me,

'You know she's a lesbian.'

Yes Mum you've told me four hundred and twenty three times.

I'd glance sideways at her. Wow. A Greek lesbian. But Mum always stopped for a chat. She did all the talking though. I was too busy holding a hand over my non-existent cleavage. And the 'Greek Lesbian' probably felt as self conscious as I looked. I'm sure she was wary of the smiling Greeks in the neighbourhood who visited her mother's deli for their kalamata olives only to go home and gossip about the Deli Woman's Lesbian Daughter.

'Maybe she just doesn't want to get married.' I said to Mum.

'No I'm telling you – someone saw her hugging another woman on the street.'

A couple of spandex-squashed testicles danced by.

'Look at that hunk in the leather shorts – what a *waste!*'

Despina screamed.

I stood up and headed for the toilets. As I weaved through the crowd a pair of skinny arms swooped down out of nowhere and wrapped themselves around my waist.

'Hey Grrl!'

Allegra sprang out in front of me wearing a tight black t-shirt with the word *bitch* sewn in silver beading across the front. Her hair looked electrified. She hugged me sloppily.

'You're drunk!' I said.

'Fuck yeah! I'm so happy!' she shrieked and pulled me through the crowd towards the bar.

'You know the person who's been sending me flowers? They're here!'

'Really?'

'Fuck *yes!*' she screamed again and I had to shush her.

'Tell him to come out of hiding – where is he?'

'He's … already out. He is … a she. A dyke.' Allegra's grin softened.

I took her hand and squeezed it.

'Grrl.' I said and surprised myself.

☆☆☆

Permission to love another woman came to me in a bank queue.

I was standing behind a pensioner who hadn't bathed in days. Mobile phones were ringing every few minutes and a baby screamed in her pram. But my epiphany didn't sneak up on me when the teller called 'next please'. It was a gradual awakening. Suddenly everything, *everyone* felt possible. Gender melted away together with my expectations of who I should and shouldn't be attracted to.

I began to enjoy women's bottoms as they jiggled down the street in front of me. I looked closer at a woman's face and touched her skin in my mind. I dreamt of Allegra and I in a spa together. Then one night, on a date with Ryder, a limo stopped beside us at the lights. The smoky window slid down and a woman looked out. Her long, blonde hair was splashed over black mink. Her mouth gleamed under the streetlights. And her eyes, electric green, inexplicably settled on me.

I straightened up in my seat.

'Like the limo Baby?' Ryder muttered eyeing the length of the car.

I didn't answer. The blonde's shiny lips had parted slightly and she was blowing me a kiss. I blinked. And then she pulled at her fur collar to reveal a bare and perfect shoulder. She stroked it with her fingernails.

'Baby?' Ryder looked at me and then at the blonde. 'Baby, *she's flirting with you!*' he whispered.

The blonde wriggled the fur off and moved closer to the window. She wore a strange pinstriped bustier that looked so tight I wondered why she hadn't turned blue.

'Oh my God.' my boyfriend panted. 'I've heard about these women, oh my *God*.'

I brushed some fringe away from my eyes and shifted slightly in my seat. My fingers wandered down to the zipper at my cleavage. I began to play with it absentmindedly.

'Get this,' Ryder continued, 'these women have clothes painted on their naked bodies and they get hired out for parties. *Huge* in New York. I think the company's called … '

She touched the curves of her painted-on bustier just as the lights changed. And I came to in time to watch her limo glide away.

'*In the Flesh that's* it!' Ryder clapped his hands triumphantly. 'The company's called, *In the Flesh*. Wanna try it baby?' he laughed.

I gave him a blank look but he was staring at the limo up ahead. ' … wonder if they franchise.' he muttered before slipping the car into first gear and driving off.

I didn't feel like I had to fuck a woman. I just realised I could – if I wanted to. But this self-inflicted permission filled me with an equal amount of dread and desire. Like a delicate paintbrush stroking pinstripes into my bare skin, the coolness of the paint gave me goosebumps at first. But I could get used to it. Question was, did I want to?

☆☆☆

While I struggled with same-sex fantasies, my career steadily climbed. I had never written so many well-received brochures, sales letters, newspaper ads, newsletters, mini-magazines. Thousands and millions and billions of words. Words that paid the bills and kept me in the lifestyle to which I had become accustomed – designer nail polish, shoes and Egyptian cotton sheets (or 'shits' as my mother used to say before she realised what she was saying and switched to saying bed linen).

As essential as advertising was to my financial stability, it was not my creative lifeblood. And all my attempts at 'playing the political games' were futile. I was not a player. I couldn't remove my personality and replace it with a full-time schmooze routine – lick this butt, worship that ego. I tried. But each time a couple of suits walked into my office, I found myself gasping for real air. Thank God for my built-in 'anti-wank-tank'. It let me take deep, pure breaths and kept me from dying a horribly superficial death.

'Client's thrilled you're working on the FauxCreme DeLaCreme campaign,' the Junior Suit said.

'Got some *spectacular* ideas?' The Senior Suit rolled up her chiffon sleeves and sat on Allegra's desk.

'We're pleased with the stuff we have so far.' she said and opened up a layout pad. Headlines leapt out. Colour swam around the room.

Senior furrowed her brow. Junior furrowed his. Senior chuckled under her breath. Junior chuckled under his.

'You're looking at the line about bottling time, right?' he laughed.

'No. Weeping plastic surgeon. Hysterical.'

Junior looked closer at the layout. 'Oh yeah, what a scream!'

Senior narrowed her eyes. Junior narrowed his.

'Right.' Senior slid off the desk and started a ladder in her pantyhose. 'You've answered the brief. It's funny. Splashy. Well *done you.*'

'Yeah good on you guys.' Junior nodded.

'Thanks.' Allegra and I exchanged looks.

'But ... ' Senior picked up the layout and examined it like she was Madame Curie.

Allegra frowned. 'Looking for anything in particular?'

' … think there's too much white space.'

' … logo should be bigger.'

' … need to make the woman look more wrinkly,'

' … FauxCreme DeLaCreme *may* help reduce the appearance of fine lines.'

'Can't say it does definitely.'

'No, legal will have a fit.'

' … and you *may* notice a visible difference in the texture of your skin.'

' … studies have *shown* not proven.'

' … want to mention the nutriphenols too.'

'Thought I had.' I said.

'Only once. Client wants it hammered home.'

' … yeah, crucial ingredient in the fight against aging.'

' … need to make women *love* the idea of Faux … '

' … can't live *without* Faux … '

'Otherwise, great work.' Senior straightened her chiffon sleeves.

'Yeah great stuff guys.' Junior nodded.

'Let's have another look this afternoon.' she said and led Junior out of the office.

'Remember the nutriphenols!'

☆☆☆

'Mama, can I tell you something?' I said.

'Are you playing with yourself again Agni?' she replied putting on the kettle.

She was referring to my last confession; the strange afternoon I admitted to using her *Judder Elite* for the relief of something other than aching neck muscles. I had to confess. My debut orgasms were so good they had to be bad, right? Mum said my bone marrow would run out if I continued touching myself 'like that'. But it was agony giving up. I'd lie in bed urging away the urges – until my hand wandered down on automatic – and then my bone marrow would come to mind. For years I wanted to be the person who invented a gauge to measure post-orgasm bone marrow levels. I thought it would make me a millionaire.

'What do you want to drink?' Mum asked.

'Coffee, sweet with milk.' I replied and sat up straight in my chair. 'Ma, there's something I've been thinking about.' I ventured.

'What you're going to wear to Despina's wedding? Make it fantastic, otherwise the gossip will kill us. Remember how ridiculous she was at her kitchen tea, ripped jeans for God's sake.' She put a heaped spoon of sugar into a mug.

'I know what I'm wearing.' I said pulling at the tablecloth.

'And?'

'I'll show you later,'

'Show me now."

'What?'

'You sly thing, show me the dress, is it inside?' She moved towards the bedroom.

'Mum!' I called after her. She turned around. 'I haven't bought it yet.'

'It's a dress?' She returned to the kitchen. 'No trousers

in church Agni.'

'I've seen other girls wearing trousers in church.'

'It's not respect.'

'God wouldn't mind.'

'It's respect.'

The kettle started to whistle.

'Do you honestly think God would be mad at a pair of trousers?'

'Any girl who doesn't listen to her mother falls. Ask Despina.' She pulled the kettle off the stove.

'What's happened now?'

'Your cousin didn't tell you?'

'No what?'

'Despina's mother warned her – I was there.'

'Warned her about what?'

'She said, don't leave the wedding invitations in your fiance's car.'

'Was his car stolen?'

'Worse! The stupid girl spilt glue over half the invitations in the back seat.'

'The back seat?' I started to grin.

'Her mother warned her, now they're ruined with the glue. Why are you smiling?'

'She's calling it *glue?*' my grin widened, 'inventive.'

'What?'

'They can get them replaced can't they?' I said.

'But she's going to lose money, why? Because she didn't listen to her mother.'

'I'm wearing a dress. Relax.'

'Bravo. What's it like?' Mum grabbed a tin of instant coffee from the pantry.

'I'll tell you in a minute,'

'Tarty?'

'What? No! It's long and it's got this, this great see-through belly bit.'

She raised her eyebrows.

' … when I tried it on in the shop the saleswoman said I looked incredible.'

'Expensive?'

'Yeah, but you'll love it, that woman did, she was uh, she was really attractive.' I filled my face with an eager smile. 'She reminded me of you.'

My mother sighed heavily. 'Don't look at me now Daughter. You should have seen me in my youth. When I walked down the street, the pavement shook beneath my shoes.' She looked wistful. 'I broke hearts.'

'I like looking at women,' I blurted.

'What?' She put the coffee in the cupboard and banged it shut.

'I mean, sometimes, I feel, you know, attracted by women.'

My mother reached for the milk. 'Lesbians put their tongues in each other's pussies.'

'Yes, no, I know that,'

'You want to do *that?*' She screwed up her nose. 'Ptoo! Yuck!'

'No, I,'

'Think of the germs.' Mum said.

'Listen,'

'Aren't you ashamed?'

'I … '

'Don't tell anyone this, not even as a joke, people

gossip!' She stirred hot water into her teacup vigorously.

'A beautiful woman in a great outfit, it's, impressive that's all.' I said brightly.

'I like beautiful women too, doesn't mean I want to lick them.' she said flatly.

'Ma!'

She passed me a mug of hot chocolate. 'Drink this. It will help you sleep.'

Up until this point my only experience of 'alternative sexuality' had been through my father's muso stories. He'd have the whole family staring slack-jawed as he drew on the technicolour memories of his years in the Latin American nightclubs of Sydney. Smouldering beauties and late nights fuelled by scotch doubles.

'I didn't do drugs, never, a couple of drinks that's all, and we could walk through the Cross at four in the morning and nobody would bother us. Different times my child, different times.'

His favourite story involved a bongo player and an exotic dancer named Babaloo.

Babaloo had red ringlets, a tiny waist and legs that 'made grown men weep'. And yet, she was a 'no-go zone'. No one in Dad's band gave her a second look – except when she took her top off and they marvelled at how great medical science had been to her. You see, Babaloo was in fact, Bob. Everyone knew it, except for the bongo player – the newest band member. He was squat, hairless and desperate for anything with oestrogen.

Dad decided to do a little matchmaking. After the last song of the night, the usual gaggle of performers gathered for a drink in the band's dressing room. Babaloo had her arms wrapped around my father's waist.

'Babaloo *please*. You know I'm not into that kind of stuff.'

'But I could persuade you,' she purred.

'No, you couldn't, but you could, persuade *him*.' Dad pointed to the bongo player.

'What's in it for me?'

'It's a practical joke Babaloo, we'll laugh, you'll laugh, and laughing keeps you young, beautiful,'

'Laughter gives you crow's feet.'

'Jesus, just do it for me.'

And that sold her.

Dad called the bongo player over.

'Babaloo, have you met Jacky?'

'Hi Jacky.' she breathed, before blowing into my father's ear and mincing away.

'She likes *you*, they *always* like you!' The bongo player gulped his scotch.

'Listen, I don't want her.'

'Sure you don't.'

'You have my word, ask the guys. Redheads aren't my type.'

'They're *all* your type!'

'Look mate, do you want her or not?'

That night the bongo player fell into bed with Babaloo. The following evening, he beat his bongos furiously. And again the next night and the night after that until one day, he left the band to be Babaloo's wardrobe assistant on the exotic dance circuit.

☆☆☆

Another conversation with Sex.

The Virgin wondered.

'There is such a thing as bisexuality isn't there?'

'Sure. Being bisexual instantly doubles your chances of picking up at a party,' Sex said.

'Funny.'

'Fact!' Sex said.

'Yeah, but what do you think about it? It can't be normal. Shouldn't people have you with, your opposite?'

'I'm asexual,' Sex said.

'But you're Sex!'

'Yes, but that doesn't mean I jump one way, or the other,' Sex said.

'What are you talking about?'

'I'm neither this way, or that. I'm fluid. I'm free. I've told you before. People can interpret me however they want, however they feel. No rules. Just me,' Sex said.

'So, we can just go out and have you with everyone?'

'If society were more permissive, bisexuality wouldn't be an issue. It would be a given,' Sex said.

'I know I have to feel comfortable with that,'

'You don't *have* to do anything. Just be you and I'll be me. And we'll get on just fine.' Sex said.

☆☆☆

'Does she like making love to you?' I smiled nervously and handed her a cappuccino.

'She calls me sex on toast.' Allegra grinned and scooped out the foam with her fingers. 'Sex with her is like extended foreplay you know? There's no rush to get anywhere, no erection calling the shots.'

'How do you, do it?'

I wanted to hear her say it.

'Tongues and fingers,' came the fearless reply. 'which is fucking ironic really.' Allegra licked her lips.

'Why?'

'My mother *painstakingly* taught me fellatio on her prized organic carrots.'

'Your mother?'

'Yep. In the kitchen under her lace curtains.'

'Wow. I don't believe that. My mother would rather chop a carrot than suck one.'

'Really Grrl? What a fucking *scream*.'

'What would your Mum say if she knew about … '

'Nothing.'

'Really?'

'Probably wished she'd given me a few cunnilingus tips too.'

My cheeks steamed red and I blurted. 'What on?'

Allegra threw her head back and laughed. 'Good question Grrl, dunno … '

'A grapefruit?'

'An orange … much sweeter.'

'Is that what she tastes like?'

Allegra closed her eyes and seemed to shiver at a memory. She looked at me and smiled.

'Sweet. Wet. Sour.'

'She makes you feel good then?'

'She's a woman isn't she? My buttons are like her buttons. She knows exactly what to do to give me pleasure.'

'Yeah?'

'Yes! And when she makes me come it's like every nerve in my body is laughing its fucking head off.'

Her nerve cells weren't worried about crow's feet. Allegra drank the rest of her cappuccino and switched on her machine.

'So what time are the fucking suits coming with the tampon jobby?'

☆☆☆

'Okay guys just to recap,' Senior Suit clapped her hands together, 'Tampons are batshit boring and icky. Need a glam ad campaign that will glitz them up. Agreed?'

Allegra squeezed her lips into a smile. 'Sure.'

'Brilliant.' Senior Suit clapped her hands again and then lowered her voice. 'We *know* you're going to *blow our socks off* ladies.' she said before strutting out of the office.

Junior Suit nodded quickly, 'Get those juices flowing!' he chirped and gave us two thumbs up before scuttling after his boss lady.

'Think I'm gonna puke.' Allegra climbed onto her desk and sat cross-legged.

'You need my anti-wank-tank.'

'Your what?'

'Nothing … suits making you sick, huh?'

'Fuck *them*.' Allegra took a swig from her cola. 'I'm not good with blood.'

'Really?'

'Really.'

'So when did you get yours?'

'Grrl, do we have to talk about this?'

'I think it's relevant, don't you?'

Allegra swallowed more cola and shook her flyaway hair about. 'I was twelve, maybe thirteen.'

'And?'

'And I got my rags. End of story.' She folded her arms.

'Come on Grrl.'

'Well fuck! I was sitting in the playground with some girls and this little shit was trying to guess the colour of our undies. He was crap and when he got to me he said, "Yours are white with strawberries." "They're not," I said. But he insisted. So I ran to the toilets.'

'And?'

'And the shit was right.' She uncrossed her legs. 'But the fuckers weren't strawberries.'

'Oh no!'

'Oh fucking yes.' Allegra's lips relaxed into a smile. 'Your turn.'

I bloomed late. Twelve came and went. Thirteen too. And by fourteen panic had set in. I was convinced – and half hoping – my first blood would come gushing through my pleated white tennis skirt during Sport. (All my friends who got their 'Ps' at school were treated to sweet tea and biscuits in the Teacher's Lounge.) Still, sweet tea or not, I wasn't in any hurry. Not like Paola Gorges anyway. At eleven, she was the most developed girl in my class with boobs, hips and stubble on her legs. When Paola got hers, she was so excited, she made sure all the kids spotted the smear of blood on her seat.

My moment came late one afternoon during *The Brady Bunch.*

I'm sitting on my parents' bed leaning against Mary, an old doll with a big face and vulgar frosted red lips. I'm giggling along with the canned laughter – picking the same thick guffaw from the same man in the audience everytime – when suddenly a sweet, pungent smell drifts up through my thighs. I ignore it. That's what little girls are made of. But the rank scent persists. So I go to the bathroom, look down at my undies and see a few strips of brown. It's dry and really not that romantic for a first period. But I scream bloody murder anyway and my mother comes flying in. She looks at my pants and instead of sweet tea I get a few sharp slaps across the face,

'I'm putting the blood back in your cheeks,' she cries and the man with the thick guffaw is let out of his can.

Tucked up in bed with a yellow facewasher wedged between my legs, I get a lecture on the dangers of men and public toilets. From now on I have to line every toilet seat I sit on with paper; hardy protection apparently against any stray sperm waiting to pounce on unsuspecting vaginas.

☆☆☆

I have never looked forward to Greek weddings. They always provide Greek families with the perfect opportunity to make the single girls feel like the last mouldy, scrunched up anchovies that no one cared to pick off the Greek salad.

'May it be your turn next!' they say, shaking your hand and planting bad breath on your cheek just as a photo of their doctor/lawyer/dentist/accountant son pops into their thought balloon.

Mummified in metres of tulle, I would be an easy target for the stream of foul-breathed well-wishers and their balloon boys.

I spent most of Despina's wedding in the toilets. I locked myself in a five-star cubicle with leather-bound doors and just sat there. I even took naps. Every now and then a woman would clickety-click in and become my temporary neighbour. I killed time by counting the number of women who dutifully contracted their pelvic floor muscles and those who 'gushed and rushed'. All things considered, my exclusive water closet was bliss. I didn't have to think. Talk to anyone. Be funny. Or charming. Or intelligent. Or good. I could just be. I only put in an appearance when Despina and her foot fetishist were leaving. As we waited for our turn to say goodbye, I saw Despina's mother whispering to Mum. She was muttering something about 'the stuff' she had packed for her daughter's wedding night. It sounded like a military exercise.

'I've packed cotton wool and pads,' she whispered and my mother nodded, a solemn expression on her face.

'You never know.' she said.

'You never know.' my aunt nodded and held up two fingers, 'I was a virgin *twice*, did you know that?'

'You told me.' Mum said and I leaned in closer.

My aunt clutched some mysterious plastic packets to her chest and hissed, 'After my first husband died you know I was only eighteen,'

My mother nodded.

'But I waited three years before I married again. And by that time,' Aunty looked around to see if anyone was listening and then continued softer still,

'I *sealed* over.'

☆☆☆

I sat in my room trying to read while Despina's mother moaned to Mum over a thimble full of extra-strength Greek coffee.

'I miss my child,' my aunt wept.

Mum tried to console her. 'This is life. You raise your children for someone else to enjoy.'

'You're right,' she agreed. 'God only rents you your children. They're never yours to keep.'

'You nurture and love them and then they leave you to lead their own lives.'

I heard my aunt burst into a fresh set of tears. 'I wish I didn't have children! Better to have one sorrow – the sorrow of childlessness – than the countless sorrows that come with children.'

'What can you do?' my mother replied.

My aunt sniffed loudly. 'You're lucky. You still have your Agni. She's a good girl.'

I steamed in my bedroom. What do you women want? Children that cling to you, strangled by your apron strings?

'But I'll lose Agni too one day,' Mum sighed loudly, 'I pray he'll be Greek, that's all. Dear God. At least she can tell him off in her own language.'

I leapt to my feet and was seconds away from running

into the living room. But what could I do with opinions as thick and immovable as the Greek mud they sipped?

☆☆☆

Who the hell was the real Agni? What was she? Little girl? Woman? Straight? Gay? Asexual? I didn't have a clue. Knee deep in a new job and new alliances, I came to the realisation that I hadn't been living 'myself'. The 'me' on show was nothing but a crazy, confused collage of all the people in my life – Mother, Father, work colleagues, friends. It felt like I'd taken fragments of their personalities and stuck them to mine in the hope they would give me some kind of tangible sexual identity.

I remember the crush I had on Prince – and why. I loved his androgyny. With his hooped earring, low cut leopard-print top and blow dried hair, flicked like Farrah's, he was the God of Sex – and I wanted to worship at his stilettoed feet. I fantasised about him and Diamond and Pearl, when I was living with my parents and he played a concert at a nearby stadium. I lay in my bed, in the late afternoon, straining to hear the snatches of suggestive lyric and bass that floated from the stadium over a few houses and into my bedroom.

The papers were full of incredible stories about Prince and his entourage taking over a prestigious serviced apartment block in the city and covering the windows in black velvet. I was wild with thoughts of lavish encounters on his huge bed, a master at work. I would give myself to him – take me Prince, let me be another instrument you are a genius at playing. I decided early on that some women were attracted to Prince because he looked like a gorgeous woman and others were repelled by him because he looked like a gorgeous woman. The duality of sexuality. A line too blurred for my father who asked the Prince band member he picked up in his cab if Prince was gay.

No, came the tired response, Prince loves to surround himself with beautiful women.

One night, in the midst of all this sexual chaos, a little girl came to me in a dream. She was a child prostitute with long, untidy brown hair. She wore fish-net stockings and an ill-fitting black leotard. Her street-smart musings seemed so strange coming out of her mouth. I was so scared for her. Out on the streets. Alone.

'Just call me kitten,' she whispered into a mobile phone and stood on the tips of her fishnet feet.

The next day I took my dream to work and told Allegra. She looked at me for a long time after I'd finished and then she hugged me.

'It's time you got out of that stranger's clothes, Grrl.' she said.

Isolated in my little room, with the garish carpet and the glow-in-the-dark stars and the door that shooshed when it shut, I decided it was time to move out. As I fell asleep, my parents began their nightly conversation. It brought the same creamy comfort and I wanted to retract my decision – persuade myself to stay in my dusty room bursting with dolls and books and childhood memories. But I didn't feel at home there anymore.

My little girl's clothes would never, could never fit me again. I felt my rose-coloured glasses slide down my nose. They weren't enough. I wanted a rose-coloured world.

# 6

# poor man's point piper

I was eight when we moved into our inner city flat.

Our new home was on the fourteenth floor of a public housing block with a view of forever. I called it Poor Man's Point Piper after an affluent Sydney suburb where the houses spill down to the water's edge and come within kissing distance of the Bridge and Opera House. On a clear day, if I stretched a little over the balcony's railing and looked to the left, I could see a healthy snippet of the Harbour Bridge and maybe a sail or two of the Opera House.

I spent my first day at 'the Point' breathing in my new bedroom with the scuffed green linoleum. It felt huge to me. I walked around touching the walls. I sat in every corner of my room. I walked around it again and again.

'There'll always be something new to explore in here,' I said out loud and my voice bounced back to me. I liked the way it sounded. So I started to sing. My notes leapt off the walls, reverberated down the hallway and made their way to my father who was out on the balcony impressing Mum with our view of the Bridge.

I felt like I lived in the best place in the world. And I was sure I'd have this view, forever.

☆☆☆

A vicious storm came out to play the day I left Poor Man's Point Piper. Wind shrieked down the streets. Clouds were stained black. And the rain spat fat, angry drops. Mum spent the whole day watching TV. She didn't get up to eat. To pee. To drink. She didn't utter a word either. I passed the time wishing my father home from work. I also did a lot of moping. Like a lost soul I wandered from room to room. The complete tour took about fifteen seconds and when I was done, I'd go back to the room I started in and do it all over again. I spent the most time in my parents' room, on their bed, staring at the things on my mother's bedside table. A folded hanky with tiny roses embroidered into the hem. Small blue bottle of French scent. Two foil cards of aspirin. A stray bauble that had lost its gold chain months ago. A silver-framed photograph of me, age seven.

I picked it up and stared at her.

I sit cross-legged in my cot-bed. I wear a toothless grin and pigtails. I hold a new Barbie. And I am basking in the emotional freedom afforded to innocent, perfect little girls.

The scene swam through my tears. I closed my eyes and leant back against the pillows. A little girl's cries filled my head. A mother's reassuring voice came …

'But you have *five* Barbies!'

'One more Mummy please … one more and no more.'

The little girl followed her around all afternoon, new Barbie in hand. She filled her ears with Mother's voice, her nose with Mother's scent. Roses. Onions. Raised her face to the kisses that flowed from Mother's mouth. Big and noisy. All over her cheeks, face, hair … Mother burst into song when her favourite Greek tune came on the radio … she whirled around the kitchen creating a million meals her little girl will eat … but her glare could frighten disobedient angels.

It was late afternoon by the time I heard Dad's key in the lock. I ran to greet him and tell him I was packed, ready to go. My father pulled off his checkered cap and threw it on a chair. His face was lined and covered in silver stubble. He sat down heavily in an armchair next to Mum.

'Stay one more night and I'll drive you to the flat tomorrow, why the rush?'

'I can take a taxi.'

Dad shook his head. 'I'll take you.' He looked at my mother. 'Tell her to stay,'

She sat motionless, staring straight ahead until she said, 'Let her go to hell.'

A sickening heat in my chest reached up to choke me. I was treating my parents like parents I didn't want to have. I was leaving the one place where I would always be protected, where I thought I would always live. In safety. In comfort. In cotton wool.

I walked into my room and stared at all my packed bags. Garbage and boutique bags bulged with my worldly possessions. I looked at my dresser. Dusty. Chipped. I gazed into the mirror I used to play rock star in, laughing and smiling at my adoring reflected fans. There was my single bed with the big doll propped up between two crocheted cushions. The sad pierrot clown on my bedside table – so many nights I'd stare at his single golden tear and wondered why it never fell. I loved the romance of having one tear on your cheek forever.

'Come on, hurry up.' Dad burst into my room and picked up the bags, two in each hand – no time to stay and romanticise with me.

'Say goodbye to your mother.'

I wanted to kiss her, but couldn't. Instead I stood by the front door and whispered,

'*Yiasou* Mama.'

She nodded slowly and I left.

Downstairs, the wind was more fierce than ever and you wouldn't have known it was only five in the afternoon. The sky was crowded with black clouds. I helped Dad load his station wagon cab. We stuffed bag after bag into the back. One pretty designer bag split and vomited its mangled contents onto the wet sidewalk. I bent over to pick them up.

'Leave it!' Dad snapped and he clumsily scooped up a couple of books and picture frames.

I felt as torn as that ridiculously fragile bag. Was I doing the right thing? Probably not. Definitely. Did it have to hurt so much? Of course not. Absolutely.

Dad started the engine and we began to drive away. I wanted to look back at our apartment block as some last minute romantic gesture. Instead, I stared straight ahead at my new life. I wanted to leave the confines of Greek expectation behind me, even though I knew it would follow me with all the other baggage Dad had jammed into his cab.

On that first night, I stood on my own balcony with a harbour view and stared at the changing scene for hours. Then I lay on my new futon bed and whispered the longest Greek prayer I knew. At first I couldn't remember past the first few lines, so I kept repeating them until I did. I fell asleep praying.

I didn't get any phone calls or visits in the week after I left. This didn't surprise me. I had paid my parents the greatest insult by leaving them. But the time had come to claim my own space of mind. Alone in my little studio flat, I slept and wrote and took long baths in strange water. The pipes in the building were old and the water ran a muddy brown colour before it cleared. The water was never pure and I'd wind up sitting in a bath of 'weak coffee' – or hot chocolate.

A month after I moved in, I decided to burn my little-girl T-shirt.

I put it in a biscuit tin and poured acetone into her folds. Then I threw a lit match into the pinkness and watched it burn. The flames rose almost immediately, their ferocity fanned by a harbour breeze. I watched, numb as the flames seared the pink over and over until at last the little fire died down. Suddenly I could see, for the very first time, what they had been doing to my shirt. Like little tongues of fire, they had licked and penetrated the folds of the shirt – in out, in and out. They moved quickly, indiscriminately, in out, in, pushing through the folds of the shirt, licking up, licking down, in and around, piercing and penetrating.

My cherry pink girl had been reduced to crumpled

cinder.

I visited my parents once a week for dinner. Initially, the remarks were the same: you look gaunt, what's happened to your beautiful face? Then we'd argue and make up again when it was time for me to leave. And so it went, around and around. Eventually, Mum came to visit me in my little studio flat carrying a huge bowl of pasta drenched in her special thick sauce.

She hugged me hard. 'You feel like a strand of spaghetti.'

# 7

## second-hand vagina

I applied for the Staff Transfer program and won a twelve month posting in Canada.

'Hello Darling.'

'Hey Dad.' I clicked my seat belt into place. 'Busy day?'

'Nah, quiet.' he said handing me a newspaper. 'You?'

'A little.'

My eyes scanned the front page. The headline blared something about the price of petrol.

'Bloody government's trying to fu- screw us.' Dad pulled away from the curb.

'You'll be alright, won't you?'

''Course I will. I've got you haven't I?' He stopped at the lights and rested an arm on the ledge of his window. A month into Summer and it was already black from the sun.

As a small child I loved to be lifted high over his shoulders. He'd swing me around and around, sleeves flapping, revealing his single suntanned arm – the other arm like chalk. Kids teased him. But up in the sky, so high, who cared?

'What have you done my baby?' he tickled my chin and spun me around some more.

I had sneaked into my parents bedroom when they weren't looking and slipped on Daddy's uniform; his checkered cap, blue striped jumper. But the finishing touch to my androgyny was Daddy's cigar. I gripped it between my teeth and ran out into the living room as the new me. Me as Dad.

In the distance a car horn sounded dissolving my nostalgic moment. I shook my head and sat up in my seat. 'Dad,' I began as he clicked on the indicator to turn left.

'Hey, hey, what do my stars say?'

'Dad I have to … '

'Your mother drove me crazy this morning. Wear short-sleeves, she said. I ironed your short-sleeved shirt, she said. Wear short-sleeves! The woman's a machine.'

'Dad listen,'

'I said I don't mind having one black arm. She said people laugh. I said I don't care.'

'You know what she's like,'

'Nag, nag,'

A motorbike moved into our lane.

'Bloody bikers. Life in their own hands … don't you ever … '

'No Dad … I,'

' … because I don't know what I'd do … ' his voice trailed off. 'come on, my stars.'

'Dad,'

'Hm.'

'Dad. Work's sending me to Canada.'

My father slowed at an orange light and turned up the

radio.

'Dad?'

A car alarm went off in a side street. And a couple of schoolchildren crossed up ahead clutching their father's hands. Dad cleared his throat.

'Are you going to read my stars or not?' he said.

☆☆☆

'*Amy's?*' Magdalene said.

'Amy's.'

'You want to have your farewell drinks at Amy's?'

'Yeah what's wrong with that?'

'That club is a *dive*.'

'It is not … it's just been around for years.'

'Which makes it – *a dive*.'

'Okay, it was great in its prime,'

'It never had a prime.'

'Come on, that's harsh.'

'Don't you want a splashier farewell?'

'What?'

'Yeah, what about uh, Steps … it's very chic and *new*. I'll have to pull some strings to get us in on a Friday night … '

'Magdalene this is *my* farewell.'

'I know Girly and it should be memorable.'

'It will be … at Amy's.'

It was the disco of choice for the sweet sixteen set when I was growing up. We all aspired to get in and mingle with adulthood. But we all lived in fear of being asked for ID. One Saturday a month, Mum and Dad drove me to Amy's. I'd sit in the back fidgeting, trying to block out the reruns of my mother's nightclub lectures.

'Don't let any man buy you a drink – they're never free.'

'If a man asks if you have a boyfriend, say no, I have a fiance.'

'But I'm only sixteen.'

'They don't have to know that.'

'What if you don't get in?' Dad said.

'I'll get in Dad, we always get in … just don't drive right up to the door.'

I tugged at my oversized satin blouse nervously. At sixteen, my wardrobe wasn't bursting with sexy clubwear. The only thing that would feel remotely at home under a glitter ball was my black leather skirt – but even that was knee-length. So I relied on my mother's clothes – a woman who had enough shoulder pads in her wardrobe to stuff a baby elephant. I usually teamed my leather skirt with one of Mum's shiny satin blouses in honey or turquoise. I'd tuck the excess length into my pantyhose, push the sleeves up to my elbows and blow dry my hair upside down for extra height. Then I'd tease out a few fake curls and snap on Mother's Alexis Carrington diamante clip-ons.

'Not too close, not too close.' I cried from the backseat as Dad pulled in right under the bouncer's nostrils.

I jumped out.

'Don't stain my blouse!'

'We'll wait here in case you don't get in!'

My parents voices snatched and grabbed at me as I joined my friends in the queue. I flicked up the collar on my blouse and pushed out my chest.

A man in a black turtleneck growled at me.

'How old are you?'

'Eighteen.'

'Star sign?'

'Virgo.'

'Pay the cashier ten dollars.'

Amy's was named after Amy Johnson – the first woman to fly solo from England to Australia in 1930. When she was eighteen, she fell in love with a man nine years older than her. They exchanged 300 love letters and as their affair dissolved, Amy wrote,

'*You don't even want the sexual love now.*'

The walls of the club were covered in giant sepia photos of her in full flying regalia. But I had no idea who she was as we sat under her gaze sipping strawberry daiquiries. And I didn't really care. To me, Amy was just a woman in a brown picture who matched the suede couches.

We slid into the couch nearest the dancefloor.

'It's packed tonight!'

'Thank God that bouncer didn't ask for my birthday,'

'Yeah I spent the whole time in that bloody queue working out what year I needed to be born in to be eighteen.'

'You just gotta look like you're flattered if he thinks your underaged that's all.'

'Shit, look it's her.'

'Who?'

'The bitch who stole Kat's boyfriend.'

'You don't know that for sure.'

'Yeah I do, you should have seen her sticking her tongue in his mouth at Sunday school – lucky the priest was late.'

'*Wow* Pan looks hot tonight.'

'He's the best DJ around I reckon.'

'That guy is such a fucking *spunk.*'

They were talking about my childhood crush.

'His name is Panayioti.' I adjusted my shiny shirt.

'Whatever … I'd pash him.'

'Hey!'

'Oh chill out.'

'Are you gonna go up to him?'

I looked over at the dancefloor. It was jammed with over a hundred sweaty bodies.

*There's a party going on right here. A celebration to last throughout the year …*

Panayioti held court like a modern day Pied Piper – with monobrow. He moved his head in time to the music, stopping every now and then to blow a kiss into the crowd.

'No way.'

'Why the fuck not?'

'Do you always have to swear?'

'Go and *talk* to him!'

'He looks busy.' I said and a bunch of girls in mini leather skirts surged towards Panayioti's turntables. He raised his arms feigning arrest and backed into a full-length shot of Amy posing with her plane.

'Here we are!' I said. 'The stomping ground of my youth.' I beamed at Magdalene who touched the corners of a sepia print on the wall and shuddered dramatically.

'This place is *screaming* for an overhaul.'

'Don't start,'

'Well it does.' she pouted and looked around. 'Who else is coming?'

'Some people from work … and maybe Alexander.'

A couple of weak strobe lights stuttered on the dancefloor. The glitterball spun like it was running out of batteries. Magdalene eyed the door.

'You do realise we're a tad early,'

'It'll pick up – trust me.' I replied and looked over to the DJ turntable. It was empty.

Magdalene moved to drop her jacket on a couch, but pulled back at the last minute.

'Is that dried *vomit?*' her voice was high pitched.

'What? Where?' I said leaning over for a closer look. 'No you idiot, the couch has just faded in that spot.' I said and sat down amongst a scattering of cushions.

'That's *vomit.*' she sniffed and put her jacket back on.

'Maybe you should've brought your disinfectant.' I muttered.

'Yes!' Magdalene perked up. 'Great idea,'

'What?'

'Alcohol! I'll get us some drinks. What do you want?'

'Strawberry daiquiri.'

'That's a milkshake Girly – let me get you a real drink.'

I glared at her.

'Okay, relax. I'll be back in a minute.'

I shook off my jacket and sat down under the watchful eye of Amy. A handful of couples sat together in booths by the dancefloor. The women looked like Russian mail order brides and they laughed loudly with the men who surrounded them clutching champagne bottles. I looked away and saw a guy with an exaggerated swagger coming towards me. He had a mobile phone to his ear.

Alexander nodded when I caught his eye.

*'I'm in a club man, yeah ... hey Cuz ... Amy's ... I know, it's ancient.'*

Alexander massaged my shoulder with one hand and sat down beside me.

'You made it.' I said when he clicked his phone shut.

'Yeah, can't stay long though.'

'Hot date?'

'You just never know.' He pushed his phone into a jacket pocket.

'You won't be able to hear that in here loverboy.'

'That's what *vibrate's* for babe.' he smiled and looked me up and down. 'Lookin' good Cuz,'

'Thanks.'

' ... which is lucky,'

'Why?'

'You'll never guess who's here.'

'Who?'

Alexander grinned. 'I don't think I should tell you.'

'Who's here Alex?' I sighed.

Magdalene returned with the drinks and Alexander's mouth fell open. I was embarrassed for him.

'Alex you remember,'

'Hi Magdalene.' he said shakily and reached for my daiquiri.

'Put on a bit of bulk since the last time I saw you Alex.'

'Like it?'

'I prefer my men weedy. But that's just me,'

'So, tell me who's here.' I repeated.

Alexander sipped the frothy drink quickly and screwed up his nose.

'Who ordered the milkshake?'

'Your cousin … who's here?' Magdalene rattled the ice in her tumbler.

'So, you still single?' Alexander slid closer to my friend.

'What do you mean, *still?*' Magdalene swirled her drink around angrily. 'God can I have some more bloody gin with my ice!'

'Bartenders can be tight bastards.' Alexander said.

'Are you going to tell me?' I insisted.

'I said gin and tonic with a *little* ice please,'

'Let me take it back for you.' Alexander said.

'Do I know this person?' I asked tapping his shoulder.

'Forget it, I'll drink it now and complain later.' Magdalene pushed an icecube into her mouth and chewed. Alexander looked on, drooling.

'Alex!' I clipped the back of his head. 'Is it a man or a … '

'Who?'

I looked up and saw a familiar face. 'Allegra!'

'Who's Allegra?' Magdalene and Alexander chorused.

Allegra lead her girlfriend through the Russian mail order brides.

'Cool place Grrl.' Allegra reached over to hug me. 'Thanks for inviting us.'

'Everybody this is Allegra and Faith.' I said and trembled as Faith kissed my cheek.

'Hi beautiful,' she said.

Magdalene hissed in my ear. 'Is she the dyke you were telling me about?'

'She's a lesbo?' Alexander muttered through his smile.

'I prefer Allegra actually.' Allegra said goodnaturedly and fluffed up her hair.

Faith settled back in the couch and spread her legs. Her hair was short and shiny and she wore a black tailored jacket with a matching t-shirt and jeans. A skinny silver chain gleamed at her neck.

'Did you guys having trouble finding the place?' I said.

'A little,'

'You should've just followed the signs to the museum.' Magdalene picked at her ice with a straw.

'Magdalene doesn't think the club's aged very well.'

'It's a dump.' Magdalene smiled.

'I've been to worse babe.' Faith reached up and stroked Allegra's face, 'haven't I toasty?'

'Fuck yeah.' Allegra grinned and kissed her quickly on the lips. 'What was that place called? You should've seen it Grrl … *so* tacky.'

Alexander patted his jacket pocket. 'What's the reception like in here?'

Faith furrowed her brow. 'Fuck what was it called … uh, Stairs, uh, Steps, yeah! Steps. Fucking *horrible*.'

Magdalene looked up from her drink, annoyed. 'Why did you go then?'

'Cousin's hens night.'

'This place, has a very, uh, fuck … a retro feel about it.' Allegra said.

Faith studied Magdalene's face. 'You have amazing eyes, uh, I didn't catch your name,'

'Magdalene.' Alexander snapped and pulled out his mobile phone.

'Right, Magdalene, yeah, what do you think babe – gorgeous eyes huh?'

'You're a fucking *flirt*, that's what I think.'

'You wouldn't want me any other way toasty,'

'Why do you call her toasty?' Magdalene asked.

'She says I'm sex on toast.' Allegra smiled.

'Toast?'

'Yeah toast. You know, cooked bread … crunchy on the outside,' Faith tickled Allegra's neck with her nose, 'soft on the inside,'

'Magdalene's on a no-carb diet.' I said and felt a sharp kick against my ankle. 'Ow!'

Magdalene sat back in her seat and crossed her arms.

'Well aren't you?' I asked rubbing my ankle.

Alexander picked at his phone's keypad. 'I've only got a couple of bars of service.'

'You were just on the phone Alex, it'll work, stop fretting.'

Faith stood up.

'Anybody want a drink?'

Magdalene sucked the ice cubes in her tumbler dry and slammed it down on the table.

'Yes please, gin and tonic … here I have change.'

'It's on me.' Faith said. 'Anybody else?'

'Vodka.' Allegra said.

'Alexander can I get you or your phone a drink?'

'Bloody service bars,' he muttered without looking up.

Faith laughed and walked off.

'So, have you two been together long?' Magdalene

asked Allegra.

Alexander chuckled in my ear. 'Do your parents know you have lezzie friends?'

'*What* is your problem?' I said.

'I don't have one, you're the one hanging out with pussy lickers.'

'Jealous?'

'Panayioti won't be impressed.'

'What's that wanker got to do with anything?'

'He's a wanker now?'

'Forget it.' I picked up my daiquiri and took a long sip. The sweetness almost choked me. 'Allegra, tell Magdalene about all your flowers,'

Alexander fiddled with his keypad. 'He's here.'

'Who?'

'The wanker.'

'What?'

Magdalene squealed. 'She sent you anemones? I *love* anemones. Roses are so 80s.'

'Faith knows her fucking flowers.'

'Alex, spit it out.'

'What?' He put his phone to his ear. 'Hello? Hello?'

'*Who's* here?'

Alexander squeezed the phone into his cheek. '*Yeah hi, can you hear me?*'

'Alex!'

'I'm on the phone,' he said.

'You said he's here.'

'Who?'

'You tell me!'

He slapped his mobile shut. 'Damn network.'

'Alex for God's sake.'

'Hm? Oh, it's Panayioti.'

Faith returned carrying a small tray of drinks. 'Who's Panayioti?'

'Hey I'm vibrating!' Alexander jumped to his feet. 'Gotta go ladies.'

I closed my eyes and let the slow thud, thud of an R&B bass drift over me.

'Aaand welcome to Amy's.' a familiar voice filled the space. 'We've got some great old grooves for you tonight, soul 80s style,'

I opened my eyes. Panayioti stood at the turntables underneath Amy and her plane. From where I sat he looked the same. But I guessed the smoke machine was just being kind.

He was the first boy I kissed. I was eight. He was twelve. And his cramped bedroom was 'the house' we played 'husbands and wives' in. He'd put on his plastic bobby's helmet and go to work and I'd stay 'home' to do the housework; tidy up his matchbox cars, straighten the posters of cars on his walls, dust football trophies. A few minutes later he'd burst through the door, 'Honey I'm home!' he'd yell and throw his helmet on the floor. Then we'd lie on top of his racing car quilt cover and kiss with our mouths closed. I always kept my shoes on – bright blue Mary Janes – and if I needed to take a breath, I'd grab hold of his shiny black hair and yank.

'What are you two doing in there? Open up!' it was Mum.

We unglued our lips and shot to opposite ends of the room as the door swung open.

'You should get your father to look at that door,' my mother said.

'Yeah, it gets stuck.' the boy muttered without looking up from his car magazine.

At my ninth birthday a photo was taken of my boy crush and I. I beamed at the camera, he stared at the cake. I kept that photo in my bedside drawer for years. It was the only photo I had of us until the night of my highschool dinner dance.

I slipped into a crème taffetta skirt and matching blouse that hinted at my sweet sixteen cleavage. I liked what peeked through the frills. Mother didn't. So she quickly found a brooch and pinned the folds of taffeta together.

I looked down at my chest and saw a small crucified Jesus in 18 carat gold.

'I don't want to wear this.' I said.

'Leave it there! It'll keep the draft out.'

I glanced at little Jesus again. He looked up at His Father.

*Why hast thou forsaken me?*

'Do I have to wear this?' I moaned, tugging at Him.

'Yes, Jesus will protect you.'

'From what?'

'The evil eye.'

The back seat. Hot and unholy feelings.

'It looks lovely,' my mother smiled. 'and you don't need to advertise.'

Maybe she was right. Maybe I didn't want him looking down my top over his prawn cocktail. But when she wasn't looking, I pulled a frill down over Christ. The doorbell rang.

'He's here my little bride! Panayioti's here!' my mother clapped her hands together.

'Mum!' I hissed fanning my cheeks.

The doorbell rang again.

'Is someone going to get that?' my father yelled from the bathroom.

Mother pushed past me.

'No, I'll do it!' I called after her.

But it was too late. She'd run down the hallway and pulled the door open with a cry of,

'Welcome my boy!'

I emerged from the shadows.

'Hi.' I smiled and yanked on Jesus.

'You look really nice.' he said and kissed my cheek.

A little shiver came and went. Fall in love with me! Forget family honour! Find the bad little girl in me!

'You too.' I replied.

'Good girls are hard to find you know.' my mother said pushing cake into his hands.

'Hm.'

'She's grown into a real beauty hasn't she?' my father said.

'Oh yes.'

And then Dad asked him how his Dad was. And Mum asked him how his Mum was.

'Fine. They're fine thanks.'

'Well we should go.' I said.

'Yes!' Panayioti said and stood up.

'Oh, a photo, just one photo!' my mother leapt to her feet and snapped a shot of history repeating itself.

I beamed into the camera. He stared at the cake.

In the car I sneaked a better look at him as he drove. He wore a charcoal grey suit with a black satin tie. And he had a very neat mullet hairstyle perfectly offset by a monobrow. I'd forgotten about that but I loved the economy of it. Who needed two?

I swooned as Panayioti hugged a corner at speed. I accidentally grabbed Jesus.

'Ouch!'

'You okay?'

'Yeah, it's just Jesus.'

'Come again?'

'Je-nothing ... I'm so excited about tonight. Apparently the restaurant is on the 45th floor and it,'

' ... revolves, I know. I took a girlfriend there last week. It's awesome.'

'Oh.'

'So how's school?'

'Good. A few of the girls are going to Amy's after dinner ... do you want to go?'

'Can't babe. I'm meeting some mates – but I can drop you off if it's okay with your parents. We can call them from the restaurant.'

'No that's okay.'

'You got a curfew?'

'Well, no, I mean ... '

'Parents can be a bitch ... but you gotta train 'em like I did.'

'Train them.'

'Yeah. Say your curfew's twelve right? You come home at five past. The following weekend stretch it to ten past.

And so on, trust me, it works.'

'Maybe I'll try that tonight,'

'You just gotta know how to play them that's all. But you're a chick, can't be easy.'

When we walked into the restaurant, I looked over at our table where all my girlfriends had stopped talking. They were staring at Panayioti like he'd just slipped off a silver screen. Giddy with pride, I pushed my arm into his.

'I'm glad you're here tonight.' I said.

'No problem Babe.' he said and snapped his gum.

My friends loved him. I knew they would. He impressed them with his knowledge of distant places …

'The Greek islands have the best nightclubs … open all fucking night.'

And wit …

'Then the midget said I'll need a ladder to lick that miss!'

I laughed and grabbed his hand. 'Keep your voice down.'

Panayioti's hand felt calloused, strong and masculine. I squeezed his fingers and when he squeezed mine I thought my clitoris would spontaneously combust. He kept holding my hand right into the next dirty joke until someone offered him a cigarette.

'Want one Babe?' he asked me.

I shifted in my seat and my taffetta made a swoosh sound, answering for me.

'I swear you are so healthy – good on you babe – wish I could stop.'

In the toilets the girls gathered around.

'He is so *cool.*'

'I think he likes you.'

'He was squeezing your hand!'

'What more proof do you need?'

'He's *so* cute.'

'You bringing him to Amy's?'

'You gotta bring him to Amy's.'

'Maybe after.'

'After what?'

'After … after our drive.'

'You're going for a drive?'

'Go for it!'

'It's just a drive.'

'Yeah sure.'

'You going to Doll's Point?'

Doll's Point. Make out Mecca. A wide strip of beach road where guys parked to take their girls 'further'. Doll's Point. Where vinyl and leather interiors meant the difference between 'all the way' or a dry French kiss in the back. Vinyl got too sweaty, too quick. But real leather, polished, slippery lambskin …

'He's *asked* you to go to Doll's Point?'

'Sure, why wouldn't he?' I lied.

We stood outside his car waving my friends goodbye.

'They're cool,' Panayioti said reaching into his breast coat pocket.

'Yeah.'

He handed me a stick of gum.

'Thanks.' I said and began to unpeel the wrapper. 'So, uh, can we go for a drive?'

He looked at his watch. 'It's getting kinda late babe.'

'We won't be out long and … Mum and Dad won't

mind, I'm with you.'

We got in the car.

'How about a quick drive through the city.' Panayioti said.

'How about Doll's Point?'

He was silent.

'Panayioti?'

'Have you been there before?' he said.

'No. This will be my first time.' I said fastening my seat belt.

Prime position at Doll's Point was the beachside spaces. And they were always full. Except for this night. But Panayioti drove into a spot on the road side.

'The beachside spots were free.' I said.

'Yeah, but I won't get stuck in any traffic when we leave from here.'

I looked around. There wasn't a single car anywhere.

'I love these seats.' I said, stroking the soft clean leather at my thigh.

'It's vinyl.' he said rather abruptly and stuffed a cassette into the tapedeck.

'No way – it feels so real.'

'Well it's not.' Panayioti chewed fast on his gum.

He reached over turned the volume up. The car filled with a low thudding beat.

'So, how's work?' I said.

'Busy, yeah busy.'

'Are you still DJ-ing?'

'Oh yeah, yeah, but I help Dad out in the chicken shop, you know, between gigs.'

'Where do you DJ?'

'All over,'

'I'd like to see you play.'

'I come on really late babe.'

'So?'

'You'd be bored.'

'No I wouldn't – I'd love to see you.'

'You are so cute.' Panayioti squeezed my shoulder.

(*Cute?* Dachshunds wearing winter coats were cute.)

'Thanks.' I looked into his eyes. He looked away.

A car cruised by with the stereo cranked up. The bass throbbed like a giant's heartbeat.

'How can that guy drive around with that music up so loud.'

'You sound like my mother.' Panayioti laughed

I cringed. 'Well, you know what I mean.'

'So I hear you're a real brain at school.'

'I just read a lot.'

'Good on ya babe.'

Our eyes locked again. He turned away – again. I sat up straighter and moved closer towards his seat.

'I was reading a magazine the other day about the colours of temptation,'

'Really.' Panayioti looked out the window and then at his watch.

'What colours tempt you – I mean, mine's uh, charcoal grey.'

He took his jacket off. 'Red. When a woman wears red, I dunno, strange things happen.'

I looked down at my crushed taffetta.

'Hey! I can't believe it.' he cried as a woman in cream jeans walked towards the car.

Panayioti leapt out, slammed the door and she jumped up on him. From the car I could just make out a few words.

'It's been so long … gorgeous!'

'What are you doing here?'

'Family friend,'

'Good deed …?'

'Meeting girls at Amy's … come?'

'Sounds … fun … '

The woman waved at me and mouthed 'hi'. I managed a weak smile and then had to watch as Panayioti kissed her goodbye on the lips.

'What a fucking coincidence seeing her here!' he said pulling on his seat belt.

I stared out the window.

'Okay, let's get you home.'

The first set of lights were red. He turned to look at me.

'So what do you want to do after highschool – probably uni huh?'

I shrugged my shoulders. The lights changed and he sped off again.

'Bet your parents want you to be a doctor or teacher or something.'

He nudged my arm. I flinched.

'Hey.' Panayioti whispered.

'What?' I said keeping my eyes on the road.

'You're pretty quiet all of a sudden,'

'Am I?'

'So uh, did you like Doll's Point?'

'Alright.' I muttered.

Panayioti turned down the stereo. 'Hey, I … '

'You better speed it up. Don't want you to be late.' I pulled on my jacket.

He stopped at another set of lights and turned to face me. His eyes were a lovely mocha colour.

'You, you're a nice girl you know,' His voice trailed off.

I started to fiddle with the clasp on my little Jesus.

'But you and me, you and me are too different babe,'

I pushed the clasp on my brooch deeper into my thumb.

' … and don't say we're not different because we are.'

'No two people are alike,' I said softly.

He pulled into my apartment block and the engine was still humming when I felt a warm trickle of blood down my finger …

… I ran screaming to Mummy who wiped the blood away and told me not to be such a cry baby. It was bad luck to cry. I asked her to kiss it better. Her lips left a bright pink smudge on my finger. She stuck a bandaid over the ribbon of broken skin. Will there be a scar? Mummy pinched my nose and told me not be silly. Then she promised my finger would 'forget' all about the cut by the time I was a big girl …

' … you'll forget about me. I promise.' Panayioti switched the engine off.

I sucked on my finger.

'I have to go.' I said.

'I'll walk you up.'

'Don't bother. Your good deed is done.' I cried and got out of the car before he could say anything.

Dad slapped him on the back.

'Have a good time son?'

'Did you take care of my daughter?' my mother stuck another noisy kiss on his cheek. 'She's a flower isn't she? A flower!'

We sat down on the couch like the embarrassed couple just back from a plastic TV date. And like all manufactured TV dates gone wrong, we didn't look at each other once in the ten minutes it took for my mother to offer coffee, ask questions about the food, tell Panayioti what a devil he was for telling rude jokes and insist he'd never find another 'flower' like me.

'Anyway,' he stood up.

'You going already?' Mum said.

'He's meeting some friends.'

'Be careful son.' my Dad said and disappeared into the bedroom.

'Thanks for tonight.' I said.

'No problem.' Panayioti said.

When he left, my mother pounced.

'Tell me!'

'He was a real gentleman.'

'That's it?'

I nodded.

'Was there anyone dressed like you, sweet and … '

'No.'

'He noticed that too, am I right? Men want good girls, I know what I'm talking about,'

In my bedroom I clamped Pillow to my face and sobbed. I tasted the cut on my finger. The saltiness had gone.

I opened my eyes just as a ray from the glitterball shone directly into my face. I blinked.

'They put too much salt in my Bloody Mary.' Faith said loudly.

'Just drink it woman.' Allegra said swallowing her vodka.

'I need another drink.' Magdalene said.

'You just had one.'

'And now I need another. Daiquiri for you?'

'No I'm fine thanks.'

'I'll come with you … this Bloody Mary sucks.' Faith said and followed Magdalene.

The mail order brides were dancing on top of a table. One bride threw a wispy scarf into the air and a man with a heavy beard stumbled towards it – but in his drunken state he pulled at the edge of Amy in her flying goggles instead. The man tugged and tugged until the corner of Amy's giant smile ripped off in his hands and he fell backwards into the couch. The scarf floated down over his face.

'Are you having a good time Grrl?' Allegra said jiggling absentmindedly to the beat.

'Yeah it's okay … you?'

She nodded cheerfully. 'It's not too crowded.'

'Hm.'

Magdalene and Faith flopped down into the cushions beside me.

'I'm going to get *very* drunk tonight. There's never a queue at the bar.' Faith took a hefty gulp of her drink.

'Not a good sign of a club you know.' Magdalene slurred.

'It might pick up.' Faith said licking the edges of her glass. 'yum, not too salty.'

'Since when did *salt* bother you?' Allegra said.

'There's salt,' Faith slipped her hand between Allegra's legs, 'and there's *salt.*' she squeezed.

'So you going to say hello to this Panayioti creature?' Magdalene said.

'Show him what he's missing Grrl.' Allegra laughed as Faith dug deeper.

I stared at the dancefloor. The man with the heavy beard bopped about unsteadily with the floaty scarf tied around his head. Two teenaged girls in lycra mini-dresses danced with their mirror reflections. And one of the mail order brides was doing the tango with a man in a shiny white suit. The smoke machine spluttered. The strobe lights had all but stopped. The Pied Piper with monobrow stood motionless against the wall.

'*There's a party going on right here. A celebration to last throughout the year-the year-the-year-the-year …* '

The tune stuttered, but no one seemed to notice. Panayioti slowly unpeeled himself from the wall and corrected the needle on his record.

' … *the year. So bring your good times and your laughter too we're gonna celebrate your party with you.*'

He retreated back into Amy's arms.

'So are you going to say hi or not?'

'He looks busy.' I said.

'I mean *look* at the state of this print,' Magdalene banged the palm of her hand into Amy's left eyeball.

'Come on,' I stood up. 'Let's move on.'

☆☆☆

My mother took me through the week's top ten tabloid murders as I packed for Canada.

'This man killed his wife with an egg beater!'

'What did he do whisk her to death?' I smiled.

'Police are *still* looking for him.'

'In kitchenware departments all over the country,' I said and kissed her neck.

She wandered out of my bedroom muttering something about taking risks with closed vaginas.

I looked over at the pierrot clown on my bedside. His single tear gleamed. Maybe I could put my life on hold; live with my parents again. At least I'd know what to expect. Even the arguments would be safe. We'd bicker, accuse and make up, then I'd say goodnight and retreat to my bedroom with the glow-in-the-dark stars and loud carpet. And the door would shoosh as I shut it behind me.

'What are you writing?' Mum came into my bedroom yawning.

'Nothing,' I said and tucked my notepad under my pillow.

'Then turn off the light and go to sleep … tomorrow's another day.'

'Tuck me in.'

'Are you a baby?' she said, pulling the sheets tightly around me. 'Now sleep or you'll never get up in the morning, you'll miss your flight … I wish you miss your flight.'

She fluffed up my quiltcover.

'I'm going to miss you Ma.'

'Yes, well … this was your choice.'

'I'll call you every few days.'

She sighed and sat down on my bed.

'You'll have children one day … I don't know when that day will come, but one day, you'll know. You'll know how a mother feels,' Her eyes filled and I reached up to her hug her.

'It's late.' she stood up quickly and straightened the quilt. 'All I'm going to say is be careful.'

I nodded.

'People are not as trustworthy as you think they are,'

I nodded again and she raised her finger.

'And no man wants a second hand vagina.'

She turned to leave.

'Mum.'

'What?'

'Aren't you going to kiss me goodnight?'

'I did that,' she said and then her face softened, 'oh, goodness sake,'

She pushed her nose, her lips into my cheek. Her breath smelled of chocolate.

Second Hand Vagina for Sale. One careful lady owner. Immaculate condition. Full service history. Looks and feels like new. Must be seen. Strictly no canvassers. Priceless. O.N.O.

☆☆☆

Another conversation with Sex.

The Virgin thumbed through the Bible.

'God said thou shalt not have you before marriage.'

'Yes, that's a classic.' Sex said.

'Is it true?'

'Depends.' Sex said.

'On what?'

'On what kind of God you believe in.' Sex said.

'Er, the usual kind – lives in the clouds wears long robes, beard.'

'I don't mean his fashion choices. Is your God kind? Or does he doom you to Hell if you orgasm out of wedlock?' Sex said.

'He's a good God.'

'Then God likes me.' Sex said.

'He *likes* you?'

'Sure. He is as you perceive Him. And if you believe your God loves you for you and not because your hymen is intact, then God likes me.' Sex said.

'And you like … *God*.'

'I can't see why not.' Sex said.

'B-but, the Virgin Mary … Angels … the Immaculate Conception for Christ's sake!'

'Yes?' Sex said.

'Aren't you miffed about it?'

'The Immaculate Conception?' Sex said.

'Yes!'

'God no. It was a marketing exercise.' Sex said.

'Excuse me?'

'Christianity was a new religion. It needed a USP.' Sex said.

'A what?'

'A USP. Unique selling proposition. And it was one of the best around.' Sex said.

'But,'

'Think about it. Which is more spectacular ... the Archangel Gabriel at the foot of your bed? Or Joseph taking you to dinner and a movie?' Sex said.

# 8

## mile high mango

Home for me in Canada was a big house owned by Honey – a sprightly seventy five year old with a large collection of wigs and five wardrobes bulging with decades of fashion.

'Dear, I can tell if a woman's wearing a wig a *mile* away.' she'd say and laugh so long and so loud her dentures almost tumbled out of her perfectly lipsticked mouth.

We lived in the house where Honey was born. She on the first floor. Me on the second. My apartment was small, but perfectly formed with a double bed, sofa and one armchair covered in tiny mint green polka dots. The wooden floors squeaked in most places. The walls were painted in a soft shade of nothing. And a small drop leaf table stood by the window like a cheerful afterthought. It was fairly unremarkable but I loved every worn inch. I decorated my bedroom wall with photos, bought a pack of red plastic plates to supplement the kitchen crockery and invested in a polyester quilt from Honest Ed's – a loud, fluorescent-lit store downtown where everything was always on sale.

Living in my own self-contained space, there was never any reason for me to pop downstairs or see Honey more than in passing. But I did, often. The stairs became our meeting place for long conversations that turned into invitations for afternoon tea and Pecan Passion cookies.

'If I had any children, I'd wish they were just like you, dear,' Honey would say and pass me another cookie.

Crunching into her fifth Pecan Passion, Honey told me about her childhood, growing up in a typical Canadian middle-class family; lots of kids, outings, parties and entertaining. Very proper and 'so much fun, dear'.

One weekend I rented *Anne of Green Gables* on video. We sat on Honey's single white bed and watched pretty, opiniated Anne with an 'e' until we fell asleep. The next day she left me a note on yellow paper. In her beautiful, turn of the century cursive she wrote,

'Thank you for a lovely evening dear. I hadn't seen Anne in years. Cookies at 3?'

This note was the first in a long series of little notes left with love. Sometimes, she left a chocolate with a note, or an orange, sometimes she left a full packet of Pecan Passion cookies with a P.S. that read,

'Make sure you share them!'

One afternoon I heard the soft thud of her cane on the carpeted stairs. I rushed out and saw her standing on the landing, out of breath.

'Did you run up those stairs?' I put my around her shoulders and guided her into my apartment.

'I wanted to show you my … wedding album.' Honey said sitting heavily into a pile of cushions. 'I just found the old thing buried under some photos of Mum and Dad.'

Honey's hazel eyes brimmed as she turned the first page.

'Look how beautiful I was,'

It was 1950 and we walked arm in arm through a garden of tulips, brushing past five bridesmaids dressed in 'springtime lilac, dear'. The photos were black and white and carefully posed. Brilliant smiles, lace brocade and a radiant bride. My landlady spent her honeymoon on the second floor of her parents' home – where Honey would live for the rest of her married life. And as her brothers and sisters grew up and moved away, her parents took more and more trips to America.

'I missed them when they were away but when they came home, I'd jump for joy!'

While her husband slept, Honey sat by the front window waiting for her parents' car. The marriage didn't last. She left him, for them.

'He didn't really love me,'

As time marched on, Honey became her parents' nursemaid. Her mother died first – in hospital. Her father a year later, in her arms on the second floor.

'He was in such pain. He closed his eyes, took a breath. That was it, dear.'

Years later I would visit Honey in hospital.

The elaborately coiffed wigs were gone and in their place limp white strands hung like a frayed shawl over bony shoulders. Honey's skin was taut and smooth. Young and refreshed. Her fingernails were painted red. On her lips the softest hint of mauve lipstick shimmered.

'You look beautiful,' I whispered and squeezed Honey's

hand.

'Oh thank you, dear, but I look a mess. Thank God Mum's here to do my hair.'

☆☆☆

'You're a peach for helping us out.' A woman in a loud orange turtleneck lead me into an office. 'I know you have other deadlines but the client's screaming and this bloody writer,'

'Is she the writer in the black glasses?'

The woman nodded, pulling up the blinds.

' … and hunchback who thinks she's God's gift to words? Got her in one.' She made space on a desk crowded with folders and stacks of A3 paper.

'Oh.' I said and pretended to search for something important in my bag.

'She's having a fucking mental health month, can you believe that? A month? She'd need a bloody decade,' The woman pushed another wad of paper to the floor.

I hooked my bag over the back of a chair. 'I've heard she spits on suits who bring her copy changes,'

'We are *account service.*' The woman glared at me.

'Right.' I said and sat down.

She handed me a small green folder.

'Here's the Cat Yum job file. Have a read. You'll get some copy changes this afternoon.'

I looked around the empty office and ran out into the hallway,

'Do I have an art director?' I called. But the lift doors had already closed.

I spent the rest of the morning stacking loose leaf paper in a pile near the phone. I gathered the paper clips and dropped them in a paper cup. Brushed eraser dust off the desk. And when I couldn't stall any longer, I switched on her computer … and searched her files. I only had to open a few before I found one containing a short story she'd written. It was a sparsely written tale about an insomniac country girl who took nightly trips into the deep dark city. The writer's descriptions were anorexic, her language simple and yet I could feel the heroine's anxieties, her fears, the wonder that filled her when she left the dusty streets of her country town and felt the cool concrete of the city beneath her bare feet. But where were the discarded hypodermics, cockroaches and glowing cigarette butts? My cheeks burned green. The writer's pen seemed to glide effortlessly from a world of organic cat food to languid scenes of forbidden adventure.

One afternoon as I keyed in the last set of changes for a hair colourant product…

*Your hair will glow and gleam from the inside out giving you glamorously gorgeous hair. Get the picture?*

… the letter 'g' kept getting stuck.

I banged on the key a couple times before turning the keyboard upside-down for a good shake. Crumbs, dust and a few dark flecks of debris showered the desk. Then I saw it, beneath the monitor, a crumpled corner of paper. I lifted the edge of the computer and yanked the paper free.

*Why do I write? Does it keep me immortal? Does it validate my existence on this planet? I could do without words. Why fret over them? The spelling, the grammar, the alliteration. Who gives a fuck? I do. Every single minute of every single fucking day. I do. My words take my mind away from the everyday. I can live vicariously through them. Why do I write? For all of these reasons and none of them. But I should write without definition, because the moment you define something, the muse will disappear.*

There was a knock on the door. And a fresh-faced suit looked in.

'I've got some more of those pesky changes for you!'

☆☆☆

Dad called, breathless, excited at some ungodly hour in the morning – Toronto time.

'We've bought a parrot Agni. George, his name is George.'

'What time is it?'

'Yeah, he talks. He says, Hello George, Hello Georgie boy. Very smart bird.'

'Dad it's really early here,'

'Listen, can you hear him? He's talking now.'

'And he's big,'

'Yeah?'

'Oh yeah big! With long feathers, green, blue, red … like a rainbow, beautiful bird. Your mother loves him.'

Mum grabbed the phone.

'He drive me crazy. All the time, *squah, squah.*'

'She loves him.' Dad repeated.

☆☆☆

Homesickness banged on my door early in the

Canadian summer.

A ferocious wind blew about Honey's house, rattling doors, windows. My memories. Back at Poor Man's Point Piper, the wind was notorious for picking up speed around the tall blocks of flats. It whipped around cars, people and animals. And as a child I loved doing battle with it. I knew I was never a match for its strength of course, but I fought anyway. There I was, light as taffeta, leaning against it, pushing, pushing, daring it to push me back. And it always did. Now, in Toronto, as the wind tore up rose bushes outside my window, I felt like I was back home. And not in a hundred year old house with antique fixtures, stained glass windows and pictures of dead grandfathers and fathers – not my own. The distance from home gnawed at me. One morning I followed a woman I didn't know for five blocks because she was wearing my mother's perfume. I wondered what I'd find if I gave in to the yearning and flew home?

Warmth. Familiarity. Family and friends there to greet me. Then, after the initial joy of seeing old faces, admiring our view, visiting my room … and after watching TV, making calls, spending time with Mum talking about everything and nothing, hanging out in her kitchen, hearing her whinge and enjoying it … after taking drives with my Dad, rediscovering our roads and being his little girl again … after being a part of their world again … after all that, what then? I didn't care. I would be happy to let familiarity breed contempt. I wanted that world back. Where were Mummy's fleshy, plump arms that cradled my head when dark moods soured my smile? Where were the silly, irrational, wise talks I had with Daddy? He'd give me his spare taxi ID photos signed with the words, 'To my darling little girl, from Daddy.' Why couldn't we return to these worlds every now and then?

I looked out the window and saw Honey in the garden. She was hammering a few loose fence pickets back into place. Her space. Her place. Keep out. Occasionally she stopped to survey the small drop of grassy land around her. It was all hers. Her home. Always was. Always would be. I pulled down the blinds and the phone rang. It was Dad. His voice was raspy, flirtatious, like a lover who missed me.

'How are you? What are you doing Darling?'

He seemed stuck in the world where I played dress-ups with his clothes. Desperate to pull me back there with him. Without me, my childhood was a wilderness of frayed memories. Come back, baby. It's warm here. No. Let go.

'Yes, Daddy, everything's fine, yes I'm eating.'

When Easter came around I visited the local Greek deli and picked up some dyed boiled eggs and port-drenched biscuits. But the eggs and biscuits had been mass-produced. Colours were flat, lifeless. Biscuits brittle, tasteless. I went to church on Easter Saturday. My religion and language connected me to my family and bridged the distance more than a sweet biscuit ever could. I stood at the door and let all my senses flood … the smell of burning incense, the glint from gold-edged icons and the huge silver bowls of sand that stood strong under the weight of a thousand flickering candles. I dropped some change into a wooden box and picked up three candles – one for Mum, one for Dad, one for Yiayia. I lit the candles, crossed myself and then stood in line for my spoonful of holy communion.

A young father stood with his little girl in front of me. I watched as he lifted her to meet the priest's golden chalice filled with port. She squirmed in her father's arms and turned away from the priest.

'Come on sweetheart,' he soothed. 'do it for Daddy.'

When I called home on Easter Sunday my parents were sitting down to lunch with an uncle and aunt. All I wanted to do was listen to them joke, talk, eat; pretend I was there. I could imagine where they were sitting, what food Mum had made. Dad would be chomping on a huge mouthful. My aunt and uncle would be taking small spoonfuls of this, a forkful of that.

I missed everything ...

... at night, while my parents slept and I watched the late movie, my eyes swept the walls in search of victims. They were small and they loved to dance with danger. When the ads screamed on I went into battle. I flicked the light on in the kitchen and as the fluorescent bar spluttered to life, I stood very still scanning the surfaces; table top, kitchen walls, green floral curtains, kitchen sink. I watched and I waited for that sudden flick of movement. That flash of shiny brown. On these nightly killing sprees, I could squash about seven cockroaches. There were two types. The fearless, quick moving slivers of brown that flirted with my slipper. And those that were literally on their last legs. They'd already gone for a deadly scamper over a Mortein-laced tile or two – and when I spied them they were clinging to the diaphanous polyester curtain with half a gut hanging out – waiting to die. I'd whip my slipper through the air, so fast it was a blur. Splat. Guts. The ad break was over. The movie was back on. At the time, I remember loathing my quest to rid our flat of this prehistoric vermin. But as I sat in my Toronto apartment, in the wee hours listening to Mum coax Uncle into having more food, I was thankful nothing lurked in the shadows. I could sit in the darkness assured that a quivering antennae wasn't poised to tickle my big toe. I could look up and know I wasn't going to see a dark shape shoot across the smudged cream-coloured walls …

'Any more cockroaches in the flat, Mama?'

'God no! I spray Mortein through the kitchen every night before we go to bed.'

☆☆☆

My parents' relationship had far from conventional beginnings …

A small boy climbed up onto the lower branch of a tree. It was lunchtime and below him a bunch of school children had gathered to cheer him on.

'Higher! Higher!' they shouted.

The boy looked down. Most of his class was egging him on, except for her. She was sitting away from the action, sunning herself. His heart wobbled.

'Hurry up! Hurry up!' the crowd chorused.

The boy looked up to see a small foothold in the trunk. He jammed his knee in and wrenched himself up and over another branch. A bird screeched overhead and he ducked, squeezing his eyes together.

'Higher!' someone yelled.

He took a breath and peered through the canopy of leaves. No sign of the bird just a thicker tangle of branches spread out like a giant cobweb. How the hell was he going to thread through that?

'How many do you see?' the cries came again.

He climbed rapidly over two more branches and began to inch along one, hugging the misshapen wood with his legs.

'Can you see them?' their voices were growing distant now but no less insistent.

He craned his neck for a better view, pushed his face through a fan of leaves and then … A couple more feet above him, in perfect golden clusters, hung the juiciest baby mangos in all of Alexandria. They bobbed about in the breeze, teasing him.

'I see them!' he punched the air.

Cheers erupted from below and a girl balancing on an old log tried to whistle through her fingers.

'Will you sit down?' a tomboy with a head of messy brown curls glared at her.

The girl attempted another whistle before jumping off. 'He is so brave.' she said.

'He is *so* stupid.' the tomboy mumbled not even looking up.

'You're just jealous 'cause he's climbing and you're not.' the girl stuck her tongue out.

'I've climbed bigger trees than that in my sleep.' the tomboy sniffed.

The boy grabbed hold of another branch. He was a good fifteen feet above the dusty schoolground now. He dug his fingernails into the trunk and jumped up onto a branch that looked like a small park bench. The mangos hung at the end. He was hunched over, steadying his breath when he felt a shudder of wings against his back. He flinched, almost losing his balance and then a white flash of pain ripped through his body. Something warm trickled along his fingers, he looked down and saw a gash in his arm.

Below, the crowd were chanting his name. He winced. The chants came again. Sweat stung his eyes, he rubbed his face and peered through the leaves. She was still looking away. More pain shot through his arm and he swooned, the chants began to fade. Her face swam through the haze and he opened his eyes latching on to a second wind.

'What's my name?' he managed to scream down into the crowd who cheered louder still.

Wiping the blood quickly on his shorts he used one arm to inch towards the mangoes. As he moved, he looked down, searching for her. She was getting up. He yanked a mango off its stem and and sent it tearing through the leaves at her. It sailed through the air and clipped a teacher's shoulder.

The boy sat outside the headmaster's office staring at his blood-splattered shorts. He heard the click of small shoes to his right. It was the tomboy. His heart wobbled. Without a word, she reached into her satchel and pulled out a flawless oval-shaped baby mango still on its stem. The boy's eyes widened.

'Don't embarrass yourself again mango boy.' she said and tossed it towards him. The fruit landed with a rubbery *thud* at his feet.

The tomboy with my mother's eyes laughed and walked away. My father fell in love.

'If you find someone who would climb the tallest mango tree for you … don't let him go.' Dad would say.

And my mother laughed, 'Or buy your own mangoes.'

☆☆☆

The door to my office squeaked open.

A man hovering near the six foot three mark looked in. He had cropped blonde hair and a thin goatee beard so fair it was almost transparent.

'Are you the copywriter working on Cat Yum?' he asked in a thick Australian accent.

'Yes and you're Australian!'

'But you can call me Zachary.' he smiled.

'Okay,' I blushed. 'I'm Agni.'

'Hello Agni.' he smiled again and set down a small backpack. 'I'm the freelance art director, they told you right?'

I shook my head.

'Typical. I was supposed to be given the grand tour of this place … get introduced, you know the deal.'

'So you had to do it all by yourself?' I smiled.

'Yep. I met a few people, swapped a bit of gossip … you're covering for the hunchbacked writer who fires spitballs at suits?'

'Yeah, she sounds nuts.'

'I think she sounds cool. Anyone who spits at a suit is fine by me.'

'They're account service don't you know.' I said.

'Account *circus*.' Zachary chuckled and turned on his computer.

I laughed, 'I like that better.'

'So *Agni* – that's an unusual name,'

'It's Greek.'

'Really? You Greek?'

'Yeah. You?'

'Sixth generation Aussie.'

'Wow.'

'Yep convict blood,'

'Nice.'

Zachary got up from his chair and came to sit on the edge of my desk. I jumped, slightly. Up close his features were quite delicate. Aquiline nose. Grey/green eyes and lips that were surprisingly full for a man.

'So is it Agni or Agnes?' he said, interrupting my thoughts.

'Huh? Oh, definitely not Agnes.' I smiled and then I had to look away, embarrassed that I may have stared too long.

'So you ready?' Zachary said suddenly.

'Pardon?' I blinked.

'Shall we get cracking on this Cat Yum stuff.'

'Yeah, right, uh … ' I fumbled around for the job file. 'Here's the brief.'

'Alrighty.' he murmured looking through the file. 'They want a '*sexier-looking*' cat? Fuck.' He screwed up his nose.

'You like cats?' I asked.

'Only in dim sims.' Zachary said before flashing a quick smile and returning to his desk.

☆☆☆

I walked into the office to find my new art director balancing a pen on the bridge of his nose. It tumbled off as I walked in.

'Damn!' he sat up in his chair. 'I'd almost broken through the ten minute mark.'

'You've been doing that for ten minutes?'

'Yeah, helps me think.'

'Hm.'

I opened the Cat Yum job file and began searching through the papers for reference material. When I looked up he was staring at me.

'Pedigree or moggy?' he asked.

'Sorry?'

'Pedigree or moggy. Which will make a sexier cat?' Zach rubbed his eyes, 'God I don't believe we're doing this, do you?'

'Designing sexy cats isn't your calling then?'

'Are you kidding? It's all I think about.'

'Try a moggy.' I smiled.

Zachary began to sketch quickly. 'You think Yum should be a moggy?'

I blushed. 'Well, yeah, er, I don't know … what does the client want?'

'Fuck the client. What do *you* think?' he said, still scribbling.

I cleared my throat.

'We can't as you say, *fuck* the client. They dictate the job,'

'Are you serious? *We're* the creatives – that's our job.

They take *our* lead.'

'That's not how they like to work here.'

Zachary jumped to his feet and began to pace the room. 'Let's brainstorm … you, me here. Let's come up with – and here's a crazy thought – a concept of our own!' he slapped his pad shut and stared at me.

'You okay?' I said.

He looked at me for a couple of seconds and then he pulled on his jacket.

'I'm hungry. Want anything?'

I shook my head.

'Back in a minute.' he said and rushed out.

When Zachary returned, he sat down without a word, tore open his sandwich bag and bit into a roll overflowing with beetroot and salad. He flipped through a magazine while he ate. One of his bites was probably equal to three of mine.

'Pedigree.' I said.

Zachary looked up at me, cheeks bulging with bread. The corner of a lettuce leaf had stuck to the yellow bristle on his chin.

'Cat Yum's star should be a sexy pedigree *diva*.' I said.

He grinned. I motioned at the rogue bit of lettuce.

'I'm saving it for later.' he grinned again and took another bite.

☆☆☆

I was hunched over my desk running a red pen through a page of copy. Mistakes and gems jumped out at me with equal energy. Client wouldn't like that. I murmured to myself. Must tone it down. Take this out. Flesh that out. Remember to include the bit about essential vitamins and minerals cats need for a healthy, balanced diet …

Something wet and spongy bounced off my head. I clenched my red pen.

'What the *heck* was that!' I said.

I looked over at Zachary. He was doubled over, laughing so hard tears shone on his cheeks.

'Very funny Zach.' I said and returned to my corrections.

'You are,' he pulled out a handkerchief and wiped his eyes, '*so* cute.'

My heart broke its rhythm but I didn't look up.

'I was just checking.' he said rolling his chair towards mine.

'For what?'

'You *never* say hell.'

'What?' I gave him a sideways glance.

'H-e-l-l. Hell. Do you ever say it?'

I put a fat red circle around the words, *pamper your pussy with Cat Yum.*

'I prefer heck. It's stronger.'

'You think?'

I turned to a fresh page. 'He-*ck. Heck.* Hell is … wishy washy.'

'Think you've just offended Satan.'

'I just don't like hell, okay.'

'As a word or a concept?'

'Do you have a point Zach?'

I looked up to find his face within inches of mine. His expression was peculiar. Neither a smile nor a frown. He blinked and I caught sight of his long silvery lashes. A warmth came and went in the layers of my skirt. I crossed my legs.

'I have a deadline doodle boy.' I said and continued with my corrections.

☆☆☆

A single halogen light shone down on the credit card slip as I signed my name. The letters were fat and looped. Rebellious. My signature had decided a long time ago never to squash itself into 'customer sign here' boxes.

'Happy with it?' the receptionist smiled.

'Yes I am. She's an amazing stylist.' I replied and handed her the slip.

'The fringe suits you – fabulous length.' the receptionist said and looked behind me at the next client who'd walked in.

'Can I help you?'

A petite redhead with a large cowlick approached the counter. A strange electrical sound accompanied her. *Tzz.*

'Hi, I have a three o'clock appointment.'

'Bikini wax right?'

*Tzz. Tzz.*

'Yes indeed.' she let out a nervous giggle.

'Just through those double white doors.'

'Good luck.' I said and smiled at her.

'Yeah thanks,' she laughed. 'can you tell it's my *first time?*'

An almighty *zap* filled the salon and a neon lit up Red's cowlick. It was beautiful.

☆☆☆

I cradled the phone's receiver in one hand as I slicked gel through my new hairstyle.

Dad's voice cracked.

'*How* short?'

'Short Daddy.'

'Your fringe was beautiful Darling, why?'

'I couldn't see through it Dad.'

☆☆☆

Zachary was running a pencil over a blank sheet of paper.

'Haven't you done the layout yet? I asked.

'No. I'm doing it now.'

'We have a meeting in twenty minutes.'

'Yes, and it will be done in twenty minutes.'

'Zach,' I looked over his shoulder. Elaborate shapes were filling the page. 'You don't have to be so detailed you know. It's just a thumbnail … client doesn't … '

'*This* is how I work.' he snapped.

'Fine.' I said and returned to my desk.

I clicked open a file on my computer. Out of the corner of my eye I saw Zach look up and stare at me for a while, as if he wanted to say something. I ignored him.

'Agni.'

'Yes.'

'I'm sorry.'

'Okay.'

☆☆☆

Another conversation with Sex.

The Virgin was uncertain.

'Have I called you away from something?'

'Yes, but that's fine. I needed an excuse to leave.' Sex said.

'Where were you?'

'An orgy. *So* much work.' Sex said.

'Too much of a good thing?'

'No. Just demanding – everybody wants to come yesterday.' Sex said.

'But that's the whole point of having you isn't it?'

'For the most part.' Sex said.

'Now I'm confused.'

'What about?' Sex said.

'I always thought you and Orgasm were natural bed fellows.'

'Nice choice of words. But no, not natural.' Sex said.

'But that's your essence, to make us soar, see fireworks, the Second Coming … to, to scream with unbridled, tongue and toe curling ecstasy!'

'Read that in a magazine?' Sex said.

'Just recently, in a sealed section.'

'Impressive. Orgasm *has* come up in the world.' Sex said.

'Jealous?'

'Of Orgasm?' Sex said.

'Yes.'

'No. We make a splendid team. But we can exist without each other.' Sex said.

'You mean I can enjoy you without coming?'

'I am the chocolate cake, Orgasm is the icing.' Sex said.

'But not everyone knows how to make icing.'

'Precisely. But you can have a lot of sticky fun trying.' Sex said.

☆☆☆

For a long time, Zach thought he lived in a town called God Forsaken.

Zachary grew up an only child in Steel City, a large Australian country town that spent most of its time caked in red dust from the local pellet plant. When an easterly blew, the dust came like chilli powder to season his mother's wet white sheets, red.

'God forsaken town!' she'd mutter, yanking the rusty-coloured sheets off the line.

'Are you close with your Mum?'

'Not really.'

'And your Dad?'

'Dead.'

'God I'm sorry.'

'It's alright. I was a kid when he died. Don't remember it.' He flicked open his sketch pad.

'I don't know what I'd do if my Dad died. It's an obscene thought, you know?'

'You adjust.' Zach said without looking up.

'Probably. Just can't imagine it though.'

I returned to my screen and tapped a few words.

'I used to draw him.' Zach said almost to himself.

'Really? Do you still have them?'

'Somewhere. Just crappy kid scribbles.'

'I'm sure they're amazing.'

'I'm sure they're not.' he said, his eyes never leaving the page.

☆☆☆

It was more parrot news live from Down Under.

'Your mother's taught him how to say *Skassai, Skassai*. Shut-up, shut-up.'

'I know what it means Dad.'

'So does George. When your mother's shouting at me, George says Skassai, Skassai. Unbelievable!'

'Really?'

'Yeah, yeah. Now I'm teaching him to say gamoto. Gamoto Georgie boy. Gamoto. Can you hear him Agni?'

'Loud and clear Daddy.'

'He's an unbelievable bird. He whistles like a man, you know. Like a man when he sees a woman. He's an unbelievable bird.'

☆☆☆

A number one pop hit filled our office with its tinny melody. And Zachary whistled along while I frantically searched through the drawers for my favourite pen.

'I could've sworn I left it here last night.' I muttered.

'Is it a shiny red pen,' Zachary said slowly, feet up on the desk, layout pad on his lap.

I narrowed my eyes at him. He continued, oblivious.

' … with a, black top, silver clip,'

' … a faded word scrawled on the side … '

'A tiny scuff mark to the right of the nib.'

'Where the *heck is it!*' I cried.

'Behind your phone where you left it yesterday.'

I whipped the phone off the desk and grabbed my pen. I sat down with a huff.

'Your goodness must be deep.'

'What are you talking about?' I sighed.

'Your goodness is hardwired.' Zachary grinned.

' … why 'cause I don't say,'

'Hell, it's only a word you know.'

'Why does it bother you so much?' I slammed a drawer shut.

'Don't get defensive … it's fun.'

' … because you think I'm *good?*'

'Aren't you?'

'Some people think I'm too good.'

'What do you think?'

'I think people should just leave me alone to be good, bad, blah.'

'Blah?'

'Blah.'

'Blah's good … I mean, bad, bad, very bad.'

I laughed and he smiled at me, his gaze lingering a little longer than usual. He looked away, embarassed.

'Know what my name means?' I said softly.

'Pure.'

'How do you know?'

'I looked it up.'

☆☆☆

I twirled the phone cord around and around my finger.

'Daddy I can't talk now.'

'Why not?'

'I'm going out.'

'Where?'

'Out.'

'Who with?'

'Dad I really have to go.'

'Where?'

'I told you … kiss Mum for me,'

'Is someone picking you up?'

'Yes,'

'Who is it?'

'Dad I don't have time,'

'Who's picking you up?'

'Someone from work. I,'

'Man or woman?'

'I'll call you later.'

Click.

☆☆☆

We pulled into a deserted carpark outside a shopping mall.

'So yeah, it was one of those 100 countries in 12 day things. Just nuts.' Zach chuckled to himself. 'God, was I tacky.'

'Okay I'll bite … *how* were you tacky?'

'We had this competition,' he took a quick drink of

water and laughed again, 'we had a contest to see who could wa-, masturbate the most in a month.'

I smothered a giggle and straightened up in my chair.

The colour of Zach's cheeks deepened. 'I came first.' he said.

'And I was *this close* to not biting,' I slapped his arm. 'You're nuts.'

'That's me.' he said quietly, looking into my eyes in a way that made me even more nervous than I already was.

'Well here we are!' I said snapping the moment in two.

'Yes,' he said taking a breath, 'here we are. You ready?'

'Well, I, aren't you going to turn the engine off?'

'Nope. We'll be back on the road in a minute.'

'Really?'

'Yup.'

I wound down my window and stuck my head out. There wasn't a soul around.

'We are completely alone.' I breathed.

'Perfect conditions.' he chirped and unrolled a packet of lifesavers. 'Want one?'

'No thanks.'

'So your Dad didn't tell you anything about this stuff?'

'No.'

'That's amazing.'

'Maybe he was hoping I'd just pick it up from someone else.'

'Brave call.'

'Do you think we should go somewhere else?'

'Why?'

'Well doing it here isn't really how it'll be in real life.'

'All journeys begin with one small step.'

'You into cliches?'

'You into stalling?'

'It's my specialty.'

'I've noticed.'

'You don't have to go through with this you know,'

'So I can still back out?'

I nodded clutching my seatbelt tightly.

Zachary rubbed his goatee. 'Maybe you're right.'

'Really?'

'This situation *does* have the potential to be more trouble than it's worth,'

'You see my point then?'

Zachary pulled off his seatbelt and reached for mine. 'Nope!' he laughed and unclipped my belt.

'Zach, let's go for a drive instead.'

'You've been there, done that.' he adjusted his seat and flicked on the radio. 'A little soothing music,'

'P-lease.'

'Don't scoff. Apparently it works.'

I pulled off my coat. 'No second thoughts then?'

'None.' he replied. 'Now wanna hop over to my side?'

'I am not *hopping* over to your side.'

'Sheesh woman, I don't have all night.' He climbed out of the car and I did the same.

Zachary looked over the bonnet of his car at me. 'Don't worry. 'I'll be gentle.'

'I can't believe you just said that.'

The distant noise of a car startled me.

'What was that?'

'Hal.'

'Who the heck's Hal?'

'The security guard.'

'I am *not* doing a thing with him around.'

'He's a nice guy, don't worry about him,'

'He might want to watch.'

'Will you relax, he'll only come around to tell us when he's locking up the gates.'

'How do you know?'

'I've done this before,'

'Oh really?'

'Yeah. I helped a sister of a good friend of mine.'

'You should start charging.'

'I've thought about it.' he grinned. 'Come on, round to my side. No more stalling.'

I climbed into the driver's seat. Zachary leaned forward.

'Okay. Put the car in reverse and drive around the carpark.'

'In reverse?'

'That's what I said.'

'Why?'

'It'll help you get more comfortable with reversing.'

'Zach I want to parallel park not drive down the street backwards.'

'And how do you get into a spot when you parallel park?'

I blushed. 'You reverse?'

'Brilliant. Now reverse.'

I spent the next hour going around in circles – in reverse.

'Slower. Slower!'

'Now will you speed it up a little grandma?'

'Make up your mind.'

'Do as you're told.'

'Yes sir.'

'Now back into that spot … slowly, *slowly!*'

At one point, Hal the security guard trundled through the carpark in his pick-up and lived up to his friendly reputation by lending us a couple of traffic cones.

'You're in good hands,' he shouted as I reversed right into a neat row Zach had set up.

'Shall we try that again?' he called out from an empty bay.

I nodded sheepishly. But on my second attempt I narrowly missed Zach's toes. He leapt out of the way just in time.

'I knew you'd regret this.' I said as he jumped back into the car cursing.

'Do I look regretful to you?' Zach's face was flushed and his little golden goatee seemed to glow against his pink skin.

'You look hot.'

'Flattery will get you nowhere.' he said and leaned towards me.

'That's not what I … '

'You have to learn to trust your feelings.' He put his hands over mine and moved the steering wheel first all the way to the left and then all the way to the right.

'Excuse me?' I said.

'There's no need for any sudden moves … don't rush it … feel your way first, feel the way the car is moving,'

A steady heat began to build up in my cheeks. I was grateful for the dim light.

'It's all about an awareness of space,' he said and then we drove around, his hands still over mine.

' … keep asking yourself, how close am I to the next car, but don't be afraid of getting too close.'

I nodded and I could feel the warmth from his breath on my face.

'If you know your car … don't be afraid, just take it slow, that's how you build your confidence.'

We came to a gentle stop near a pole.

'Okay. Shall we try it one more time?' he said.

'Let's call it a night.' I said. 'You look like you've had enough – and so have I.'

'No, we're on a roll. Come on, one more reverse and I'll take you home.'

I breathed out loudly. 'Okay.'

'Right, reverse slowly, but not too slowly past the pole, use it as a guide … keep it on your left as you go, okay,'

I nodded. 'When do I speed up?'

'You won't need to … the car will move into the space without speed, it goes a little down hill here. Ready?'

'I think so.'

'Okay go.'

I put the car in reverse and backed out slowly at first, then I accelerated just a little until I could see the pole getting closer and closer and closer …

'Watch where you're going!' Zachary cried.

'What!' I slammed on the brakes and the car jolted. 'Don't shout at me.'

'You were about to hit that pole for fuck's sake!'

'Must you swear.'

'I had to get your attention, alright? I'm sorry.' he

slammed the gearstick into Park. 'Fuck,' he muttered.

I flicked off the radio. 'I wouldn't have hit that pole Zachary.'

'Yes you would have.'

'No, I … '

Zachary smothered the rest of my protest with his lips. His kiss was soft and slow. And long-awaited. Hal's pick-up rattled past.

'I'm lockin' up kids!' he called.

That night I dreamt of a giant mango tree.

# 9

# fifteen minutes

Another conversation with Sex.

The Virgin was adamant.

'I want to be in a huge loft on a huge wrought iron bed with rain pounding the windows.'

'I do love a good rainstorm.' Sex said.

'Er, this has nothing to do with you.'

'It has *everything* to do with me.' Sex said.

'I want the *rain* to be pounding. Rain. Do you understand?'

'Perfectly. You want to be pounded. It's a metaphor.' Sex said.

'And next you'll be telling me I want a man with a small penis if I fantasise about a rainshower.'

'Now you're getting it. But I do love a good rainstorm.'

☆☆☆

'So what's this movie about?' Zachary whispered, leaning over me to get at the popcorn in my lap. His scent was sweet and spicy.

'The usual story, girl meets boy. Girl loses … '

The lights dimmed and the soundtrack exploded.

'Ssh, it's starting,' he said.

The opening titles faded in and out of a beautiful Tuscan landscape. An orange sun dropped behind a farmhouse and a boisterous family gathered at a long wooden table laden with fat bottles of olive oil and wine.

'Stunning place.' Zachary whispered, pressing a small kiss in my hair.

'Hm.' I replied handing him the popcorn.

A barefoot girl smiled at a curly-haired boy. He returned her glances and they met in the moonlight. Thunder rolled overhead, they paused to kiss. Aunts and mothers gathered at the wooden table to cluck with approval. He brushed against her breasts. She confessed virginity with a look. And I strained to catch Zach's expression. Her pink mouth broadened into a smile, baring all her teeth. He tangled her hair in his fingers. And in the distance her family applauded. I chewed on my lips and curled my legs beneath me. At first, our elbows were touching. Now I had inched as far away as possible. My body was a denim-clad ball stuffed down into the seat. A new sun splashed over the green hills and the penultimate scene unwound. I squashed myself down further into worn velour and stared, poker-faced, at the seven foot tall images mid flagrante. I didn't even flinch for popcorn. She perspired sweetly, her face turned towards a misty Tuscan horizon. He spread her legs, stuck quick kisses all over, and pushed. She moaned, kneading him. Then, it was over. The barefoot girl emerged, radiant. Cheeks ever so slightly rouged. Post-coital makeup like new.

I wanted to throw my popcorn at her. Whaddayamean there's no pain? Whaddayamean there's no embarrassment, no fumbling? How can you look so blasé after first-time sex?!

The credits rolled, lights came up and I unravelled slowly from my pins and needles.

'Tuscany's *incredible.*' Zachary said standing up and brushing bits of popcorn from his jeans.

'Yeah.'

He slipped his hand into mine. 'Ready to go?'

I nodded, limping out with him. And he wrapped his arm around my waist like we were already lovers. We strolled in silence along a busy street and stopped for a milkshake in a 50s style diner where I sucked up the sweet bubbles and tried not to look at him.

'Don't move.' Zach said suddenly plucking an eyelash from my cheek. 'Top or bottom?'

'Pardon?'

'Is your eyelash stuck to my finger or my thumb? Top or bottom?'

'Is this some kind of bizarre ritual?' I laughed.

'If you say top and your eyelash *is* on the top you get to make a wish,'

'And if it's on the bottom?'

'The wish is mine.'

'Sounds fair.'

'So top or bottom?'

'Uh, top.'

'You sure?' he shook his hand.

'Hey!'

'Top?' he kissed my nose. I nodded.

Zachary separated his fingers and there, stuck to the tip of his finger was a dark lash.

'Now make a wish and blow it away.'

I closed my eyes and wished hard. 'There.' I said triumphantly.

'What did you wish you for?' Zachary said stroking my face.

'If I tell you it won't come true.' I smiled.

We lay down on my bed. I circled his mouth with my tongue.

'That's nice.' he murmured.

I looked up and saw the spectre of my virginity flutter down over me like the 'old lady' shawls Yiayia would crochet and make me wear in church because it was 'respectful'.

Zachary stroked the shirt from my shoulders, kissing skin where cotton had been. And when I sat naked on his hips, it felt so natural. He ran his fingers over my lips. And I inhaled him as he moved down past my face, my breasts, coming to settle between my thighs. His mouth cupped me, tasting gently over and over until I came. I squeezed my eyes shut as the flutters in my stomach rose higher and higher. And I exploded. Everything around me, inside me dissolved. I felt his lips again, quietly encouraging me to fly again.

☆☆☆

I stood outside a sex shop for women called *Hush!* I was

goin' in. Only this time, I was comin' out with a purchase – noisy or not.

The shop had a distinctly red décor. A red leather couch, red lamp shades, red rugs. Even the parrot sitting on an open perch in the corner was red. Only the walls were lined with black leather shelving. And one shelf in particular caught my eye. It had a row of rigid-looking vibrators all lined up under a sign that read, *Glow*. I decided to take a closer look, but I only managed to take a few steps before something long and rubbery smacked me in the eye. I leapt back and looked up. It was a penis mobile; lots of the suckers fell free from bouncy black elastic. I heard a faint giggle and turned to see a woman with a wild halo of tight black curls smiling at me.

'I'm sorry for that,' she said in a French accent, 'people always bump into it.'

'Maybe you should hang it somewhere else.'

'We think it is – how you say – well hung.' she giggled again and her curls shook.

'Right.' I smiled and looked over her shoulder to the *Glow* display. 'What are they?'

'Oh fantastique,' the woman clapped her hands. 'Come,' she said.

The vibrators under the *Glow* sign stood neatly in a black box. Up close they had a strange green tinge. The sales assistant flicked a switch and the dicks were plunged into darkness.

'Watch zees.' she said and within seconds the penises glowed in the dark.

She reached into the box and clicked one on. The vibrator obediently began to shiver and shake.

'Very clever.' I said, 'but not really me.'

The French girl frowned. 'You want vibrator, non?'

'Non, I mean yes. Yes.'

'Very good. We have very large range. Come.'

I followed her to another black leather shelf where a smaller gaggle of dildos grazed. They ranged in size and colour. Shape and texture. Lots of plastic, circumcised heads teamed with rubber balls and rings.

'They all wipe clean.' the woman announced and reached for a particularly menacing phallus in black rubber. 'Zees is *very* popular.' she said and when she clicked the monster on, something undulated under its dark, elastic skin. It was a penis possessed, and, frankly, not that arousing. I shook my head.

'No problem.' the girl said cheerfully and lead to me another display.

'Do you sell the Judder Elite?' I asked.

'Pardon?'

'Never mind,' I said and another rubber wonder caught my eye, '*What* is that?' I pointed to a dildo that looked like a drag queen had designed it.

'Oh, cest magnifique. I have zees one.' she said, plucking a fuschia-coloured penis from the shelf.

It had a transparent middle filled with pearls and when she turned it on, the pool of pearls rocked and rolled.

'Wow. And this is for, er, inside?'

'Oui, in, out, on clit.'

'Right,' I said and pressed the whirring head against my palm.

The French woman shook her head and smiled, taking

the pink appliance from my hand. 'Like zees,' she said and placed the penis at the tip of my nose.

My whole face quivered. The salesgirl winked, 'sensitive non?'

I nodded. 'But it's still not the right one.'

Call me old fashioned, but I preferred the least phallic of vibrators. It didn't need to have diamonds or pearls, or a make believe network of veins crawling all over the latex to make me come. Just good, reliable vibrations.

And then I saw it. It was the ultimate in vibrator chic. Sleek. Compact. And very, very French. It was a real, live honest to goodness Lipstick vibrator that could easily pass as one of Chanel's finest in your designer clutch.

The French girl gave me a nod of approval. 'Zees is good *and* beautiful.'

'Can I test it?'

'Oui.'

I twisted the lipstick on – it was red, of course – and placed it on my nose.

'Yes,' I smiled, 'Yes!'

☆☆☆

I reached into my purse and pulled out a crumpled magazine page. The colours had faded, but I could still read the words. The page came from the thick glossies I pored over as a teenager; the shiny worlds of airbrushed women and crease-proof fashion. But I cared little for the makeup tips or advice on buying the perfect sling-back. I bought the magazines for one thing. The sexual problems column.

*When we have foreplay I make a small incision in my boyfriend's scrotum, insert a straw and inflate his testicles. He loves it. Is this dangerous?* Confused Paddington

*My boyfriend is on a low sodium diet. Is there any way I can make my cunt taste a little less salty? I really want to please him since he does so much to please me.* Anxious Surry Hills

*I love going down on my lover and I always swallow but a friend told me cum can be fattening. Is this true?* Weight Watcher Kings Cross

I liked to pretend I was Confused from Paddington or Anxious from Surry Hills. It didn't really matter who I was. I wanted to own their problems, at least until I turned the page. It was my way of imagining adulthood.

Every month, the magazine published a 'star letter'. It was usually a meaty, frequently asked question and the writer won a fountain pen for her efforts.

*I'm a virgin and my boyfriend and I are planning to have sex soon. But I'm terrified. I think he's too big for me. My friends tease me and say I won't find the 'right size'. And I know there's no such thing. But what if my vagina really is too tight for him? Will sex hurt? I just want my first time to be the best time. Help!* Vagina in Panic Redfern

*Dear Vagina in Panic,*

*Relax. Take a bubble bath. Light some candles.*

*First intercourse is generally uncomfortable but it can be painful if you're nervous. Your vagina might clamp shut or even go into spasms. It could also dry up and cause chafing when the penis tries to enter; not the best housewarming for your first guest.*

*If you're really anxious, make a date with your gynaecologist. You can have your vagina examined and an assessment made on*

*how difficult intercourse will be. The doctor can also use lubrication, anaesthetic and a speculum to open you up. Some gynaecologists even offer a hymen-removal service.*

*So dive into some bubbles, extend the foreplay and feel those juices flow! Your vagina will self-lubricate, expand and lengthen and comfortably accommodate even the biggest boys.*

*As for your first time being the best time. Lose that fantasy now. Your first time is unlikely to be your best sexual experience. Great sex is much more than just penetration – it's foreplay, it's orgasm, it's designer lingerie.*

*So. Whether you opt for the speculum or scented candles, make sure it's your choice.*

*Good luck!*

Expand. Lengthen. Cold metal objects. It was like reading about carry-on luggage. I scrunched up the page and buried the Vagina in Panic at the bottom of my bag. I glanced at the time. It was ten to nine in the morning. Zachary wouldn't waltz into the office until way past the hour. I still had time for a little surfing. I typed in the word 'sex' and the usual array of soft porn sites sprang up. Eventually I landed on,

*The Easy A–Z of Sex*

I scrolled.

*Lubrication. The vagina is a miraculous muscle capable of self-lubricating as arousal increases. A woman's body takes approximately eight minutes to produce the lubrication necessary for smooth intercourse.*

My fingers tightened over the mouse and I scrolled a little further skimming over *orifice, pregnancy, testicles, urethra…*

*Vaginismus.*

I stopped – and soon wished I hadn't.

*Vaginismus affects 1% of women. It is generally the involuntary tightening of the pelvic floor which results in either the inability to penetrate or painful intercourse.*

*Vaginismus can affect women who have a fear of sex and the act of penetration. These fears may be due to the overprotection of parents or the secrecy with which sex and intimacy was handled. Fear of the unknown and frightening stories about painful sex can also result in vaginismus.*

*… when a penis is poised to enter the vagina, the muscles surrounding the opening contract dramatically making the entrance to the vaginal canal feel like a wall …*

'Good morning!' Zachary breezed in, dropping a kiss on top of my head.

'Hi!' I jumped.

'You surfing?' he said.

I nodded and began to scroll quickly.

'It is an absolutely *glorious* day.' Zachary threw his backpack to the floor and sat on my desk. 'I'm thinking you, me, gourmet sandwiches, picnic blanket … ' he moved his lips over my cheek.

I whipped around in my chair. 'Did you know the typical person spends 600 hours having sex between the ages of twenty and seventy?'

'Wha-?' Zachary almost fell backwards onto my desk.

'Yeah, it's true,' I clicked the mouse absentmindedly over and over.

'Keep the cursor still.' Zachary leaned in for a closer look at the screen.

I pushed him back.

' … th-that's twelve hours a year, one hour a month

and fifteen minutes a week.'

'*Fifteen* minutes a week?'

'That's what it says.'

'Then it must be true.'

'Don't you believe it? Don't you think you're typical?'

Zachary smiled to himself and grabbed an apple from my desk. 'Depends.'

'On what?'

'On what your definition of sex is.'

'Sex, sex … you know, man, woman, rolling around,'

'Rolling around?'

'Does it matter?' My voice squeaked.

'You coming down with something?'

'What? No. Answer the question.'

'Hm?'

'*How* do you define sex?'

'How do I define sex?' Zachary settled back in his chair and stroked his goatee. 'hm. How do I define,'

I jumped in. 'Penetration Zachary. Sex is penetration. Right?'

'Ah yes, that old chestnut.' he crunched into the apple.

'Well spit it out.'

'What?' he said between mouthfuls.

'What's your average?'

'Based on a decade? A year?'

'Oh for goodness sake,' I steamed.

He climbed onto his desk and crawled towards me on all fours.

'Wanna bite?' he smiled.

'Will you get down before someone comes in!' I pushed his face away.

He laughed and crawled backwards to his chair.

'Statistics are only an average.' Zachary nibbled around the apple's core and then threw it over his shoulder into the bin.

'Well, maybe the statistic refers to sex in its purest form.'

He laughed loudly. 'In its *purest* form?'

'Yeah, you know … true sex includes an orgasm right? So,'

'True? Purest? What is this?' he laughed again. 'Tell me, are *you* typical?'

I squirmed in my seat. 'No.'

'And neither am I, so that can only mean one thing,'

'We're not normal?'

'We're not a statistic.' Zachary flicked on his computer and turned to email.

I simmered in my seat for a moment, folded and unfolded my arms and said,

'Do you like bubble baths?'

☆☆☆

His wasn't like the flaccid, fleshy examples I'd seen dripping in Fanta years ago. It was like an animatronic penis. A strong and flexible freak of nature. It bent backwards, forwards, and kept a perfectly straight line like a fat ruler without the inches – or with I guess. I couldn't look it in the eye at first. Or touch it. I let it rub against me though. And I was amazed at how something so hard could feel so smooth against my skin.

Zachary sat back and folded his arms behind his head.

Something shiny, like expensive silky thread trickled down his skin.

'Did you just come?' I asked, wide-eyed.

'No baby,' he smiled, 'you'd know if I did.'

I reached out and felt him – tentative. My fingers faltered for a second and then I pushed his penis, bending it back onto his stomach. My eyes darted up to his face.

'Does that hurt?' I asked.

'Nope.' Zachary replied shutting his eyes. 'It's nice … '

I kept my fingers pressed into the head, pressed into his stomach and when I let go, his cock sprang back down like a catapult. I gasped. Zach laughed and then I pushed it back again. Let go again. Pushed it back again. Again. And again.

'Having fun?' Zachary grinned.

Yes. Fun. It was like some bizarre executive toy – hours of pointless fun.

Well, almost pointless.

☆☆☆

We opened our eyes to the dazzle of snow-coated rooftops, streets and cars. Zachary leapt out of bed and ran to the window.

'Baby, it's snowing!' he cried and did a little on-the-spot jig.

'Too cold.' I whimpered and pulled Honest Ed over my head.

'Come on Baby the snow's calling us!'

'Can't hear it,' I mumbled from my foetal position. But he yanked the quilt off again.

'You're *not* missing this.'

Out on the snow-caked street, commuters stared as my boyfriend ran through the snow screaming, 'Woo-hoo!' clad only in his T-shirt, shorts and sandals. I shivered. Thermals, polar fleece, woollen scarf and an angora hat pulled down over my ears and still the icy breeze managed to creep under my skin.

'Baaaaabyyyy!' Zachary shouted as he scrambled on top of a snowbank. 'Live life on the edge with me!'

'Only if I don't fall off!' I called back and buried my chin into the folds of my scarf.

And then I lost sight of him. I called out. Nothing. I ran a few steps down the street and peered into the distance. He was gone.

'Where the hell,' I muttered.

I heard footsteps behind me and whirled around in time to see Zachary crunch a handful of snow into my face.

'Bastard!' I shrieked and tore after him. When I caught him we fell into the snowbank and laughed so hard I forgot about the cold and the ice and the wet.

'I love you.' he said and pressed his lips against mine. They were so warm.

☆☆☆

'Well?'

His fingers slid through me. I was wet enough. He began to stroke and I hummed a soft tune, stretching out for him, the indulgence awesome. Laying back, I let the feelings wash over and through me. Sweet, sweet flavours.

Up and high I came.

'You have nothing to worry about.' I whispered.

'What do you mean?' He propped up himself on an elbow.

'You and Lipstick. There's no competition.'

'What a relief.' He made an exaggerated sweep of his brow.

'Because,' I continued, 'I'd never turn down a good organic orgasm – like this.'

'I'm so glad,' Zachary said.

'Not,' I added, ' … that there's anything wrong with genetically modified joy.'

☆☆☆

The morning light danced through the blinds. I closed my eyes and raised my face to the sun. It was warm, energising. I had one month left in Toronto. But I didn't want to think about it. I took a breath and thought of him instead. Right now he was standing in a queue waiting to order my hot chocolate, his cappuccino. He'd come whistling down the hallway soon, poke his head around the door and sing,

'Office Service!'

Then he'd close the door behind him with the back of his foot, set our hot drinks down and kiss me quickly, quickly on the lips, my hair, my neck and then, without uttering a word, pick up his coffee and take a seat at his desk as if nothing had happened. I smiled at the expectation and opened up a women's magazine. One word greeted me.

*Yes!*

It looked like the newest word in the English language. Eager to please with its truth. Stuffed full of promise. Hiding nothing. Pure. Clean. Honest to goodness. I ran my fingers over the bold fuschia-coloured block lettering.

'Yes.' I whispered and grinned to myself. 'Yes.' I said again and uncrossed my legs.

A shrill voice startled me. 'Good you're here.'

'Oh hi.'

The woman with the loud tangerine turtleneck stood over me. I wondered whether she ever wore anything else.

'She's not coming back.'

'What?'

'God's gift to copy … she's not coming back.'

'Has she resigned?'

'Something like that.'

'What about her stuff … she's got files on this computer.'

'She's coming in on the weekend to get them.'

'Right. Uh, does that mean we can stay in this office?'

'You and that sexy Australian?'

'We uh, yeah.'

'You like him?'

'We, we work well together,'

'I've heard.'

'Excuse me?'

'Tell him to come and see me when he gets in.'

'Is everything alright?' I asked but she was already halfway down the hallway.

The door creaked open and Zachary came in with our

drinks. His face was grey.

'I thought you were a suit.' I jumped up and squeezed his body. He pulled away.

'These are hot.' he said plainly and placed a styrofoam cup of hot chocolate on my desk.

I followed Zachary to his desk and pushed my face into his neck as he shook off his jacket.

'Don't,' he shrugged me away and sat down. 'Someone could walk in.'

'Since when has that bothered you?' I said.

Zachary ignored me, flipped open a layout pad and began to draw. I returned to my desk and pulled off the lid on my hot chocolate. Curls of steam rose up into my face. I glanced at him. He was still scribbling. I looked down at the frothy head on my drink. It was sinking fast.

'Have you ever had a hot chocolate froth goatee?' I asked.

No reply.

'You could spoon the froth off,' I took my cup and sat on the edge of his desk. 'and … '

I looked down at his pad. A messy-looking Big Ben stood tall albeit slightly wonky.

'It's got a kink in it baby.' I said laughing softly. 'It's good though.'

His pencil scratched at the clock's face, filling it with numbers.

'Is this part of a new brief?' I said.

He rubbed his finger into the grey lead smudging a shadow behind the clock. 'No.'

'Okay.' I pressed my lips together. 'Uh, that suit with the big mouth came in a minute ago.'

He looked up.

'And?'

'She wants you to go and see her.'

'Right.' he said and returned to Big Ben.

'What's wrong?'

He shook his head.

'Zach?'

'I'm going there.' he said quietly, poking a pencil into Ben's face.

'To London?'

'Yeah.'

'Wow.'

He glanced up at me quickly. 'You okay?'

'What? Yeah, why shouldn't I be?'

He looked away again. 'I don't … '

'I never thought we'd go away together so soon though.' I ruffled his hair.

'It's not like that.'

'It's not like what?' I rested my head on his as he dragged his pencil across the paper.

'You don't understand.'

'Don't you think they'll let us take time off together?'

'No.' he replied. More shadow piled up behind Ben.

'We'll just give them plenty of notice, I'll have to tell my parents too, can't wait for those fireworks,'

'I'm going alone.'

'Why?'

He stopped shading. He looked like he was about to say something.

'What's wrong?' I said.

'Everything.'

I snatched his pencil away. 'Stop with the cryptic shit and tell me what's going on!

'I'm leaving.'

'You're what? Where?'

'I've had a job offer at a London agency.'

'And you said yes?'

'I applied for it before we met ... I never thought I'd get it,'

'When do you leave?' I stared at the deflated froth in my cup.

'The London office called me last night after I dropped you off.'

I banged my cup down on his desk, chocolate liquid flooded Big Ben. 'So when do you leave?'

Zachary pushed his chair back and stood up. 'Day after tomorrow.'

'Great.' I looked down.

He put two fingers on my chin, lifting my face to his. 'Come with me?' he said softly.

'Yeah right.'

'We can do it,' he said.

'No we can't.'

Zachary grabbed my hands and squeezed them in his. 'It could be *amazing*. London's great, and we'll explore, you and me,' he looked in my eyes. 'We can't break up the team.'

I pulled my hands away. 'I can't just pick up and follow you to London.'

'Why not? It'll be an adventure ... live on the edge remember?'

'*No*.' I stepped back further until I was up against the

wall.

Zachary stared at me with a helpless look in his eyes and my heart broke. Now would be the perfect time to cry, I thought. Delicious self-pity. Regret at opportunities missed. Anger at the words left hanging in mid-air. The fear of letting go ripped through me. I swallowed my tears.

'Come back to the apartment.' I whispered.

'What?'

'Let's go home.'

'Now?'

'Yes!' I stepped away from the wall and clutched his shirt. 'Let's go home.'

'Baby, what for?'

'I – we should … ' I tightened my grip. 'We should have sex.'

'Are you serious?'

'Yes!'

He stepped back. 'This is nuts.'

'Don't you want me?'

'What? No! I mean yes, yes.'

'Come on then,' I reached for his jacket.

'No. *No*. That's *not* how it should be for you,'

'Let me decide how it should be for me.' I snapped.

He reached out to touch my hair. 'Come with me to London Baby,'

I flinched. 'You can't order me around Zach!'

'You've just ordered me to fuck you for the first time, what's that?'

My eyes fell onto the magazine page.

*Yes!*

The word looked desperate now. Overdressed and ridiculous in its fuschia skin. I walked over to my side of the office and swung my backpack on.

'Could you please not swear ... ' I said softly.

'Where are you going?' He rushed over.

' ... and please don't call me.'

The answering machine blinked one message when I walked in. I dropped everything and ran to press play.

'I'm counting the days Darling!' my father's jolly voice smothered me.

☆☆☆

I spent the first night without him wrapped up in dreams of death. A pretty girl in a lilac bridesmaid dress skipped up to me.

'Have you heard your Dad died?' She wasn't smiling or crying. Her face was plain.

I burst into tears and drifted into another dream where Yiayia was dying. I remembered her wonderfully warped ideas of nutrition. Each time I visited her, she'd usher me into her big old kitchen and pop a cube of fresh butter in my mouth.

'This is good for you my baby.'

In the final part of my dream, I stood in a bathroom with my father. He was bare-chested and smiling. I was hysterical. I couldn't bear to part with him. Daddy, don't go! But he was oblivious to my tears. In fact, he didn't seem to know he was dead until I told him. When he realised he had to say goodbye, his face morphed into a woman's and he started to stroke his chest into the shape of two breasts. I cried myself awake.

☆☆☆

'I will be your mirror,' she said and handed me a hot cup of cranberry tea.

I decided to see a therapist a month before flying home. She sat back in her armchair and with a cool smile, asked me to start anywhere.

I sipped my tea and then I just talked … and talked about the snow outside, the city skyscrapers, her colourful drawstring pants, the room's décor, the guilty pleasure I felt when, as a little girl, I enjoyed Daddy's warm hands rubbing lavender-scented talcum powder into my skin … the battle to forge my own path, be my own woman and not the one my mother wished me to be … the smorgasboard of movies on offer in North America … and my moment of terror when Mum moved out of our apartment because I refused to cancel my trip to Greece. While she had her seven day tantrum at an aunt's house, I did my first load of laundry, made mushroom soup from scratch, kept the apartment clean and watched Dad play endless games of Solitaire, using it as a form of fortune-telling; if the cards turned out, Mum would be home soon.

'Did things change when she came home?'

'I stopped doing the laundry.'

I remembered watching a spectacular sunset on Santorini, without feeling anything. It was as if a cloud had come to settle over me.

'I don't think you were depressed,' my therapist noted and her eyes settled on my mouth. I was trying not to cry.

'Symptomatically you may have appeared so, but you

were just in the process of breaking away and becoming you.'

When I talked about leaving home, my eyes overflowed. I looked at her, embarrassed at the way my mouth twisted out of shape each time I tried to hold back tears. Her eyes filled too, though her smile remained. I wanted to hug her.

'You've been too hard on yourself,' she said blinking a tear away.

Stop judging you. You the little girl. You the woman. You the virgin.

# 10

## the neon sign short circuits

Back in Sydney and I was greeted by a public housing nightmare.

The foyer of our apartment block was being renovated and the glass doors had been freshly vandalised the night before. Shards of green glass had been swept up into the corner. Mum picked her way through the glass tut-tutting and Dad called the culprits 'bastards – but the police will fix them up.'

Poor Man's Point Piper didn't feel the same. I no longer appreciated the grittiness. Didn't feel proud of its urban-jungle feel anymore. We stepped into the lift and I reached for the 'close door' button. Dad stopped me.

'It's broken.' he said and pressed the 'emergency stop' button instead.

The doors closed and the lift shot up to the fourteenth floor in seconds.

Walking into our living room, I saw images of me everywhere. On one cabinet Mum had created a shrine to me. Photos of me had been stuck haphazardly to the wooden veneer. In another corner, several frames of wood, silver and brass showed off my smile. And on the coffee table, a bunch of fabric flowers with fake drops of dew had become the final resting place for another grinning shot of me. Every space displayed my likeness. It was as if I had died.

☆☆☆

'Say hello George!' Dad beamed beside the parrot's cage like a new father.

George eyed me suspiciously and began to pace up and down the floor of his cage. Hopping from perch to perch. Nibbling at his birdseed as if he hadn't been fed for days. His chatter, incessant. Repetitive.

'Hello George. Hello Georgie boy. Hello Georgie, beorgie, keorgie.'

I decided George was Woody Allen with feathers. He was also the only parrot I knew who could wolf whistle.

'He loves women. Oh yeah.' Dad smiled and sat down for a snack next to George's cage. 'Watch this,' he smirked, taking up a forkful of rice.

My parents' first priority when they sat down for a meal was to hand George something, anything from their plates. A pea, some fetta, a grain of rice – all followed by a sip of cola served in a teaspoon. There was no ignoring George. He'd hop onto the top perch and flap his long rainbow-slashed wings, repeating his name over and over until his needs were met.

'You spoil him Dad.'

'So what?' he replied, pushing a teaspoon of coffee through George's bars.

☆☆☆

Magdalene sat in the corner of a café twirling her hair, reading. I hardly recognised her. Her regulation black had gone and in its place was pink. Lots of pink. She looked like a puff of fairyfloss had thrown up on her.

Magdalene's gaze wandered from her broadsheet and she saw me.

'Agni, Agni!' She jiggled up and down in her seat. 'Over here!'

'What's this?' I laughed kissing her cheek.

'Little girl chic.' She jiggled again and the miniature candy-cane clips in her hair quivered.

'You're *kidding* me.'

'Ha bloody ha. Do you know how expensive this look is … see these?' She pointed to her shoes; pink and round-toed 'flatties' with bows. '$600. But they're kid leather.'

'Naturally.'

Magdalene flicked her hair dramatically and almost sent her candy-canes flying into someone's short black.

'So how *are* you? Glad to be back? Parents driving you nuts? You know parent-angst is *so* hot right now.' She ripped open a packet of bubblegum. 'Want some?'

'No thanks.'

Magdalene sipped her soy-latte and spoke quickly.

'So, I can't *stand* the thought of a man touching me right now. Can't stand it. Last night I was at a ball and about four guys asked me out. I wasn't interested in any of them. A year ago they would've been four sex options. Can't be bothered now. The guy who gives me reiki massage seems interested,' she dropped a sugar cube into her cup. 'he's *so* full of sunny, positive *shit*. Not interested.' She took another gulp of latte and pulled a face.

'What's wrong?'

'Too strong.'

'He's too strong? The bastard.'

'Not him. This.' She swilled her latte around. 'Waitress! You know he described his last girlfriend and she sounds like *me*. Tried to *save* her from herself. That's probably what he's planning for me. *Not* interested.'

A waitress with a chin stud wandered over. 'Yes?'

'A soy hot chocolate.' Magdalene snapped without looking up.

'Yes sir.'

'*Excuse* me?'

'Grande or Petite?' The waitress smiled sweetly and her stud gleamed.

'Petite.' Magdalene turned to me. 'So yeah, I'd rather stay miserable.'

'Well, Toronto was great.' I said, to no one in particular.

'Oh God, what an ego-maniac ... how *was* Toronto?'

'Great.'

'What do you mean *great*, great, that's such a colourless word.'

'Okay back off. You're not at work now counsellor.'

'Oh God who am I kidding?' Magdalene frowned and pushed a stick of bubblegum in her mouth. 'I mean *look* at me,' she moaned, 'I'm dressed like a five year old, I'm sweet, I'm chaste, I'm pink ... fuck ... I'm a *fashion* victim.'

A capri-clad blonde flashed an annoyed look at her. Magdalene adjusted her candy canes like a spoilt child.

'Do I have *desperate* in fluorescent all over me?' she said.

I smiled at her. 'Not in fluorescent.'

The waitress returned with a diminutive drop of hot chocolate served in a tiny white cup.

'Petite … ' she began.

'Yes fine.' Magdalene took the cup and sipped it like a cocoa addict.

The waitress gave her a dirty look and walked away.

'You need a good *fuck*.' I said under my breath.

Magdalene almost choked on her gum.

'Oh – my – God.' she said, her grin widening.

'What?'

'You did it didn't you?'

'Did what?'

'God, I'm gonna explode! Did you do it or not?' she spluttered.

'Huh?' I looked around the café, 'Oh, yeah, yeah, no big deal. It was about time.'

'Well, *hallelujah!*' Magdalene gave an exaggerated wave of her arm. 'I thought you'd die with cobwebs on your hymen, woman. Hey! You're a woman now!'

'Ha. A woman. Yeah, thanks.'

'Do you know,' she peered into my eyes, 'I thought you looked a little … different.'

'It's that obvious?'

'Like neon.' she said and blew a large pink bubble.

I went home to find a postcard of Big Ben from Zachary and my parents poised to interrogate. Who is he, does he speak Greek, what's his blood type, can we see his birth certificate, a sample of his urine perhaps?

I read Zach's postcard twenty times before falling asleep with Ben under my cheek.

☆☆☆

Dad was standing at George's cage watching him as he weaved and bobbed seemingly in time to a Greek song.

'Look Agni he's dancing!

'He's bored Dad.'

'No, he's dancing I'm telling you.'

'You should let him fly around the room a bit.'

'His feathers have been clipped.'

'Why?'

'I don't want to lose him. He's a tropical African you know.'

'What's a tropical African?'

'That's George.' Dad replied, blowing at the parrot's feathers.

'You should let him out Dad.'

'He's alright. Look his bars are quite far apart … it's not like a real cage.'

'Have you ever let him out?'

'Of course, sometimes. He flies. But you know your mother … doesn't want mess.'

'I have something else to clean now.' Mum called from the kitchen.

'Your mother follows him around with that dust buster when we take him out.'

'You want cockroaches too?' she snapped.

'Hates that buster. And your mother's blender too.'

'Ah yeah. Can't stand the noise,' Mum laughed. 'Squah, squah and now he says, *Skassai!*

Dad chuckled. 'He's an unbelievable bird. Hello Georgie boy.'

The parrot inched along his perch until his beak touched my father's nose.

'He loves me you know.' Dad said.

☆☆☆

It was a sultry Summer night. The kind of heat where, if you could, you'd peel your skin off to cool down.

I tiptoed to the balcony door and stood in the light breeze. George tittered quietly in his sleep. I looked through the bars and admired his plumage for a moment before settling down into an armchair just under his cage. Another breeze laced with a neighbour's joint reached me just as I undid my belt and silently pushed the Lipstick down to my crotch. George let out a soft chirp in his sleep. I took another breath and clicked 'on'.

My trousers muffled the whirr. I leant back and moved my Lipstick around, up and down. A warmth washed over me and the sensation deepened. I pulled my trousers lower, exposing half of the Lipstick together with its sound. Georgie stirred. I clicked it up a level and the volume increased. George fluttered awake and stared, wild-eyed.

Squah!

I hardly noticed. Close to oblivion now; up and down I moved the Lipstick.

Squah! Squah!

Louder and louder the buzzing came and the vibrator now inched over the top of my trousers.

Squah! Squah! Squah!

George paced backwards and forwards along his perch, flapping his wings against the bars.

Buzz. Flap! Buzz. *Skassai!*

But all I could hear was the buzzing. All I could feel was the beginning of sweet, sweet release. Closer, closer, any second now. But …

Squah! Squah! Squah! Squah! Squah!

Focus lost, I yanked the lipstick out of my panties and while it still buzzed in my fingers I raised my hand to try and soothe the parrot.

George pushed his beak through the bars and attacked my hand.

'Ouch!' I cried, losing the grip on my Stick.

I watched in horror as it clattered through the bars, straight into the birdseed. That's when George went ballistic. His shrieks sounded like someone was ripping paper into a megaphone. Feathers and seed were flying. Suddenly the light was flicked on. And there I was, trousers down around my knees.

'You try to kill him?' My mother rushed to the cage. 'What's *that?!*'

My Lipstick was bobbing away in the seed like a miniature jackhammer while George beat his head against the bars.

Mum grabbed a kitchen towel, opened the cage and recovered the Stick. She furrowed her brow, 'What is this, shaky Chanel lipstick?'

'Not exactly Ma.'

'Switch off, off!'

I snatched it from her and flicked a switch. And then with one last exaggerated shudder of his wings, George stopped shrieking.

'You don't have shame?' she said.

'No.'

'Very nice,' she said and passed George a teaspoon of cola to calm his nerves.

But as Mum reached into his cage, George made a strange purring sound before whipping around and pinching her hard on the finger.

'Naughty Georgie! You see what you done – you make him wild.'

'He's always been wild. He wants to fly Ma.' I said and turned to go to bed, hoping I'd heard the last of this episode. But as I padded away I heard her mutter,

'You're going to run out of bone marrow.'

☆☆☆

Allegra's new home was a large commercial studio space above Dong's Karaoke Bar. It was a huge, ridiculously bohemian room complete with tall dust-caked windows, scuffed wooden floors, exposed electrical wiring and fluorescent bars screwed onto the ceiling. Stuff was crammed into every available nook and cranny; boxes, crates, paints and canvases. But on the wall, presiding over all the chaos, was a giant painting of a beautiful naked woman lying on a bed of flowers.

'Who painted that?'

'My friend, Lady Liz. I call her that 'cause she's such a

fucking girl. Gorgeous.'

Allegra pulled me towards her makeshift kitchenette, the shower cubicle hidden behind a plastic curtain scattered with stick-on stars, the washing machine in mid-cycle, the park view, the fridge covered in magnetic poetry. It really was a stunning space and as we sat chatting, I had visions of turning Allegra's rundown box into a trendy cavern of polished wooden floors and track halogen lighting.

'Fucking ugly.' she said when describing the end of her relationship with Faith.

'I went home without her, locked myself in the house … she comes banging on the window at fuck knows what time, stone sober, I let her in she starts screeching and pulling at the bedclothes says it's her fucking bed so I grab the mattress, push her onto the balcony and lock the door, next morning she gets up, surrounded by all her shit and she can't remember a fucking thing. That kind of shit happened all the time,'

'You loved her?'

'Of course, but she was a complex … troubled … violent thing,'

'Did she ever hurt you?'

'She threw a pair of scissors at me once.'

'She's crazy … '

Allegra shrugged, 'We both were. She just hurt herself more in the end.'

I watched as she piled a plate high with rocket leaves and drizzled olive oil all over them.

'Are you still, you know?' I ventured.

'Am I still … '

'You know, bi,'

'No. I'm unbiased.' She shoved an oily leaf into her mouth.

'What?'

'It's my new word. Want some salad?'

'I just ate.'

Allegra tore off a section of crusty bread and dipped it into the pool of oil in her bowl.

'Haven't I told you about my new word?'

'No.'

'Well … just like the word 'woman' doesn't ring true for me,'

'Hang on, you don't like being called a woman?'

'Nope. I don't identify with gender.'

'Can't wait to hear this.'

Allegra pushed another piece of bread into the olive oil and smiled.

'I don't think of myself as a woman like you.'

'What?'

'Yeah, I,'

'You think of me as a woman?'

She nodded. 'Don't you?'

'Well I, sometimes, no, well, Magdalene calls me Girly,'

'Magdalene should get a fucking girlfriend.'

'And you call me Grrl!'

'It's a sound Grrl, not who you are.'

Allegra wiped up the remaining green juices in her bowl. 'Anyway I can't relate to the word 'woman', just like I can't relate to the words straight, gay, *bi-curious*.' She pretended to gag.

I laughed and picked up a piece of bread. Allegra handed me a small, yellow bottle, 'Drizzle some olive oil on it Grrl.'

'Thanks.'

'So, what was I saying? Oh yeah … um, none of those fucking labels felt right, so I invented my own.' Allegra turned her bowl over triumphantly. 'I am *unbiased*!'

She pulled open the fridge and grabbed two bottles of spring water. A small white magnet clattered to the floor. I moved to pick it up.

'Don't worry. They're always falling off … here.' Allegra handed me a bottle.

'Thanks.' I said peering at the scattering of poetry on the fridge. Rectangular-shaped magnets of short, fat and long words covered the top half.

*apparatus thick pubic slide juice clinch bare murmur and a drunk orgasm in the night*

Allegra smiled. 'I got the Erotic version.'

'Yes you did.' I said and began to move a few of the squares around.

'You going to write something?'

'No, just tidy them up.'

'For fuck's sake, the magnets aren't meant to be tidy – write something!'

'Maybe later.' I said and sat down. Allegra shrugged and joined me on the sofa.

'So you like my space?'

'I think it's great.'

'Me too.'

'You're lucky.'

'Fuck luck!' Allegra shrieked and pulled me up from

the sofa. She spun me around and around. 'You make your own luck Grrl!'

We fell to the floor in two giggling heaps.

'You're glowing,' she said suddenly.

'It's hot in here.'

She laughed and curled her legs into a lotus position. 'No Grrl, you look different.'

I pushed my legs up to my chin and hugged them. 'Believe me. *Nothing's* changed.'

She looked at me for a moment before pressing a palm to her heart.

'Real change happens here,' she said and then pointed to her crotch, 'not here.'

I walked over to the fridge and picked up the magnet that had leapt to its death.

*Girl*

I stuck it back up on the fridge and formed a new line next to *bare murmur and a drunk orgasm in the night.*

*the girl flutters away*

☆☆☆

No one tells you what it's really like.

I couldn't even understand the *concept* of someone's body part inside me. Were it not for the fantastic hype, sex would be seen as just a bizarre shoving of parts into other parts.

I felt a twinge of hot, burning pain.

My eyes flew open. I was hot. Shivering. Are you in? Yes. Joy then, devastation. It's over. It's beginning. Baby oil trickled down my thighs. The bubbles in my champagne flute floated to the top and exploded. He moved deeper into me. I slid my palms up and down his back, careful not to change my position, open my legs any wider. He stroked my face. Okay? He kissed me. I nodded and tears flooded my vision. You? Yes. You're beautiful. No. I'm making such a fool of… His lips came down onto my cheeks. Ssh. He pressed deeper. A small stinging pain came and went. He raised his body off mine. I looked down at the sheets. They were striped red. So was he. I gasped and moved to wipe him clean. He grabbed my hand and bundled me up in his arms. A fresh sheet covered us.

'Sleep.' Zachary said, 'sleep.'

☆☆☆

He kissed the back of my neck while I stared at my reflection in the mirror.

'I look different.' I said.

'No you don't.' he said cheerfully. 'You're still gorgeous.' He kissed me again. 'I'll be in the bath. Call me when breakfast gets here.'

I called my mother.

'Your father was just about to call the police!' she screamed and I had to pull the phone away from my ear. Zach popped his head out of the bathroom,

'You alright?'

I nodded and blushed putting the phone back to my ear. Another screech came.

'We haven't heard from you all night!'

My voice was soft, 'I was with him, you know I was

with him, I told you.'

*'He's an old friend, we're going to catch up. He's in town on business.'* I said.

*'Isn't that lipstick too bright? Isn't that dress too tight for a friend?'* she said.

'I never dreamed you, *you* would drop everything, one call and you're his?'

'Mama,'

'Do you believe he wants to marry you? You believe in fairytales?'

'I needed to see him.'

'You dropped us.' came my father's tired voice.

*I switched off my bedroom light, the stars glowed back to life and my door shooshed as I shut it and made my escape.*

'He called you from the airport and that's it! Where's the *respect?*'

'It's here Mama, it's here. *Yiasou.*'

I hung up the phone. Breakfast had arrived.

☆☆☆

The shower was running hot.

I stood with my legs apart watching the blood drop and dissolve into the water at my feet. My veins tingled. No magazine fills you in on the bits of flesh that hang around after first time sex. And even if they did they'd probably dress it up in the season's latest sequins and feathers. I reached down between my legs and felt a blood-engorged piece of flesh, plump, like a grape. It just hung there. Pull it, I thought. Let the blood flow and move on. Pull it. So I did. Gently. Pain came with a new warm gush of blood that fell to the shower floor. I moaned and pulled again. More blood. Less courage. I stepped out of the shower.

'It's your hymen.' the doctor said.

Twenty-eight years old and I didn't know the fundamentals of the humble hymen.

Mum was reading her newspaper when I walked in.

'You found your way home?' she said, her eyes didn't leave the page.

'Yes Ma.' I said and sat down.

'Good,' She rustled the paper and kept reading.

'Where's Dad?'

'Working.' She turned the page noisily.

'What's for lunch?'

'Leftovers.'

'Going to bingo today?'

She ripped a section of the newspaper and threw it at me. 'See what happens to women who trust the world?'

The headline screamed something about a twelve year old who had been raped on her way to school.

'Ma she's not exactly a woman.'

'The world is evil and you're sleeping with a stranger we haven't met.' She looked up. 'Why are your eyes red?'

'I'm not a virgin.' I said suddenly, not knowing how else to announce it.

'Well, that's not news.' she said and returned to her paper. 'Look what this man did to her, he's an animal!'

'Ma, are you listening to me? I had sex for the first time last night.'

My mother folded her paper away and looked at me

with the wide eyes that terrified me as a child. 'Happy now?'

I didn't say a word. My mother relaxed her glare. 'You're a woman now.' she said with a strange and new tenderness.

'I've just come from the doctor,' I began to sob. 'I woke up this morning, we did it this morning and there was more blood on the sheets, not much but … and then in the shower, more blood and I was scared … the doctor said not to worry.'

I burst into tears.

'What are you crying girl? It's bad luck to cry. Don't be silly. It's natural. This is what happens. Tonight, before you go to bed, sit in a tub of warm saltwater. It's nothing. Wait till you have a baby. This is nothing, just sit in the water. The salt will calm the wound – it's a wound you know. Having first sex is worse than having baby. At least with childbirth you get anaesthetic.' She passed me a handful of tissues.

I blew my nose rather noisily and looked at my mother through wet eyelashes.

'Is he good looking?' she asked with a small grin.

'Who?'

'This man.'

I nodded.

'Come on, I'll make you some coffee.' she said and I followed her into the kitchen.

☆☆☆

Mum was whispering to Dad as I walked into the

kitchen.

'I don't know how I'm going to face the man who's fucking my daughter.'

When she saw me, she jumped and yanked open the oven door, 'Yes, yes. Everything be ready for the prince soon.'

Half an hour later, the dining table ached under the weight of pastry triangles stuffed with spinach, a white soup with fat meatballs floating in it, lamb cutlets, peas, chips, slabs of fetta, salad, bowls of olives, taramosalata, tzatziki. Zachary's eyes dutifully popped out of his head when he arrived.

'Wow. This look amazing.' he said and handed my mother a bottle of wine and flowers.

Mum hugged the flowers but waved the wine away. 'I drink only beer.'

'You didn't tell me.' Zach looked at me.

'You didn't ask.' I said.

'But I like wine,' Dad took the bottle. 'Thank you.'

'There's so much food. Anybody else coming to dinner?' Zachary put his arm around me.

'You only.' Mum said taking her place at the head of the table. Dad sat down in the chair beside her, next to George's cage.

'Hello Georgie! Hello Georgie boy!' he chirped.

'So this is George the famous parrot?' Zachary ventured.

'Yeah. Have a look, have a look.' Dad slipped a small spoon filled with cola through the bars. George squawked appreciatively and pecked at the brown liquid until it was gone.

Dad was delighted. 'He's so *smart!*'

'What a parrot, huh?' Zachary said nudging me.

'Parrot? He's a human being! And he *loves* women,' Dad said.

'Oh yeah?' Zachary smiled and looked at me, 'does he flirt with you?'

Dad laughed, 'All the time.'

Mum spooned some mash onto Zach's plate. 'You happy with Agni?' she said suddenly.

'Mama!'

Zachary nodded. 'She's a wonderful woman.' he replied and stroked the back of my neck.

Dad looked over at us for a moment before filling another spoonful of cola for George. 'She's my little girl.' he said in a voice I could barely hear.

'See?' I said and Zachary just grinned, his mouth too full to reply.

Mum stiffened. '*Always* a baby for us. Even 40 years old, still baby.'

Dad turned from George. 'We just want her to be happy, that's all.'

'I *am* happy.'

'You take good care of her, I'm sure.' Dad said.

'Agni is a big girl. She can take care of herself.' Zachary replied. 'Did you make these?' he said picking up a filo triangle.

My mother waved her arm over the spread. 'I make *all*.'

'Can you cook like this honey?' Zachary winked at me and I slapped his arm.

'Agni like the flower … a pure girl,' my mother said, 'like this,' and she handed Zach a bowl of white soup with meatballs.

'She's like a meatball?' he grinned at me.

'Just try the soup.' I said.

'I already have.' Zach looked into my eyes making me blush.

'And?' I gazed at him.

'Not bad.'

'*Really.*' I smiled.

Mum tapped the edge of his bowl with a large spoon. 'Leave the sweet eyes for now, try your soup before it be cold, come on.'

'What sort of soup is it?' Zachary asked my mother.

'Special lemon and egg soup – I make,' Mum patted her chest and then she turned to me and said in Greek, 'he would never have tasted anything so good in his village.'

'What did she say?' Zach asked between meatballs.

Mum shot me a look.

'Mum's wondering if you've ever had anything like this in Steel City.'

'God no. Everything different there. Small country town.'

'Ah, you see.' Mum said, satisfied. 'This avgolemono.'

'It's delicious.' Zachary swallowed a mouthful of the soup. 'Just like Agni,' he whispered.

My father looked up from his food and tapped the bars of George's cage loudly.

'Hello Georgie boy!'

'You say, avgolemono.' Mum said.

'Mama he's eating now.'

'He can say, *avgo-lem-o-no!*'

Zachary cleared his throat. 'Avgo-lem-o-no!'

Mum scowled. 'More practice, you be good.'

'One day,' Zachary said and helped himself to a dollop of taramosalata, 'You know, my mother cooked everything with lard.'

'That's pork fat Ma.'

'Yuck!'

'Ma.'

'No, she's right. Lard's horrible. Your food is very good.'

'Ah, you see.' Mum repeated and then said to me in Greek, 'he's no idiot. He knows pure things when he *tastes* them.'

I glared at her. 'Mum says you obviously have good taste.'

Mum looked at my father, 'She's telling him everything I say in Greek.'

'Leave her alone. It's fine.' Dad said, 'Zachary have a look at George now,'

The parrot snatched a pea from my father's fingers with his claw.

'See how smart? Unbelievable bird.' Dad gushed again.

'Like a human.' Zachary nodded and kissed my cheek.

After Zach had left, Dad came up and gave me a hug.

'He's a nice man. Very polite. As long as he takes care of you.' he said.

Mum said she was too busy with her dishes to talk. But that night, as I fell asleep under my stars I heard her say to Dad,

'Don't worry, slowly, slowly I will teach him Greek.'

☆☆☆

I stood in my bedroom and told the stars goodbye, packed my books in boxes and pushed them in the corner of my crowded little room.

'I'll be back.' I whispered.

'Be careful,' my mother squeezed me and her perfume crept into my clothes. 'you will be in a, a defuck relationship now.'

'You mean defacto.'

'Defuckto, defuck, what's the difference. People will still talk.'

'Let them Ma.' I kissed her on the forehead.

'Did you say goodbye to Georgie? He'll miss you – *a lot.*'

'I know Daddy.'

'Anyway, call us when you get to London.' Dad said, hugging the breath out of me.

'I will, I will.'

'And remember what I told you.' Mum raised her eyebrows.

'What did you tell her?' Dad said.

' … that a man should know his woman only from the waist down. What goes on from her waist up is … '

'What does that mean?' Dad said.

'Never mind.' Mum snapped.

'I have to go Daddy.'

'Bye bye Baby.' Dad pulled me into his arms again. 'If it doesn't work, come home.'

And then he reached into a bag and handed me a framed picture of the little girl who danced for her dinner many, many years ago.

☆☆☆

We had sex and the word *fuck* was in my mouth and in my head. I loved how it felt.

Fuck. Fuck. I said it over and over. Fuck loud, strong and clear. Fuck, like I wasn't afraid anymore. Fuck, like I had given myself permission to enjoy the feel, the taste of it on my tongue. I woke up feeling clean. There was nothing dirty or shameful about me – or fuck. I reached over for him, but he was already up and gone. Probably by the pool, I thought burying myself under his pillows.

Zach burst into the bedroom.

'Baby wake up! Let's go … I've gotta show you something!'

'We're on holiday.' I mumbled from under his pillow.

' … come on Santorini is *stunning* this time of morning.'

'I'll see it this afternoon.'

'No, you have to see it *now*.'

I opened one eye. He stood over me smiling. His cheeks were smudged black.

'You been playing in a volcano?' I rubbed my eyes and sat up.

'Come and *see*.' he grinned and pushed a t-shirt into my hands.

'Let me find a bra.'

'No time.' he said and pulled the t-shirt over my head.

A strip of silver mist dawdled on the horizon and the squeaky clean sky was already crammed with sunlight, as our motorbike curled around the cliff road.

'Where are we going?' I screamed over the engine's roar.

But who heard? And minutes later, with sleep still in

my eyes, I was staring at messages of puppy love 'written' in white pebbles by the side of the road. We had zipped past these tributes dozens of times before teasing 'the romantic fools' who had made them.

Zach wiped his brow and pointed to a particularly large message. It was a deafening declaration spelt out in pebbles that looked like giant's teeth pressed firmly into black volcanic sand.

*I love you.* The sign read.

'I had to steal other people's pebbles.' Zach confessed with a sheepish grin.

# 11

# the case of lost virginity

I lost my virginity.

I waited and waited at the baggage carousel. Suitcases in tartan, vinyl and leather spun around and around. My virginity was nowhere to be seen.

I went to the lost baggage section to file a report.

An attendant in her 60s peered at me over her bifocals.

'What does it look like?' she muttered in monotone.

'It doesn't look like anything.'

'I'm sorry Madam, we need a description.' she pushed a carbon sheath under a fresh page in her red ringbinder.

'Well, I don't know. I never studied it.'

She frowned and wet the tip of her pencil with her tongue.

'Any distinguishing features? Freckles? Scars?'

'Goodness no! It's perfect.'

'Colour?'

'Um, pink, yes pink. It's pink – sometimes dark, sometimes light, but mostly pink.'

'Does it have a name tag?'

'Well, no, it doesn't need one. It's unique!'

'That's what they all say.' she said under her breath.

'Look it's old, I've had it for a long time,'

'Fine.' she ripped out the carbon copy. 'you've lost one perfectly old and unique pink virginity. Is that correct?' she narrowed her eyes over the bi-focals.

'Yes.' I said.

'Fill in your name and address on this form. The airline will ring you if a virginity fitting this description turns up.'

'What are my chances?'

'Slim to none.' she said and handed me my carbon copy.

'But virginities don't just vanish into thin air – someone must have it!'

'No one has it Madam. It's just *gone.*'

'Gone?'

'Yes Madam. Now if there's nothing else,' she looked over my shoulder. 'Can I help you sir?'

'Yes, good morning, I seem to have lost my libido.'

# 12

## a mouthful of breast

The phone rang and rang and rang. It sounded like an angry parent. Come on, answer me! The phone rang and rang again. Now it was a needy child. Please, talk to me.

I looked at the time it was just after two in the morning. Zachary snored beside me. I slid the covers off, careful not to wake him, and ran out into the living room.

I picked up the phone. 'Hello!'

'Darling! How are you, how is the boy?'

'What's wrong?'

'Nothing's wrong. We just,'

'Do you know what *time* it is Dad?'

'Here take Mum.'

'Your father is driving me crazy, how are you my love?'

'Mum, do you know what time it is?' I repeated.

'Your father said it's only eight at night.'

'It's two o'clock in the morning!'

'Oh God! I told him, I told him we shouldn't call,' she called out to my father. 'it's the middle of the night there, are you insane? Your daughter was asleep. He's making me crazy.' she sighed.

'Mum I'll call you back tomorrow.'

'Yes, go back to sleep, what did you cook today?'

'Mum, tomorrow,'

'Tell her about Despina.' my father called out.

'What's he saying?' I rubbed my eyes.

'Be quiet, I can't hear your daughter!' Mum yelled in my ear.

'Ma!'

'Wait, your father wants you, here take the phone madman.'

'Despina's pregnant.' Dad blurted happily.

'Huh? That's great,'

'Isn't it? Soon it'll be your turn hey darling? You can't leave your father grandchildless.'

'Dad, it's really late,'

'Never too late for babies.'

'Dad,'

'Take your mother.'

'Your father hasn't stopped talking about you,'

'Tell her about Alexander and his mobile,' Dad called out again.

'What's he saying?' I was wide awake now.

'I can't have two conversations at once!' Mum shouted.

'Ma.'

'Tell her about Alex.'

'Your cousin got a mobile phone bill for $3,000.'

'For a year?'

'A month! His father's helping him out. See children get into a mess and who runs?'

'Wow, okay Mum, let me go now.'

'And the hooker!' My father yelled. 'Tell her about the

hooker.'

'And he's fallen in love with a prostitute.'

'A real one?'

'What do you think a plastic one? You are so naïve daughter – wake up!'

'I don't want to Ma it's two in the morning,'

'Oh Christ, okay love, go. Call in the morning.'

'When will she call again?' I heard Dad say.

'Shutup I'm talking!' Mum said.

'I'll call in a couple of days,'

'A couple of days? Okay, alright, goodnight.'

''Night Mum, love you, night.'

'Wait your father wants you again,'

'Darling, good night, sweet dreams, say hello to the big man.'

'Goodnight Dad, I will, bye.'

☆☆☆

I jumped out of bed and padded into the bathroom. 'I have a lovely post-coital glow.' I said.

Zachary pecked my shoulder. 'So would I if I had twelve orgasms.'

'Jealousy will kill you Zach.'

'Yeah, yeah.' He started the shower.

I touched my cheeks. 'You know what? I'm going to market a new blush and call it Post-Coital Glow'.'

'That's great Baby.'

'Yeah, Post-Coital Glow … *look like you've come – all day!*'

I followed Zach into the shower and stood still while

he rubbed a bergamot-scented shampoo into my hair.

'Or what about, *because it was worth it.*' I laughed and slipped on an exfoliating glove. 'Ready?'

'Yes, please.' Zachary grinned and turned his back to me.

'You're a back-scratch slut.' I said.

'I love it when you talk dirty.'

☆☆☆

Mum sounded impatient.

'What have you cooked for dinner?'

'Nothing, we're getting takeaway.'

'That's all poison. Cook something quickly,'

'Ma, I've just come home from work … I don't feel like it.'

'Then cook in the morning instead of wasting time at the gym.'

'You'll never get pregnant with too much exercise!' Dad called out.

'Tell Dad to be quiet.'

'Your daughter wants you to be quiet – the truth is too bitter.'

'Ma!'

'Stick a few lamb chops in the oven, put some olive oil on the top,'

'Ma,'

' … a few vegetables sliced or chopped it doesn't matter,'

'Mum,'

' … and in an hour you have a beautiful meal. It's not

hard.'

'That's the door Ma.'

'Who's at the door?'

'Who's at the door?' Dad called out.

'Ssh, I can't hear what she's saying!'

'The Chinese is here.'

'Chinese? Yuck … they blow their noses in the chow mein.'

'You eat their garlic prawns.'

'That's different.'

'How?'

'Garlic kills germs.'

'Alright Ma,' I sighed, 'there's the door bell again. *Yiasou.* Kiss Dad for me.'

☆☆☆

'Where have you put the passports?' I called to Zachary from the bedroom.

'Somewhere, uh, maybe in the wardrobe. I'll look when I get back from the gym.'

'Don't worry, I can do it.'

'No, I'll do it!'

I wandered out to the living room where he was putting on his runners.

'Whatcha hiding?' I curled up behind him and wrapped my arms around his waist.

'Lots.'

'I've seen shots of your perm in the 70s baby, you can relax.'

'I'll find the passport when I get back.' he turned

around and kissed me. 'okay?'

I nodded.

I opened the wardrobe and found a box of photos buried in the back. A faded kaleidoscope of memories; dog-eared and peeling.

Little Zachary peers out from under a tangle of sun-bleached hair. His ears stick out, his smile is small. He has one hand on the bonnet of a truck. His other hand clutches the scruff of a siamese. His mother stands beside him, squinting in the sunlight. Her arms are crossed and she wears an apron covered in lemons, limes and red dust. Now Zach is at a school cricket match with a plaster on his forehead. And over there, under a collection of report cards, Zach's sitting at the edge of a breaking wave, surrounded by foam. I pushed my hands a little deeper into the box, some dust escaped and I sneezed. And there was Zachary again, no more than seven, maybe eight years old. He's balancing a sketch pad bigger than him on his lap – well-worn crayons are spread out at his feet and his grin lights up the whole photo. In the background a plump man with a heart-shaped mole on his cheek looks on with a grin to match his son's.

I flipped the shot over. The inscription read,

*Pa's Da Vinci.*

I held the scene up to the light. The man shared Zach's white-blonde hair and green eyes.

I pushed even deeper into the box and pulled out a black leather portfolio. The edges had cracked with age and when I clicked it open, a wad of sketching paper fell out. A couple papers were creased into messy quarters –

the work of a child in a hurry. A few other sheets lay flat, covered in scrawls of houses sitting next to impossibly tall trees. And there, tucked into a side pocket, was a school exercise book stuffed full of more sketches. They were of the plump man in Zach's photo; lovingly detailed images of him mowing the lawn, tinkering with an engine, holding up a long fish by a riverbank. Some scenes were in pencil, others in a leaky blue biro. Large fatherly grins and crinkly smiling eyes were marred by unexpected splats of ink. But even imperfections were signed. Every illustration had a curly letter Z at the bottom together with the date.

I turned to the last page in the book. It was crumpled and ripped at the corner. Little fingers had glued a piece of clear cellophane over the illustration. And stuck behind the plastic was a smudged scene in pencil of the same plump man dozing in an armchair. His heart-shaped mole had been outlined, twice. There was no signature.

'What the hell are you doing?'

I jumped, sending the book flying across the room. 'You scared the shit out of me!'

'*What* are you doing?' Zach repeated grabbing the exercise book from the floor.

'Your drawings are beautiful.' I pointed to the book. 'They're of your Dad, right?'

'Wrong.' He stared, unblinking.

I stood up. 'But, you've written Dad beside a couple of them.'

'Are you done in here?' he snapped.

'Baby,' I touched his face. His eyes were shiny. 'You okay?'

'I said, are you *done?*'

I nodded and he pushed past me to the box of photos on the floor. I watched as he stuffed the exercise book back in the folio, back in the box. Then he crammed the lot into the wardrobe again.

'Do you remember him?' I whispered.

Zachary turned around and his face went soft for a second. And then, coming to, he rubbed his eyes and spat,

'No.'

Then he left the room.

☆☆☆

The coldest hotel in the world was the setting for our one year anniversary.

I looked out the window as we flew over Northern Sweden bound for the Ice Hotel. All I could see was white. Miles and miles of snow. The best 'middle of nowhere' I'd ever seen. Zachary squirmed in his seat like a restless toddler about to sit on Santa's knee. I smiled at him and rested my head on his shoulder. I couldn't think of anything to say. I felt about as frozen as the wilderness we were flying over. What was supposed to happen when couples turned one? How was I expected to behave? I felt awkward and green all over again. I winced at a pang of old virginity. It was like a missing limb. Gone but not forgotten.

'Almost there baby!' Zachary said and I jumped.

'You okay?'

'I'm nervous.'

'What about?'

He looked into my eyes, delightfully oblivious to my inner shit.

'Th-the landing. I'm always nervous about landing.' I stumbled.

'Don't think about it … just let go … it'll be over before you know it.'

'That's what I'm afraid of.' I muttered.

'What?'

'Put your arms around me and squeeze.' I said and shut my eyes.

'Come here then,'

The plane landed with a soft shudder.

'How was that?'

'Soft.' I replied and opened my eyes.

'It was hard to organise … snow on the tarmac, skilled pilot, light snowfall,'

'Yeah, yeah,' I smiled.

When we walked off the plane, we were greeted by King Winter. A large and jolly-looking man in a flowing coat of reindeer skins, silvery beard and crown of icicles.

'Welcome to snow and Winter!' he boomed and instantly I believed he helped his cousin Santa train elves in the Autumn.

A representative from the Ice Hotel greeted us next in his dark brown fur hat and ear flaps. He took one look at our leather boots and jackets and sniffed,

'No good.'

Next thing we were padding through the snow in thick rubber boots and bright purple snow suits. In the distance, a dozen or so huskies leapt about on their leads.

'Can you believe this?' I shouted over the barking.

'It's magic!' Zachary yelled back and lifted me into the sled.

I grabbed at my fur-trimmed hat. 'I don't want a frozen head!'

'You won't freeze,' he laughed and threw a reindeer skin over my lap.

With a loud whoosh we were off. The dogs were silent as they sped through fields of untouched snow. We rode through snow-capped forest glades. It was like gliding through an enchanted world. Every now and then, our huskies lowered their heads to scoop up mouthfuls of snow.

'What happens when the dogs get old?' I asked our driver, Yann.

'They go to the big dogsled in the sky.' he smiled sadly and quickly yelled something in Swedish to his pack.

When we pulled into the village of Jukkasjarvi, we had our first glimpse of the Ice Hotel – a giant igloo with thick wooden doors sheathed in reindeer skins. I thanked Yann who bowed politely and said 'Adieu.' Zachary shook his hand, we patted a few of the dogs and then we raced each other to the Hotel's entrance.

We pushed open the doors into a surreal wonderland of ice so clear and pure it seemed to glow blue. Huge, round columns stretched up over our heads. Two men stood at a transparent reception desk. And little fibre optic lights pulsed red, green and blue inside the bellies of giant female figures sculpted in ice. Padding down the snowy, candle-lit hallways we muttered 'wow' over and over again. And then we stopped and looked at each other. We breathed out slowly and saw our 'wows' form into wisps of mist in the –5 degree air.

A serious look crossed Zachary's face. 'I have to play.' he said.

'It's freezing out there Zach.'

'Try and stop me.'

It didn't take long for my lover to morph into the planet's tallest five year old. And as the sun set over Jukkasjarvi, we chased each other up and down embankments, took photos, made snow angels and licked the outdoor ice sculptures almost losing our tastebuds.

'What are you doing?' I said.

Zach pulled out a sketch pad and sat down opposite a row of sculptures shaped like giant diamonds and animals.

'I have to get this down.' he said shaking off his right glove.

'Now?'

Zachary nodded and rough outlines began to take shape quickly on his page.

'Aren't you hungry?' I sat down beside him and rested my head on his shoulder.

'Nah.' he replied.

I bent over and blew hot air over his drawing hand, red and raw.

'Thanks baby.' he whispered and continued to sketch rapidly.

Soft lines filled the blank paper. An icy expression here. A spike of frozen fur there. He gazed at the sculptures for a few moments then returned to the page each time with renewed fervour.

'You love this don't you?' I said as he began a fresh sketch.

'It's a fun thing … I can manipulate shapes, lines, perspective sometimes,'

'Feelings … '

'Yeah feelings too … a great illustration, drawing whatever, can touch people in a way that photography can't.' He looked at me. It had begun to snow and his lashes were tipped with tiny snowflakes.

'Will you draw me?' I said in a small voice.

Zach brushed the flakes from his eyes and returned to his sketch pad. 'No good at people.'

'You are too, I've seen your stuff.'

'I just dabble Agni.'

'Come on, give yourself a little more credit,'

'It's *just* a hobby.' he said, pushing the lead deep into the page.

'You are really gifted,' I touched his face. 'I know it … '

Zach stopped drawing. And I continued, 'Your Dad knew it too, didn't he?'

Zachary slapped his pad shut. 'Can we drop this please?'

'We never talk about your father. Why?'

'Because there's nothing to talk about.' He stood up.

'I care … '

Zachary reached over and put his lips on mine. 'We didn't come here to talk about ghosts. All that matters is you and me.'

That night we curled up in a family-sized sleeping bag on our queen sized slab of ice. Me in my woollen stockings and turtleneck. He in his birthday suit.

'Do you love me?' I whispered from my foetal position. But he had already fallen asleep.

The next morning, our room was bathed in an eerie blue light. I stared at it until my nose got numb and I had to disappear back into my furry cocoon. Deep in the warm folds I heard a whisper,

'Happy Anniversary Agni.'

I blinked into the darkness. 'Who's there?'

'It's King Winter … and I have an icicle for you.'

'You sure it hasn't melted?' I whispered.

'No. It's enchanted.'

'Really.'

'Mmmm,'

Zachary pulled me closer. His skin was warm and soft. I flicked his nose. 'Ice is a real passion killer,'

'So we'll warm up … '

'The expression is a *hot bed* of action … '

'Oooh, so witty.'

'These stockings ain't comin' off.' I said and flung the reindeer skin off the bed.

'Jesus woman!'

'Cold?' I laughed.

Zachary pulled the skin back over his body and whimpered. 'Well at least kiss me happy anniversary.'

I kissed him on the mouth. 'Happy anniversary.'

We spent the day on a snowmobile safari zipping over frozen rivers and little hills that looked like wedding cakes. We stopped for a salmon soup lunch cooked for us over a fire in a tiny wooden hut. And then, as the sky turned a deep shade of pink, we headed back to the Hotel closely followed by a herd of reindeer and their shepherd – a small black dog who yelped like mad from the back seat of his master's snowmobile.

Back at the Ice Hotel, a wedding was about to take place. We padded into the Ice Chapel in full snowmobile attire and sat a few pews from the front. The groom arrived soon after us clad in a brown tailored jacket with exaggerated lapels.

'Do you think he's trying to look like an extra from Starsky & Hutch?' I whispered and Zachary laughed out loud. I poked him.

'Ow!'

'Ssh! We're not invited. Let's keep a low profile.' I adjusted the zip on my purple snowsuit.

'Purple is not the colour of low profile Agni.'

'Doesn't matter … let's try and blend in.'

'We need to be wearing a few dead animals to *blend in*,' Zachary said as a woman with a fox's body slumped over one shoulder walked down the aisle.

'Let's just be quiet then.'

'Do you think he's getting cold feet?'

'Zachary!'

'Come on that was funny,'

'What makes a person get cold feet anyway?' I whispered.

'Inappropriate footwear?'

I glared at him.

'I don't know, nerves, uncertainty … what's your point?'

'I didn't feel like sex this morning,' I blurted and pulled my hat down over my ears.

Zachary stared at me for a little while. Then he looked

away.

'Well aren't you going to say something?' I hissed.

'Can't.' he replied looking straight ahead.

'Oh Baby, it's not that I didn't want you. I just, I … say something!'

'Can't.' Zachary repeated.

'Baby,' I tugged on his sleeve.

'You said we should keep quiet.'

'Don't mess me around,' I smacked his padded arm. 'What are you thinking?'

He smiled, 'It's okay,'

'Okay?'

'Okay.' Zachary turned back to Starsky.

'But it's our one year anniversary, we, we should be having mad, crazy passionate sex all over the place … in the snow,'

A man wearing a bear's paw as a hat looked over at me. I lowered my voice.

' … behind the ice sculptures, in the restaurant,'

'Snowsuits on or off?'

'I'm serious!'

'So am I.'

Zachary's big green eyes widened and he touched my face.

'So am I.' he repeated.

'I'm afraid I'll make a mistake and this … this will be over. Like yesterday, that stuff about your Dad, I didn't mean to interfere, but, I care you know,' I looked at the smudged snow beneath my boots.

'I know,' he said and lifted my face to his.

My eyes grew hot and the tears came. One by one they

trickled down my red cheeks. Zachary wiped them away with his fingers. I blew my nose loudly.

'So much for low profile.' he smiled.

And I giggled. Then I cried again, caught helplessly in that strange moment of emotion that's neither sad or funny. Just true.

Zachary put his arm around me.

'You're stuck with me. Get used to it.'

'No cold feet?' I sniffed, my bottom lip still trembling.

'My boots are thick. It's Starsky you have to worry about.'

We booked into a chalet with huge skylights above our bed that night. We made love and afterwards spent hours looking up at the stars hoping the Northern Lights would 'switch on' just for us.

'Eskimos believe the Northern Lights are a bunch of Gods playing football with the head of a walrus.' I whispered, stroking his hair.

'Hmm.' Zachary murmured and buried his head deeper into my shoulder.

'Isn't that magical?'

'Hmm.'

'Magnetic forces, my butt … the Northern Lights are *magic*,'

'Hmm.'

' … just like King Winter.' I breathed out and promptly fell asleep.

☆☆☆

'And take your oils, here, you'll need an extra sketch

pad just in case. You'll probably use all your HB pencils too,'

Zachary stared at me from across the bedroom. I was oblivious, stuffing his backpack full.

' … couldn't stand your whinging if you didn't take your Snoopy eraser, and if you feel like charcoal, I bought … ' I felt his arms on my shoulders.

'Hey,' Zachary's grip was firm. I looked up into his face.

'I'm always saying goodbye to you.' I whispered.

He hugged me. 'You are *such* a drama queen.'

'I'm Greek,' I sobbed into his shoulder. 'It's my legacy.'

'I'll only be gone three weeks. We've been apart for longer, right?'

'Yeah.' I sniffed.

'Then what's the problem?'

'You, you might meet another artist at the retreat … long legs, silky blonde hair,'

'I hope so, guys in beards bore me now.' he smirked.

'It's not funny.'

'Yes it is.' Zachary handed me a tissue.

'I could come with you … I'll, I'll write, you'll hardly notice I'm around.'

'Then what's the point?'

' … we'll take long walks when you're not working … you and me, you'll love it.'

'Agni.'

'Mm?'

'Is your mother going to fend for herself in big bad London?'

'Who?'

'Agni.'

I wiped my nose. 'I forgot about her.'

'When does she fly in?'

'I told you, tomorrow afternoon.' I lay down and stuffed a couple of pillows under my head.

'I can't believe your Dad isn't coming.'

'He couldn't get the time off work.'

'He's a cab driver!'

'Well, I don't know.'

'I think he just wanted you to spend some time alone with your mother.'

'Don't know, don't care.' I pouted.

'Come on, it might be fun.'

'It'll be a drama.'

'Possibly.'

'We'll clash.'

'Most likely.' He closed the flap on his backpack.

'She's going to drive me nuts.'

'Probably. But it'll be a good time for both of you.'

'Bah humbug.' I rolled over on my side.

He flopped down next to me and pulled me in close.

'Come on,' he said, stroking my hair. 'this was your idea, wasn't it?' he put a girlish lilt in his voice, '*you're talented Zachary, it's not just a hobby Zachary, you're amazing Zachary …* '

'I don't talk like that.' I made a face and he hugged me.

'If I can come up with some good, fresh stuff, I might get that Arts grant, and then, I can blow the agency job,' Zachary lifted my chin. ' … we might get a little nook in Tuscany somewhere, we'll write and draw, eat olive oil,'

My pout began to melt. 'Promise?'

'Cross my heart.'

☆☆☆

I heard my father flipping through his paper.

'The world's going crazy. Droughts, suicide bombers,'

' … too many boybands,' I said.

'What?'

'Nothing.'

'That's why your mother didn't want to fly,'

'Because of the boybands?'

'What?'

'Nothing.'

'Your mother loves you, you know. She has a bit of a temper, but deep down … '

'I know.'

'We love you.'

'Yes Dad.'

'When are you coming home Darling?'

'Soon. I promise.'

' … it's just that I look around at everyone who has every-thing … I have nothing.'

'You have Mum.'

'That's different. I want my child home with me.'

'I know.'

'When are you picking your mother up?'

'I'll leave in an hour.'

'Good,' and then he dropped his voice to barely a whisper.

'It's *killing* me not having you home.'

☆☆☆

Perfume counters have always been places of worship for Mum. I love them too. It's where my beautiful mother comes to life. As a child, I remember her rushing from counter to counter, eager to drown in her favourite French potions. No patch of skin was left untouched. And when she ran out of space on her arms, she'd push down her v-neck to accommodate another spritz or seven.

'Stand still.' she warned.

The spray was cold and sudden. It trickled slowly down my neck and I didn't dare flinch, desperate to keep every last drop of scent from sliding down my skin.

'You're my big girl!' Mum pulled me onto her hip and kissed my face.

Like a sweet-smelling confection in high heels, My mother had a scent I could follow forever. It was never anything I could clearly distinguish, I just knew it was Mum. I felt like the cartoon character whose feet leaves the ground as she trails behind the heady aroma of homemade pie.

'This way,' I said linking Mum's arm with mine. 'You'll love this.'

Everything was shiny. Spotless glass counters stretched out ahead of us littered with multicoloured glass bottles. Coiffed women hovered nearby with gold name badges and varnished smiles ready to spray any bare wrist they saw. The latest citrus-laced summer scent choked the air,

*Long-lasting and evocative, the intricate bouquet of a French country garden bottled. Set your senses free, lose yourself in the joy of fragrance. The joy of you.*

'Would you like to try?' A sales assistant with mascara clumps like small flies pounced on us. Mum held out her wrist. Spritz!

'It contains the pure, essential oils of flowers found in a French country garden.' the woman trilled.

My mother nodded and flared her nostrils. 'Cat piss.' she whispered. I giggled and pulled her away.

Strong lights beat down on us. Shoppers pushed past carrying bright yellow bags.

'This is the biggest cosmetic department in Europe Mum.' I said taking her hand. It felt small in mine.

As we dodged bargain-hunters and prams, Mum made a pilgrimage to a dozen different perfume counters. She sprayed the testers dry and bewitched assistants into handing over all their samples; tiny glass vials that were gone in a splash down her cleavage. I ran my nose over her cheek. She was bathed in a pricey, pretty stench. I grinned.

'You like the store Mum?'

'Well,'

'It's bigger than our department stores back home isn't it?'

Mum sneezed.

'Wanna take a break?' I said.

She shook her head and then I lost her to another hapless sales assistant.

'This is a classic eau de parfum madam.' The woman held up a dark bottle shaped like a ball.

My mother's face lit up. 'This one's my weakness.'

'Take a card.' The assistant said spraying a sliver of cardboard.

Mum pointed to the bottle. 'I prefer … ' she said.

The woman reluctantly surrendered the tester. My mother quickly coated her palms with the scent and jammed them up against her nostrils. 'Ah!'

'We'll take one thank you.' I said and the assistant's tense grin softened.

We sat down in a little café. Mum sniffed her arms. 'I smell like a brothel!' she laughed.

'A very expensive one.' I said.

'It's only money.' Mum shrugged.

'That's what I say!'

'I know.'

I grabbed my mother's hands and kissed them. 'I've missed you.'

'Me too.'

'How's Dad?'

'Your father's the same. He's getting older, more annoying,' she stirred her coffee. 'He misses you. You're his soft spot.'

'I know.'

A waiter appeared at our table. 'Something to eat ladies?'

'Mum?'

'No thank you.'

'We're fine for now thanks.' I said.

The waiter took the menus and left. I watched him as he walked into the kitchen.

'What are you looking at?'

'He looks like Zachary.'

'You're dreaming.'

'No – look at him again.' I insisted.

Mum drained her coffee cup. 'Whoever's hungry, dreams of bread.'

'I'm not hungry.'

'Really? You don't miss him?'

'Maybe ... doesn't mean I'm hungry for him.'

'Your pussy isn't even a *little* bit ticklish?'

'Mama!'

'What? You're in a defuck relationship.'

'It's defacto.'

'Same thing.' She looked away. 'Where's the toilet in here?'

I studied the faint pink stripes on the tablecloth. 'Why did you come to London?'

'What?'

'Why did you come now Ma? Why not last week, or six months ago? Why now?'

'I'm here now, what are you talking about?'

'Dad told me,'

Mum's face darkened. 'Told you what?'

I took a breath. 'You didn't want to visit while Zach was in the flat,'

Mum began to shake her head no and then she stopped. 'That's *right*. I have nothing to hide. You are in a defuck relationship.'

'*Defacto*.'

'I don't care, it's not decent.'

'It's decent for me.'

'You deserve to be married.'

'I'm not ready.'

'When you will be ready? Despina's expecting her *second* baby and you're still not ready.'

'So?'

'People are talking.'

'What people?'

'People.' She pursed her lips.

'Well I don't care what these *people* say.'

'You live with people, not animals. You have to care.'

'I'm happy where I am now.'

'What if he leaves you?'

'Marriage won't make him stay.'

'Divorces are more respected.'

'That's bullshit.'

'Bullshit. Bullshit. Everything is bullshit. Thank you very much.'

'Mama,'

'You know more than me.'

'Mama,'

'The camel is 100 years old, the baby camel 150.'

'Don't start.' I motioned for the bill.

'Do what you like, I don't care. You'll be crying.'

'No I *won't*.'

'Bravo.' She stood up abruptly. Her yellow shopping bag fell to the floor.

'Your perfume.'

The waiter arrived with the bill. 'Thanks.' I said averting my eyes.

Mum pulled on her jacket and grabbed her shopping bag. 'What do you want for dinner?'

'I don't care. I'm going to the gym.' I dropped a ten pound note on the little silver tray.

'I'll have cutlets and chips ready when you get back.' she said and walked away leaving a trail of stale perfume for me to follow.

☆☆☆

I stared at the bank of video monitors.

A pop star in 'spray-on' silver hotpants shook her body down, down, down to the ground. The camera came in close. Her lips bulged red like roasted peppers.

I looked at my watch.

'Is the trainer running late?' I asked the receptionist.

'Yeah, but she'll be here soon – would you like to go and come back?' she said.

'It's okay I'll wait.'

I settled back in my chair. The pop star stuck her silver bottom out and swung it from side to side. A languid bass beat cradled her exaggerated swing. Mahogany cheeks spilled out all over the lens …

… my mother sucked her teeth. 'Look at that, look, *that!*'

'What?' I said dialling Zachary's Artist's Retreat.

'Why doesn't she take them off too?'

'Don't you like them?' I teased.

'Do we need to see her bum?'

'It sells more records.'

'Look, l*ook!*' my mother leaned forward just as the pop star bent over to stroke her ankle. 'ptooo!' she spat at the TV screen.

'Her shorts are nice.' I put the phone down and joined her on the couch.

Mum stared at me in disbelief. 'Would *you* wear them?'

' … with the right shoes.'

'Bravo. Bravo.' my mother crossed her arms.

' … she's got a great bum too.'

'She's got a great bum?'

'Yeah.'

Mum threw her hands up in the air. 'You've gone mad.'

'Well she has!'

'Aren't you ashamed of yourself? A woman of your age... what would Zachary think?'

'He'd think she has a great bum too.'

'Bravo.'

'What's the big deal?'

'I think you need to pack your bags and come home – as soon as possible.'

'There'll be bums there too.'

The pop star spun around on her platforms, kissed two fingers and slapped her butt.

'Change the channel please.' Mum said.

I pointed the remote control to the screen. The pop star grabbed a silver top hat and slammed it down over her crotch.

'She's amazing isn't she?'

A small black woman sat down next to me. Her afro was tightly woven into little plaits And her eyes shone like black buttons on an expensive suit.

'Yeah, uh, incredible er, butt.' I said.

'Yeah,' the woman grinned. 'you here for the fitness assessment?'

'Oh! Yes, yeah... sorry.' I stood up quickly and shook her hand.

'Don't apologise... blame it on her butt. I'm Daisy.' she smiled.

I blushed. 'Oh, hi... yeah, I just have thigh envy.'

'You have thighs.' she laughed.

'They could be thinner.'

'I'll be the judge of that. You ready to go?'

'Yeah, I-I'm already changed.'

'Great. We're just downstairs.'

I picked up my bag and followed her into the gym. There was nothing pretty or delicate about Daisy. She wore an off-the-shelf deoderant – the kind that burns your brain if you sniff it quickly. Her shoulders were broad, arms thick. Muscle was etched into every nook of her brown skin. I scratched my forehead.

'Have you always worn your fringe so short?' Daisy said taking my pulse.

'Er no – brave move huh?' I replied and exhaled noisily.

'It suits you … ' she said looking at her watch.

'Oh, thanks … your, er … your plaits are cute too.'

She frowned. 'You have quite a high resting heart rate.'

'Really?'

'Under any stress?'

Well. My mother can't pronounce defacto. I'm lusting after silver hotpants. I'm missing my boyfriend. I'm killing my father.

'No.' I replied.

'Okay. Let's put a heart rate monitor on you.'

She handed me a snake-like contraption. I had to wet it and wrap it around and under my breasts.

'Shall I do it here?'

'Not unless you want an audience,' she laughed. 'Let's go to the change room.'

We walked down a hallway together and into a large white tiled room. I turned on the tap and let the water splash all over the band.

'You only need a couple of dabs … here.' She took my heart rate monitor and moistened the rubber strap. 'Wrap it around and click the fastener in place. Okay?'

I nodded.

'All yours.' she said and turned her back.

I fumbled under my crop top.

'Can you manage?' she asked.

'I just … ' I pulled up my top and she turned around just as my left breast squeezed out. I squashed it back in again. ' … so awkward … '

'Take your time.' she said looking away. 'I want an accurate reading of your heart.'

'Okay, just, trying to find the snap.' I mumbled and continued to struggle. 'Oh *shit*.'

I felt warm fingertips at my back. Then a small twist in my skin, a push and a click and …

… the sound of a million heartbeats reverberate against the tiles. She pulls me close. Every square inch of her skin like butter. Let me show you. Reveal you. My mystery and modesty shatter with every beat. I am on show. She sees inside me. I touch her face. Lips leaves heat on my skin. A kiss in the crease. A trace of my spine. And inside I jolt like I've just come down the steepest rollercoaster. All lovely tangles tight and wet. I let go. Tongue tiptoes, skimming, light and uncertain. Her flavour, heavy. Heart beats loud for all the world to hear…

'That better?' Daisy said, adjusting my top.

I nodded.

'Cool,' she smiled, 'let's go.'

☆☆☆

'What took you so long?'

Mum stood at the dining table, hands on her hips brandishing a lamb cutlet.

'I was at the gym.' I said and flopped down on the couch.

'All this time?'

'Yes *all* this time.'

'Alright, don't eat me.' she held her hands up in mock protest.

I squeezed my eyes shut and counted to ten.

'Yeah, close your eyes.' she taunted.

'I have a headache Ma.'

'You kept me waiting like an *idiot*.'

She stomped about the kitchen shoving cutlery into drawers and pushing bowls into saucepans where they didn't belong.

'Your chips are cold now.' she said with her back to me.

'That's what microwaves are for.' I pulled up a chair at the table.

Mum whirled around. 'Watch that tongue. I'm not your slave.'

'I didn't ask you to cook for me.'

'That's the thanks I get?'

'Mama.' I sighed piling a few limp chips on my plate.

'*Call* me, tell me you're running late.' her cheeks were red.

'Just … '

'Is this how you treat your *beloved?*'

I pulled a film of cling wrap over the chips. 'It's not … '

'I don't know why I break my back to cook,'

'Then don't!' I jumped to my feet. 'Stop whinging and close your mouth.' I ran to my bedroom.

'I'm changing my ticket in the morning!' she yelled after me. 'You can stay here and defuck day and night!'

'Good, go home!' I screamed.

A few hours later I emerged from the bedroom to find Mum sitting on the couch staring at the TV. Her eyes were red and she clutched a ball of tissue in her hand.

'I put your dinner in the fridge.' she said without looking at me.

'Okay. Have you eaten?'

'You know I don't eat lamb.' her voice broke.

'So what did you eat?'

'Nothing. Do you think I have an appetite?'

'You have to eat something.' I said.

'I'm not hungry.'

I pulled off the cling film and picked away at the tired food on my plate. Mum came over and sat down opposite me.

'Is it tender enough?' she said as I cut up a cutlet. 'it was tender when I cooked it.'

'It's yummy.'

'Thank God.' She threw her hands in the air dramatically.

I smiled and reached into the fridge. Her face softened as I handed her a small tub of Greek yoghurt.

'That's my weakness.'

'I know, eat it.'

She blew her nose noisily and took the yoghurt. I chewed on another biteful of lamb. The sweet flesh melted easily in my mouth.

'This is the best.' I said.

Mum nodded. 'No one cooks like your mother.'

'No one.' I agreed.

We sat in silence for a few minutes.

'How was the gym?' she said at last.

'Okay. That pop star was on again.' I smiled.

'With the lovely arse?'

I nodded. She hid a grin.

'Eat your food.' she said.

☆☆☆

A thousand cultures collided at Greenfields, my local deli.

Pink Egyptian pickles in chubby jars sat next to bags of Basmati rice. Greek shortbread stuffed with crushed almonds lined the shelf above the fresh packs of chopped up sugar cane. My mother scratched at their styrofoam tray.

'We used to stick straws in them and suck their juice when we were kids.'

She smiled at the memory and continued to move down the aisles naming exotic spices, herbs and tangy sauces. She picked up a bunch of chilled green leaves shaped like marijuana.

'You crush the leaves, mix them in with chicken stock, add garlic, cumin, seasoning,'

'Ma, go and talk to the shopowner in Arabic.' I interrupted, pointing to a stout man with a bald patch as he greeted another customer.

'*Ahlan mous-ahlan!*' Welcome!

'The man looks busy. Come and look at this.'

I followed her to a shelf filled with cartons of apricot nectar and several small bottles of ouzo. Mum studied the label and screwed her nose.

'Forget it, it's not the good stuff Agni.'

'It's still ouzo.'

'No, water.'

'How do you know?'

'I know.' She put the bottle back on the shelf. 'You always liked expensive ouzo.'

'I hate ouzo.'

'You didn't when you were small.'

'You gave me ouzo when I was a baby?'

'When you were teething, I rubbed it into your gums. You loved it.' She smiled and moved down the aisle.

We turned the corner. A small dark woman with familiar little plaits was sniffing a mango. Something inside me jumped.

'Mama, Ma go and tell the shopowner you speak Arabic … come on.' I nudged her towards the counter.

'What am I going to say to the man?'

'You'll think of something … go, I'll wait here.'

Mum's eyes landed on a green vegetable sparsely covered in fair-coloured fur. 'Okra!'

Daisy turned around suddenly and waved when she saw me.

'Do you know her?' Mum whispered as she grabbed a handful of okra.

'Hm?'

'She looks like a man.'

Daisy came over and put a hand on my shoulder. 'I

didn't expect to see you here.'

'It's my neighbourhood.'

'Really? Lucky you, I love this shop.' She looked at my Mum. 'Hi, I'm Daisy.'

Mum smiled vaguely. 'Hello.'

'This is my mother. She's visiting from Sydney.'

'Do you like London?'

Mum made a face. 'So, so.'

Daisy laughed. 'I know what you mean.'

'She likes London too much,' Mum pointed at me, 'stupid.'

'No, she's beautiful!' Daisy laughed again.

My whole body blushed. 'Haven't seen you around the gym lately.' I said.

'I resigned, I'm moving to Egypt believe it or not.'

'You Egyptian?' my mother asked.

Daisy nodded.

'Ah!' Mum's eyes lit up.

Within seconds the two women were swapping small talk in guttural tones. The shopowner looked over at us and smiled.

'*Mabrouk!*' my mother said and turned to me, 'Your friend is going to marry.'

'Wow, congratulations.' I said.

'Thanks,' She looked back at the fruit section. 'She was here a second ago. Honey!'

A slender woman wearing a white linen dress wandered over and slipped her hand into Daisy's. Mum dropped her okra.

'Hi.' I said. 'I know Daisy from the gym.'

'Yeah, hi how are you?' The woman smiled.

'You speak Arabic?' Mum said.

'No but I want to learn.' She looked at Daisy who gazed warmly at her.

'Maybe you can teach her.' Daisy said to my mother.

'Very hard to learn.' Mum said and picked up another handful of okra.

'I know.' Daisy's girlfriend nodded. 'I keep telling her.'

'Well it was nice to meet you.' Daisy smiled.

'Okay.' Mum nodded.

'Good luck in Egypt.' I said

We watched them pay for their mangos and leave hand in hand. I turned to my mother. She was busy squeezing the okra.

'See?' She looked at me.

'What, aren't they fresh?'

'Even a lesbian's ready for marriage.'

'*Ahlan mousahlan!*' the stout shopowner shouted to another customer.

☆☆☆

I wandered into the bathroom holding a red box with a white bow tied around it. Mum was covered in suds.

'Okay I found the box. Now what?'

'Open it.' she said.

'Is this for me?

'Yes.'

'Why Ma? It's not my birthday.'

'Doesn't matter. Open it.'

I untied the bow and gently lifted the lid. Inside, nestled in white tissue, were a pair of orange suede shoes.

I gasped, 'Ma are these your famous suede heels?'

'You remember?' she said with a soapy smile.

'I thought Papou made you throw them away.'

'My father was mad. These shoes cost me a month's wages!'

'They're a dancer's shoes, aren't they Ma?'

'They're a fool's shoes.'

'No Ma.'

'Quiet.' she said and her eyes filled. 'I don't want you to wear them. Just look at them to remind you what colour regret is. Live your life, Agni.'

Mum reached for the shower gel and slid halfway down the bath. She looked up at me. I was still reeling. 'Come on, help.' she barked.

I knelt by her.

'Ax,' she sighed, rubbing shower gel into her skin. 'If these breasts had a mouth.'

Mum stretched her short chubby legs out in front of her. Her skin was like milk, puckered perfectly at the knees and along her thighs. Her arms dimpled and flabby from too many sweet coffees in the mornings. She looked like a well fed china doll. Mum rubbed the gel quickly and clouds of rose-scented lather filled her cleavage.

'These breasts fed ten babies a day when you were born,'

'Ten?' I laughed handing her a sponge.

'I had *so* much milk – even after I fed you – nurses brought me more babies to feed.'

'What was wrong with the mothers?'

'Dry. No milk! And the babies, tiny, tiny, like skinny mice.'

'I have Dad's boobs.' I said rubbing her back with the excess suds.

'Don't be stupid. Wait a little,' she said. 'wait till you're pregnant.'

'One day.'

'One day, two days, a hundred days,' Mum sighed.

'I can't wait to have your grandchild.'

She glanced at me quickly. 'I'll be in the ground when that happens.'

'You're so *dramatic.*' I splashed some water in her face.

'Hey!' she scooped some bubbles out of her ear, 'when are you going to grow up?'

'When you let me.' I smirked.

Mum raised her eyebrows. 'When I *let* you?'

I nodded.

'Did you ask my permission to leave home? No. Did you ask for permission to have a defuck relationship? No.'

'Defacto Mama.'

'You are *over* grown up.' Mum wrung out her sponge.

'You wish I was still a baby don't you?'

'Not a baby… maybe two or three years old.'

'Wasn't I a good baby?'

'You bit my nipples. Naughty bebe … burped blood like a baby vampire.'

'You always dressed me up in the best clothes,' I said.

' … like the daughter of Onassis. The best shoes, best dresses,'

… she propped me up on a shelf beside her ornaments and figurines, draped a few glass beads around my neck …

' … like a doll. Everyone loved you.'

'You took a photo of me on that shelf.'

'Ah yeah.' she smiled.

'I had that photo on a wall in my flat.'

'Mm.'

'You came and visited me at my flat in Sydney. Remember?'

'I remember. It was a nice little flat.'

Mum slipped deeper into the bubbles. 'Oh! Pull me up … your mother's getting old.'

'No you're not.' I helped her up, catching sight of a sparse mass of pubic curls through the frothy water.

'Where have your ringlets gone Mama?' I grinned at her.

'Age.'

'Or does Daddy eat them?'

My mother laughed loudly. Her eyes creased in the corners and she gave me a soapy kiss.

'I'll miss you.'

# 13

## eyelash wishes

'I needed that.' I breathed out and disappeared into the crook of his arm.

'Hm.'

'It's *necessary* sex.' I said.

'Yes baby.' Zachary folded his arms behind his head and closed his eyes.

'I mean … it's such a relief, you know?'

'Hm.'

'There's nothing rude about it is there?'

'It's a beautiful thing.' Zach murmured.

'To, to want to have yummy, sweaty … to actually *feel* like sex?'

'I *love* the way you are.' Zachary pulled at the sheets until they covered us both.

'Sometimes I used to feel queasy after it.' I whispered so he wouldn't hear.

Because little girls didn't have sex. Little girls didn't feel that insistent pulse between their legs at the sight, at the smell of sex. Little girls just didn't.

☆☆☆

The bright lights of advertising had dimmed for Zachary soon after he returned from the Retreat. So he resigned to concentrate on his art. I was earning enough to support us both. It was a nice arrangement, at first. I went to work. He stayed home to paint … and play Domestic God.

'You do realise you're a house husband now.' I joked as the oven timer buzzed.

Zachary looked up him from his chopping board. 'Know what I'm learning?'

'What?'

'This cooking thing is all about timing.' He dashed to the hob to stir a creamy concoction.

'Any news from the Arts Council?'

'Nope. They're taking their friggin' time.' he muttered throwing chopped garlic into a bubbling liquid.

'It'll happen baby.' I hugged his waist.

'Are you going to help or are you going to talk?'

'What's up with you?'

'Nothing, it's hot, I'm hungry,'

'Diddums.'

He glared at me.

'Alright I'll go and change,'

'Hurry up, this'll be ready in a minute.' he called after me.

We sat down to dinner. Zachary lit a tealight candle.

'Done with your miffed moment?' I said.

'Sorry.' he replied and pulled me close for a kiss.

'No one's asked you to be the a la carte King Zach.'

'I know,' He sliced into a chunk of crusty bread, 'Home made herb bread Madam?'

'I'm serious.'

'I know, I enjoy this okay.'

'Did you do any painting today?'

'I had to keep an eye on the bread, you wouldn't believe … '

'Zach!'

'What?'

'There's nothing wrong with takeaway.'

'Pricey poison.' He shuddered.

'You *love* takeaway.' I crunched into a potato. 'This *is* delicious though.'

'Bravo.' he said in a mock Greek accent. 'Hey, your parents called this morning.'

'And?' I said with my mouth full.

'Your mother gave me her moussaka recipe.'

'You're kidding me.'

'She says I should mince the meat myself.'

'How much time do you have to waste?'

'Maybe she has a point … I mean, what do they *really* put in that mince?'

'Meat Zachary.'

'But what *sort* of meat?'

☆☆☆

The alarm screamed in my ear.

'Come on Agni get up!' Zach called from the living room.

I wandered out to him with one eye still closed. I fell into his arms. 'Tired.' I mumbled.

'We've gotta stop those late nights Baby,'

'Mm.' I murmured into his chest. 'I'll go take a bath.' I said.

'A shower will wake you up.'

'Can't.'

'Why?'

'It's dirty.'

'Well excuse me for not being more efficient.'

'Relax. A bath will be fine.'

'I'm home I should clean.'

'You should get a grip.' I said and tweaked his ear, 'You coming for a bath?'

'I've gotta cook breakfast.'

'Your loss.' I yawned and padded away.

As I put on my makeup I could hear Zach whistling and bacon crackling. I reached for my eyeshadow.

'Ready!' Zach called.

'Coming!' I replied, blowing away the excess powder from my compact.

'Come on it's getting cold!'

'Okay!'

I ran a little mascara over my eyelashes. Zach charged into the bedroom. I jumped.

'I've put a lot effort into this.' he said.

'Alright!'

I sat at the breakfast table glaring at him while he cracked a few silly smiles.

'When are you going to snap out of this?' I said pushing a bit of bacon onto my fork.

'What?'

I shoved the bacon into my mouth and chewed quickly. 'This domestic superman routine.'

'Someone's gotta do it.' he said and poured me a glass of juice.

I pushed it away. 'You need to get out of the house today.'

'Yeah like that can happen.'

'Why can't that happen?'

'Because I have a bathroom to clean and a kitchen floor to mop.'

I put my fork down and stared at him.

'What's wrong with your bacon?'

I picked up my plate and carried it to the kitchen.

'I can do that.' He called out after me.

'No.' I called back.

'Well let me take you to work.' Zachary picked up the keys.

'I can walk.' I snapped and pulled on a leather jacket.

'It's raining Agni.'

'I don't care, I want to walk.'

'In the rain?'

Five minutes later I was sitting in the passenger seat. 'I won't be treated like a child Zach.'

'Don't be such a drama queen.' he said sliding into peak hour traffic.

'And don't patronise me.'

'I'm not treating you like a child.'

'You are.'

'Am not.'

'Yes you are.'

'Am not.'

I clenched my fists and punched my thighs. 'You're *smothering* me!'

'Am not.'

'Stop it!'

'Okay, maybe I lost a little perspective.' he said taking a back street.

'A little?'

Zach touched my shoulder. I flinched.

'You're not listening. I don't need you to care of me, cook for me, clean for me like I can't do it for myself … *I'm not a child*, not a child, okay? It's like fucking déjà vu.'

'Calm down.' Zachary pulled up outside the agency.

'No I won't calm down and I won't get up on time, I won't eat all my breakfast, I won't be wrapped in bloody cotton wool Zach.' I buckled with those last few words.

He leaned over and grabbed my hand. 'Baby, what's wrong with taking care of you?'

'Can't you see?' I sobbed, squeezing his hand. 'You're turning into *them*.'

Zachary sat back in his seat. 'Bullshit. That's bullshit.'

I reached into the glove box for a tissue. 'It's so obvious.'

'I'm *not* your parents.'

'Well you're doing a bloody good impersonation.'

Zachary shot me an angry look. I ignored him and we sat staring at commuters as they cowered under umbrellas before making a final burst into an office tower.

'They're like lemmings.' he said softly.

I threw my seat belt off.

'Where are you going?' he said.

'I'm late.'

'Here,' he reached for a paper bag on the back seat. 'I made you a sandwich.'

I took the bag. 'When was the last time you painted people Zach, real people?'

'Do you want it or not?'

I threw the sandwich in his lap. 'I've got a client lunch.' I said and left.

☆☆☆

A familiar voice laughed into the machine. I grabbed the phone.

'Despina! Hey how are you doing?'

'Hi Cuz, love your machine message.'

'Thanks. How's everything, how are the kids?'

'They're fine, getting bigger.'

'Yeah? I really miss you guys.'

'How's Zachary?'

'He's fine, working on his painting.'

'Really?'

'Yeah, he'll probably make a living out of it one day … he's great you know.'

'Wow, good luck to him. My husband spends all day with feet for his living.'

I laughed. 'It's something.'

'Yeah. Hey, Alexander just came in … Alex, Agni's on the phone.'

'Yo.'

'How are the women Alex?'

'Wonderful.'

'Yeah?'

'Plentiful.'

'Is that it?'

'Well there's nothing more I can disclose at this time.'

'Really.'

A high pitched beep broke up our line. 'That's my mobile. I'll pass you back to Despina. See ya.'

'We're going to get my brother a mobile implant for his ear this Christmas.'

☆☆☆

I snapped on my rubber gloves and poured some dishwashing liquid into a sponge. Zachary handed me the dinner plates.

'You going to fill the sink up?' he said.

'No.'

'You're wasting water.'

'So?' I scrubbed a plate clean and rinsed it. Steam rose from the dish. Zachary gave me another plate.

'How was work?'

'Fine.'

'Are you busy?'

'No.'

'What did the client say about your radio script?' he handed me a couple of glasses.

'Nothing. Will you just leave everything at the side!' I shouted.

'I'm trying to help.'

'Well don't.' I squeezed more soap into the sponge and attacked the kitchen bench. I scrubbed the speckled formica like it was covered with day old egg yolk.

'It's not that dirty.' he said.

I continued to scrub. Suds spilled over the side.

'Hey.' Zachary pulled me gently away from the bench, 'come on,'

I dropped my gaze to the floor. He tugged my gloves off and sat me down.

'You're right.' he said softly.

'Can't hear you.'

'I said you're right.'

I folded my arms.

'I've been getting a little carried away lately.' he said.

'A lot.'

'Okay a lot. But, I,'

'You're stalling.'

'I'm getting to the point okay?'

'No, you're putting off your work for me … I'm your excuse.'

'You're the best one around.' he grinned.

'Forget it.' I stood up.

'Okay, okay, sit down.'

'Zach, my parents put the emphasis on me when I was living at home. It was always me.' I jabbed my chest. '*where* are you going, *what* are you doing, *who* is he, she, *why* are you late, *when* you are doing this, *when* are you … '

I stopped mid-sentence. Zach's face had darkened and he didn't look like he'd a heard a word I said.

'I'm kidding myself.'

'What are you talking about?'

'This,' he swept his arm through the air, 'here … the pictures I pretend to draw, the dreams I try to have.'

I moved to touch him, 'Baby, your art is … '

' … contrived, still-life bullshit!'

'Don't say that,'

Zachary shook his head and stared into space. A tear crept down his cheek. 'I failed him.'

'Who?'

He exhaled like a tired old man and began to sob.

'Baby,' I tried to cover him with my arms, he shrugged me away.

'He said he was dog-tired,' Zach wept. 'but I ran up to him. Look what I drew Pa, look!'

Zach wiped his eyes as if he were seeing something for the first time. 'Look.'

'So he took my sketches and he sat down, didn't even take his shoes off … and he started looking at my drawings like he was studying them, like they were the most amazing fucking things he'd ever seen … I hid my nose in a sketch book … I always did that when he looked at my stuff … well Pa? I said. But he was quiet. And then the next minute he's snoring and my sketches are sort of shaking on his chest … so I grab a pencil and start to sketch him … his face, those tiny creases in his forehead, the heart mole … I'm drawing so fast it doesn't bother me that Mum's in the bedroom talking to the sheets again, "God forsaken town Lawrence! Clean sheets too much to ask for!" I look at Pa. He's not moving, not even snoring anymore, he's just there, just sitting, so still, and then he makes this noise like a bad cough or something. But I keep drawing don't I? Can't tear my pencil from the page, no, because I've got to get the fucking perspective right.'

Zachary's eyes filled again. He wiped them away, angry

at their interference, and continued,

'Mum runs out of the bedroom with her damn sheets. "Look!" But Pa doesn't move. She shakes his shoulder. He still doesn't move. Now I'm crying and I don't know why … Pa's dog-tired, I scream. And now she's screaming too, shaking him over and over, everything's so *loud*, "How long have you been sitting there?" she yells. I don't know I say, I don't know … '

Zachary's voiced trailed off and he looked at me, confused, back from a tangled place in time.

'Last thing the man saw was my stupid fucking scribble.'

I prised open his arms and pushed myself in. He immediately grabbed hold of me.

'I'm an idiot.' he whimpered.

'No.'

We lay down together.

'We'll be okay.' I whispered in his ear. 'Ooh, don't move,' I plucked a stray eyelash from his cheek.

'Top or bottom?'

He shrugged his shoulders.

'Come on killjoy, top or bottom?' I said.

'Bottom.'

I opened my fingers. The lash clung to the top. 'No, hang on, it's really on the bottom.' I stuck my fingers together again.

'Come on it's yours.' he said.

'No,'

'It's *yours.*'

'Okay.'

I made my wish and nuzzled my face deep into his chest.

‘I love you.’ I said from the folds of his shirt.

‘What did you wish?’

‘That would be telling.’

☆☆☆

On Valentine’s Day I came home to a heart-shaped apple pie. Zach had written our initials in pastry on the top.

‘I made it myself.’ he beamed.

‘It’s gorgeous.’ I leapt up on him. He caught me and buried his face into my neck.

‘So are you going to tell me what your eyelash wish was last week?’ he said, brushing his nose against my cheek.

‘Nope.’

‘You sure?’ his eyes were wide and beautiful.

‘Positive.’ I smiled.

‘Come on, what did you wish?’

‘I’m not telling you!’ I pinched his chin.

‘You believe in eyelash wishes?’

‘I’m not telling you Z,’

‘Well do you?’

‘What’s happened?’ I squirmed in his arms.

Zachary squeezed me. ‘I got it Agni!’

‘What?’

‘The grant, I got it!’

‘Woo-hoo!’ I screamed and covered his face with kisses. ‘I told you, I *told* you!’

‘We’re going back to Sydney!’

‘What?’ I let my feet touch the floor.

‘Sydney, remember? Big prawns, sunshine?’

'I thought you applied for a European grant.'

'No it was *a* grant.'

'So it could've been anywhere?'

'Yep.'

'What about Tuscany?'

'What about it?'

'You said we were going there.'

'It was always an option.'

'Oh.'

'We got lucky Baby.'

'Yeah.' I sat down.

Lucky. The man I loved was ready to take me home to the city I loved. I could have my homemade apple pie and eat it too. But that's not what I wished for.

'I'm not ready to go home Zach.'

☆☆☆

'*Qantas flight 415 now boarding for Sydney.*'
Zachary walked towards me holding two plastic cups.

'Your hot chocolate madam.' he smiled and sat beside me.

'Baby, you're flight's boarding.'

'Yeah I heard … it can wait.' he said, putting the cups down.

'Zach come on,'

He touched my lips. 'Ssh.'

I put my head on his shoulder. 'Have you got everything?' I said.

'Not everything.'

I glanced up at him, he was staring at me, eyes full of

tears.

'Don't Zach. You promised.'

'Can't help it.'

'Try.'

'You asked me to choose,'

'I don't want to go through this again.' I wiped a tear away and took a large sip of hot chocolate. 'Ow!'

'Is that chocolate too hot?' he said reaching for my cup. 'I'll get you more milk.'

I pulled away. 'It's fine. I'm a big girl.'

He looked away. 'What are you going to do?'

'Wait till it cools down.'

'I meant when I leave,'

'I know what you meant.' I took a breath. 'I don't know… might go freelance, maybe do a little of my own writing.' I put my head back on his shoulder.

'You've always wanted that.' he said touching my hair with his lips. I felt a chill.

'How do you know?'

'I just do.'

'I'm probably crap at it.'

'Don't think so.'

A large family with four trolleys of luggage hurried by screaming at each other.

'Light travellers.' he nudged me. I nudged him back. 'If I send you some stuff to read, will you read it?'

He nodded. 'You know I will. And when you're signing autographs in a huge bookstore somewhere, I'll be the tall guy in the back cheering you on.'

'You can't cheer at signings.'

'Can too.'

*'This is the final call for all passengers flying Qantas flight 415 to Sydney . . . '*

Zachary took the cup from my hands and crouched down between my legs.

'I gotta go.'

I nodded. His face was a beautiful blur through my tears.

'You know,' he toyed with my fringe, 'you still can't parallel park properly.'

I let out a strangled little laugh. 'Think I need more lessons?'

'Definitely.' Zachary's eyes began to fill again.

'Know any good teachers?'

'I'll get back to you.' he said quietly and pulled my face towards his.

I stayed and watched Zachary's 747 as it taxied away from me. The plane took off. It climbed over a couple of clouds and then he was gone. Raindrops skidded across the glass pane. I imagined them as tears.

I found a rectangle of thick paper under my pillow that night. It was a portrait of me, asleep. I stared at myself. Heart-shaped face. Little brown daggers of fringe poked skyward. Messy brushstrokes swept detail into my lashes, brows and lips. I turned the sketch over and saw an an inscription. It was written in leaky blue biro.

*'I love you. Z.'*

☆☆☆

Sirens wailed. Cars swish-swooshed down wet streets.

The phone rang.

'Alexander's engaged.' my mother said.

'What?'

'And do you know who he's marrying?'

'Who?'

'That prostitute.'

'You sure she's a prostitute Mama?'

'Yes, I'm telling you, yes.'

'What's Uncle saying?'

'What can he say? His blood pressure is sky high. Despina almost lost her baby.'

'She's pregnant again?'

'Yeah, an accident. Why did she want another baby? Three children. I don't know.'

I heard my father in the background. 'Tell her about Zachary.'

'What?' Mum said.

'Zachary, you know, the … ' Dad insisted.

'Alright, alright, be quiet, I can't hear your daughter and you at the same time.'

'What's he talking about Ma?'

'I keep forgetting to tell you.'

'What?'

'Zachary means 'sugar' in Greek.'

'Yeah.'

'Does he know that?'

'I don't know.'

'You should tell him.'

# 14

# belonging

I leaned over and kissed the Virgin's Icon.

As a child I was lifted up to Her face. The jewels in her crown dazzled me. Her serene beauty flawless even under a hundred lip prints. She was *Panayitsa* or, Little Virgin Mary and my moment with Her was always fleeting. A quick kiss and I was back on my feet struggling on tiptoes eager for another look.

The strong smell of incense reassured me with its spicy familiarity as I took my seat. I closed my eyes and saw the little girl waiting for her turn to 'catch the smoke' like Mummy had taught her. The priest swept past in long purple robes 'throwing' incense into the hands of the faithful. She reached up and scooped the smoke curls from the air, drew them into herself and made the sign of the cross. The smoke was always elusive and I never thought I caught enough of it for my prayer to be heard.

The incense burner jingled. I opened my eyes.

Endless fronds of smoke unfurled into the congregation. They reached out to me. I swept them up, guiding them into my prayers. I crossed myself and looked up into His face. He returned my gaze from His home in the domed ceiling. His arms were stretched as wide as the dome itself. It comforted me to think he could stretch his arms even wider if the dome were bigger. I studied his eyes. Watercolour blue. I wondered how dark-skinned Christians related to this Aryan image. Would they be so devout if they knew their Messiah probably looked more like Moustafa who owned the kebab shop?

A queue for holy communion began to form and the priest spoke…

'Your daughter is an innocent.' he says and now I'm a toddler fidgeting in my mother's arms.

Days before my 1st birthday I was carried into the sacred space behind the altar; the male domain where bearded men muttered ancient prayers over large books sheathed in gold and gems. Where bread was blessed and crumbled into golden chalices of wine. Females had always been considered 'unclean', unworthy of setting foot in this inner sanctum.

'Father are you sure?'

'Bring your child to be blessed.' he smiled.

I dabbed a tissue to my eyes and went to stand in line for holy communion.

☆☆☆

'I wanted to be here for Easter, but no flights.' Dad kept his arm wrapped around my shoulders.

'Doesn't matter Daddy.'

'We haven't spent Easter together for years you know.'

'I know, but you've enjoyed being with me these past few weeks, right?'

'Zachary loves you.'

'What's that got to do with anything?' I laughed.

'I'm just saying.'

I took my father's hand luggage. 'I think you have to check in here.'

'You know he visits every week. Your mother cooks him dinner,'

'You've told me Daddy.' I reached into his coat pocket, 'where's your ticket?'

Dad stopped. 'Come home with me now.' he said suddenly.

'Dad,'

'Come, I'll buy you new clothes in Sydney.' my father spoke quickly, he fumbled around in his jean pockets for his wallet, 'look, I have credit cards,'

'We've already talked about this.' I handed Dad's ticket over.

The ground stewardess smiled. 'Do you have a ticket Miss?'

'I can buy her one now.' Dad pushed me aside, slapping down a card.

The stewardess looked confused. 'Excuse me?'

'I'm not flying today. It's just my father.'

'Let me … ' Dad elbowed me again.

'Stop it.' I hissed in Greek.

'Sydney's a long way from London.' the stewardess smiled knowingly.

My father nodded sadly. 'What can you do?'

I pulled up a chair in the café and put a newspaper down on the table.

'Daddy I got you a paper to read on the plane.'

'English rubbish.' he sniffed and pushed the paper aside.

'So did you like London?' I asked cheerfully.

'It was alright. Cold.'

'I know and it's Spring!'

'And you love it here better than Sydney.'

'I don't.'

'Then what's the problem? Come … oh I don't know,' his voice trailed off.

I didn't say anything.

'Everyone loves you at home … even George misses you.'

'I know,' I smiled.

'Zachary can make moussaka like your mother now.'

'Yeah?'

'She doesn't like it of course … you know your mother – he doesn't mince his own meat she says,'

I took his hands. 'I'll come home soon Daddy.'

'You keep saying that.'

'I will.'

'When?'

'I don't know.'

A girl skipped into the café on a plastic rope followed by her father.

'Beautiful little girl.' Dad said pulling his hands away from mine.

I nodded. He reached into his hand luggage and presented me with a faint blue box.

'I wanted to look at this with you on the plane home,' he said.

It was my baby album. 'Have you had this all along?'

'I told you. I wanted to look at it with you on the plane,'

'Daddy.' Something grabbed at my throat.

' … but you're stubborn. Like your mother.'

He turned to the first page. Vanilla escaped and there she was. A pink baby in mother's fashionable arms. A toddler swinging her leg over a dog. A tomboy playing dress-ups with Daddy's clothes. A tiny feline fatale in Mummy's pantyhose. The nervous bellydancer, hands held high dancing for her dinner. There she was. A tightly wrapped up bundle napping in a taxi to the strains of an Italian lullaby.

'You used to hum like this … Hm. Hm.' he laughed softly. 'You were such a smart, baby. Very, *very* smart.'

'How did you know I liked the song?' I asked as the final call for boarding came.

'I knew,' he smiles, 'I just knew.' He closed the photo album and handed it to me.

I leant over and kissed him hard on the cheek. Dad grabbed the newspaper.

'Does this rubbish paper have any star signs?'

☆☆☆

I never kissed my little girl goodbye. She just slipped her hand into Daddy's and blended away into my memories.

There she is straddling the family German Shepherd.

There she is chasing boys with her plastic gun. She's cuddling a bottle of hot chocolate with Mummy now. She's in Daddy's taxi, in Daddy's clothes now. There, there little one.

There, there.

## the end